BAY OF ARROWS

Other Books by Jay Parini

Singing in Time (poetry)

Theodore Roethke:
An American Romantic (criticism)

The Love Run (novel)

Anthracite Country (poetry)

The Patch Boys (novel)

An Invitation to Poetry (textbook)

Town Life (poetry)

The Last Station (novel)

BAY OF ARROWS

BAY OF ARROWS

JAY PARINI

Henry Holt and Company New York

Published by Henry Holt and Company, Inc.,
115 West 18th Street, New York, New York 10011.
Published in Canada by Fitzhenry & Whiteside Limited,
91 Granton Drive, Richmond Hill, Ontario L4B 2N5.

Library of Congress Cataloging-in-Publication Data
Parini, Jay.
Bay of arrows : a novel / Jay Parini. — 1st ed.
p. cm.
I. Title.
PS3566.A65B3 1992 92-8331
813'.54—dc20 CIP

ISBN 0-8050-1676-7

First Edition—1992

Designed by Claire Naylon Vaccaro

Printed in the United States of America
Recognizing the importance of preserving the
written word, Henry Holt and Company, Inc.,
by policy, prints all of its first editions
on acid-free paper. ∞

1 3 5 7 9 10 8 6 4 2

For DEVON, who makes every word possible

Out of the crooked timber of humanity,
no straight thing was ever made.
—Immanuel Kant

PART ONE

Chapter 1

The cacique and his high priest had never seen anything like it. The three caravels had stood all morning in the ultramarine bay like great seaworthy beasts, while petrels swarmed their riggings. Even from a good distance, one could make out the peculiar costumes worn by these mysterious sailors who had appeared from nowhere.

"They are ancestors, returning to claim our kinship," the high priest said, explaining what could not be explained. Because he seemed to know what he was talking about, the cacique decided to make the ultimate sacrifice.

His only daughter, the princess, was admired by the whole village. Her smooth skin, wide black eyes, and easy disposition made her much coveted by all the young men of the tribe. In the company of her elders, she spoke softly, keeping her eyes fixed on the ground ahead of her. She offered sympathy at every turn, selfless to a fault, without the slightest trace of affectation.

"I will give the great white gods my daughter," the cacique announced, barely restraining his tears.

He ordered the princess to bathe, then to allow the older women to anoint her with palm oils as she sat in the ceremonial *dujo*, an ornately carved chair used only by the cacique and his family on special occasions. Her nose was pierced by an elderly woman, who daubed the small incision with juice of the soursop to dull the pain; a gold ring was put into her nose, one of the few in the tribe's possession. Through all of this the princess remained serene. It was her understanding that the great white gods would transport her to heaven in a chariot of fire.

"Yocahú will preserve you," her father said, referring to the spirit of the manioc root, which had preserved his family for many generations.

Everything was set as the afternoon deepened. The phantasmagoric ships blazed on the water. Clouds dispersed, and the sea became a sheet of hammered gold as the invaders huddled in small boats, waving flags and singing an unfamiliar tune as they approached the shoreline. The cacique noticed that one man stood in the stern of the first boat with his arms folded, his chin jutting forward in the salty breeze.

The princess was naked now, her black hair pulled back behind her ears, her wrists tied to a stake. The white men caught sight of her from a considerable distance and began to row more quickly. It had been a long time since they had seen a woman—any woman—and this one, or so it seemed from afar, must be among the most beautiful women in the whole of Cypango or India or wherever on earth they happened to be. Their comments were made so that the captain (a prude) would not overhear what they said.

The captain's faithful translator, Luis de Torres, sat in the boat behind Columbus, ready to intercede for him in Arabic, Hebrew, or Latin. He was especially good at Latin, but he imagined that these untutored inhabitants of the Indies, remote subjects of the Great Khan, would probably not have mastered the intricacies of his favorite classical tongue. He was not even sure about their Arabic. Would it be the same dialect that he had learned from an elderly Moor in Algeciras? He had tried to explain about dialects to Columbus, but the captain was oblivious to such distinctions. His own language, a racy Genoese dialect, merged with odd bits of Spanish or Portuguese, depending on the company.

Not far from shore, Columbus leaped over the side of the rowboat, stepping boldly through the ankle-deep waves and pushing forward onto the white beach, where he promptly fell to his knees—as he had done at every landfall since arriving in the New World. He kissed the hot sand and crossed himself several times. Rodrigo de Escobedo, his scribe, took note of everything.

The Taino princess stared bravely ahead. Her watery black eyes gazed at the great white ancestor who approached in shiny black boots and vermilion trousers. He stopped a respectful distance from her and knelt once again, this time kissing the wooden cross that dangled from his neck. He seemed entranced now, praying, muttering to himself: *Sit nomen Dominus benedictum, per Jesum Cristum, salvatorum nostrum.* His hands fluttered across his chest in a sign of the holy cross. Then he stood, princely himself, lordly erect and proud. He moved ceremoniously toward the gleaming girl.

She was awed by his narrow eyes and russet beard, so unlike anything she had ever seen before. His breath was foul and hot as he swayed above her; his right hand reached toward her face, and he pinched the gold ring in her nose between his thumb and forefinger.

"It's gold," he said, turning to the men behind him, his eyes peppery and red. "The ring is gold!"

Chapter 2

"It's gold!" Geno cried, sitting up in bed.

"Go back to sleep," Susan whispered in a hoarse morning voice.

Geno reached for the little notebook that he always kept beside his bed and scribbled a few lines. Later, he would see how much of the dream he could reconstruct.

It was early April, with snow in patches on the fields. In the distance the white peak of Mount Isaac was just visible. Milo, just six, had been wakened by his parents' talking. Now he padded down the bare hallway in sleeper pajamas, the flap at the back hanging open. Still mostly asleep, he stood for a long time beside his father, Chris Genovese, without speaking.

"You awake, darling?" Geno asked, touching his cheek.

"Daddy, I think it snowed last night!"

Susan Worthington rolled over, her back set to protect her from the commotion.

"Look outside!" Milo said. "We can build a snowman! Come on, Daddy!"

"I don't think it really snowed," Geno said.

Susan groaned. "Can you guys carry on this dialogue somewhere else?"

"Let's go downstairs," Geno whispered, rubbing a hand across his face as if to pull off the mask of sleep. He twisted his lips, trying to activate the muscles of expression. He would prop Milo in front of a video—*Home Alone* or *Crocodile Dundee*; that would keep him for an hour or so before breakfast, during which time he could read whatever it was he was supposed to teach that day or jot witty comments on a yellow pad, some of which would emerge as spontaneous, offhand remarks to his special seminar on modern poetry. On lucky mornings, he might even draft a brief poem of his own before breakfast—or add to the sequence of poems about Columbus that had, for months, been obsessing him.

Before long, he stood at the kitchen sink with Milo watching him from a stool behind the breakfast counter.

"You don't want to watch *Home Alone*?"

"I've seen it twenty times."

"Or *Crocodile Dundee*?"

"I hate that movie."

Geno sighed, dumping a day-old pot of Irish breakfast tea into the drain and studying the strange pattern it made, a disruptive swirl of fattened tea leaves. In the British manner, he heated the pot with a swish of boiling water before trying to make more tea.

"Let's go outside, Daddy!"

"It's too early, damn it!" he said, cracking the joints of his fingers one by one.

"Don't yell at me."

"I'm sorry."

"We can go skating on the pond. It's perfect."

"It's just seven, honey. Maybe later, huh?"

Milo did not, of course, have any sense of time. He had gotten brand-new skates the week before, for his birthday, so he wanted to skate, even though winter was slipping behind them.

"It's too early, so forget it," Geno added.

But he sensed a familiar lack of conviction in his voice. When it came to Milo, he could not say no. (And he was only marginally better with James, who was ten, although Geno prided himself on having gotten James "under control.")

"I'll get your skates from the garage!" Milo shouted as he disappeared around the corner, still in his pajamas.

Not fifteen minutes later they were outside, Milo in a lime-green snowsuit, Geno in snowpants with a puffy down vest over his red flannel shirt. From the southeast, a V-line of Canada geese appeared with a honking noise that echoed along the Champlain Valley. The ground was frozen, with stalks of milkweed and mullein stuck like arrows in the crusty snow, but the air smelled of thaw—a faintly damp odor that brought hope to the wintering heart.

The pond was milky gray now—a weirdly translucent eye—with a foot-high rim of snow ringing it like bleachers. The black limbs of a willow stood like a gallows in the middle distance.

"Mommy doesn't like to skate, does she?"

"She does so."

"I don't think so," Milo said. "Whenever I say, 'Let's go skating,' she says, 'Get lost.' "

Geno knew that Susan had a thing about this pond. "It might *look* frozen," she had said to James and Milo only yesterday. "But the ice is thin. If you want to skate, Daddy or I will take you to the indoor rink at the college."

He hated it when Susan was the sensible one, and when he—once again—was just another child, irresponsible, in need of mothering. But the pond *was* frozen. Before putting on his skates, he stepped onto the ice and leaned, hard as he could, forward; there was no give at all. He pushed farther out, testing, his eyes searching for splintery cracks in the slick surface.

"Get your skates on, Daddy!"

"Be patient!"

Geno took off his gloves to lace Milo's shiny black skates before turning to his own, which were ancient relics—the same ones he had used in the late sixties, at Dartmouth. (He remembered those gin-fueled, midnight parties on Occam Pond with a shudder, a dream-image from another life or, more likely, a scene from some forgotten black-and-white movie with a script by a third-rate admirer of F. Scott Fitzgerald.)

"Your skates are dirty," Milo said.

"It's just a little rust. Won't slow me down at all, sweetie. You watch me go."

Why was he showing off for a six-year-old? He felt the

foolishness of it all as he skated, backward, toward the center of the pond, pretending he was playing for the Bruins. With an invisible stick, he shot his imaginary puck across the glassy pond. "Goal!" he hollered, trying to catch Milo's eye. Looking up, he saw the farmhouse blazing in the pink-and-orange sun, its windows filled with fiery light.

"Watch *me*!" cried Milo, rushing toward the other end of the pond with a low, zigzag sway.

It all happened so fast. Swiveling, Geno saw the boy tumble in the slow motion that engulfs all accidents, that holds the moment, flylike, in its thick goo. Geno's panic was followed by a quick but hollow smile, as if a flicker of confidence were ignited and extinguished at the same time and supplanted immediately by a loss of hope, all premature, and the rush to salvage something from the wreckage.

Milo had managed to find the one bad spot on the ice: the pond's soft fontanel. He had pitched, with only the slightest gasp, through the glassy surface. What upset Geno more than anything else, in retrospect, was the fact that the boy hadn't even cried for help.

Only a few nights before, he had put Milo to bed with a book about a kid who fell into a frozen river; in that particular story a dog had rescued the boy by dragging a branch to the spot where the boy had gone through. The dog—one of the improbable sons of Lassie—held the branch in his teeth and pulled the boy back onto solid ice. It had seemed, as Geno read it, possible that such a thing could work, and now he scanned the shoreline desperately for a branch. "Shit," he heard himself crying. "Shit, shit, shit."

Then he caught Milo's eyes: the look of helplessness, as if he had sunk beyond panic into something like acceptance. It was the worst thing he'd ever seen.

Instinct guided him now, and he found himself taking off his skates and rushing across the pond in his stocking feet. The thought occurred to him that he should lie down and extend a hand to Milo, but the ice looked horribly thin around the opening, so he jumped. He knew that he would hit the bottom quickly and bounce up again; it should be simple enough to rescue Milo by grabbing his arm and lifting him onto hard ice. The water was hideously cold, but he could stand it for all the time he would need.

Milo had managed to keep his head above water, and Geno caught him under one arm and rolled him over on a ledge of ice. He followed himself, carefully, and kept them both rolling until the ice seemed firm enough to stand on.

"You okay, honey?" he asked, kissing Milo rather frantically on his icy cheeks.

The child's blue lips merely quivered.

Geno carried the stunned boy to the house in his wet stockings, the soles of his feet tingling and burning as he stepped through the snowcrust.

Later, in a hot bath, with the weeping child huddled against his chest, he wondered what to say to Susan about all of this. It was not the sort of thing she would take lightly, and this did not seem the right moment in their marriage to return to the topic of his incompetence as a father.

Milo would describe the incident in his own way. Perhaps he should just let that account float out there, then he could either ratify, modify, or negate whatever was said. A child's version is always distorted anyway. Or perhaps he should confront the thing bravely and get the rhetoric on his side from the outset.

"That was a lot of fun, wasn't it, Daddy?" Milo said, his small voice barely audible. It was one of those trial sentences that children will occasionally set in motion, unsure of their aerodynamics.

"Yes," he said, firmly. "It was lots of fun."

Chapter 3

NIGHT-FISHING OFF SAVONA

Out with a sunset land breeze,
sailing with a wind
that frills the margins of the grape-deep sea,
that lifts the skirts of water
to expose bare knees of pinkish rock,

the brassy surf reflects my face
as, turning to the edge,
I'm tempted to believe the world is bounded,
that a wall exists beyond which
none may pass unaided.

In the falling sun
I watch a solitary tern implode,

its memory of fire.
All night, to Corsica and back, I light the torches
under firefall stars,
filling my nets with fresh sardines,
libeccio *with oily, green-gold eyes.*
So much life gleaned and gathered in the web

of my confection. Back:
a salt spray fizzing in my eyes, the cobalt sea
becoming russet-tinged, then redder,
calling into port at Portofino, Nervi,
Cogoleto, then Savona, where

the woodfires crackle on the docks
and barrels swell with fish like money,
and that blessed saint, Andrea, welcomes me—
a naughty child who's taken
something that was just not mine.

Chapter 4

Spring takes a campus by surprise, with euphoria like helium filling the lungs of students and faculty alike. The faculty, for their part, find themselves digressing in class, full of extempore riffs on the nature of freedom or the freedom of nature, while students lie in the grass and write poetry for the first time. The air is full of bird song again, and stereo loudspeakers are turned to the windows of ivy-dribbled dorms face-out. Music drifts through trees whose greenness is fragile as the first beard of an adolescent boy.

Geno sat beside the creek that passed through the Barrington campus, his back propped against a big rock. He studied the ice floes that gathered, compacted, split, and melted in slow motion, taking in the cool air and icy sun. Somehow, the sight of melting ice did not comfort him as it had in the past. It reminded him, too painfully, of that terrible moment when Milo slipped, so quietly, into the not-quite-frozen pond.

He pushed the image of Milo out of his mind with a fierce thrust. It was not his habit to dwell on unhappy things. Better to let them fade, slip away, evaporate. Perhaps he was, as Susan argued, afraid to face things. Fine. He was afraid. And he would not face them, not today, when spring was breaking into existence with a primal vengeance, taking over the earth again.

His face banked upward like a flower desperate for light, and Geno could feel the sun's sharp edges on his cheeks and forehead. He wondered how much longer he could stand to live in such a northern climate, since he loved the light. He and Susan sped off to the Caribbean nearly every winter for a couple of weeks, and two years ago he'd taken a semester off without pay in the Dominican Republic, maintaining that he had to do research for the long poem on Columbus he'd been planning for ages. They lived in Santiago, in a little adobe hut on the edge of town, and they had loved it: the succulently moist air, the endlessly blooming flowers, the crisp blue skies and brief tropical showers. Geno had wanted to stay, but that was impossible.

For a start, he and Susan had no money to speak of. Her family was rich, but she would have to wait for any inheritance. And Geno depended totally on his salary. What he wanted, desperately, was a windfall, and he was constantly plotting ways to get it. He had been the only person in America to lose money in real estate in the mid-1980s, largely because the apartment building he'd bought was built over a long-abandoned toxic waste dump. To recover his losses, he'd tried to write a thriller in the form of an epistolary novel about a gay KGB agent who had fallen in love with photographs of a young CIA agent; the Soviet offered to become a stool pigeon in exchange for nude pictures of the American agent. No one offered to publish it. More recently, he'd bought a book about speculating in gold. The world, especially the Third World, was full of it. The Andes, for instance, offered unlimited resources for prospectors, and one could buy penny stocks in mining companies that specialized in finding gold in these remote areas. According to the book, these stocks could appreciate a hundredfold in just a few years. Geno planned to get his hands on some of them as soon as possible, and he'd even thought about approaching his father-in-law for a loan.

The book on his lap, however, was not about gold. It was the *Collected Poems* of Yeats, and it lay open to "Vacillation." Geno had gotten this famous poem by heart, but he loved to see it again in black type, substantial, retrieved from a vague scatter of brainwaves where it was held in aural but not visual memory. The poem is about brief but transcendental chunks of time—moments of ecstasy. Geno loved those chunks, but they had become less and less frequent since his fortieth birthday a few years ago.

Academic life had grown heavy, full of "enemies." Bracketed, provisional enemies. They were the temporary ones necessitated by academic politics, and these days academic life *was* politics. Overt politics—not like in the fifties, when people thought that the Arts and Sciences were pure and unassailable. Now all knowledge was tainted. The tain in the mirror was exposed. Bias was everywhere and acknowledged; or, if it wasn't acknowledged, there was someone trying to pry that acknowledgment loose. "Yes, I am a prejudiced son of a bitch," they wanted you to say. "I am a bigoted, racist homophobe." Geno did not really mind this turn of affairs. Or, at least in the imagined version of himself on display in the mental theater of his own inward actions, he pretended not to mind. He was a privileged white male, after all. He had gone to a fancy college, Dartmouth, and got his D.Phil. from Oxford. He was a professor of English now at Barrington College, and his book on modern poetry, *The Decline of the Modern*, was not only celebrated within the narrow confines of the profession—it was actually *good*.

This afternoon he wanted to think about nothing but William Butler Yeats. Quite often it was his dissatisfaction with another poet—a poetic father—that provoked verses of his own: his own voice combating older voices, commenting on or, best, transfiguring them. He always said in class that there was no such thing as a new poet. There was only the language itself, or Language, which courses through the arid plains of humanity like a great river. Tributaries may form, or swirls and eddies, but it is all one flowing substance. A poet throws himself into the stream, baptizes himself, comes up renewed. He is born again, and each real poem is both a fresh birthright and a fresh epitaph.

Geno took out his little notebook and wrote "a fresh

birthright and a fresh epitaph." His seminar would like that. He sighed now, thinking of his seminar. Was teaching really the best way to spend his time?

The seminar took place in Milton House, which had not—as everyone assumed—been named for John Milton, the poet, but for Milton Mirsky, an alumnus who had made his millions during the Depression in women's underwear. It was the home of the English Department, and it stood in a little glade of its own in what, perhaps a hundred years ago, was a cow pasture. Like most buildings at Barrington, where architectural homogeneity was a goal of sorts, it was a mixture of Tudor and Scotch Baronial, with leaded windows, protruding eaves, and vast granite turrets. "Botton the Weaver meets Sir Walter Scott" is how Geno described it.

The longtime chairman of the department was Billington Baloo, known as Chap. A large, tawny-faced Southerner whose Ph.D. from the University of Virginia was not worn lightly, he referred often to Thomas Jefferson by name and would doubtless have quoted him at length had Jefferson ever said anything quotable. His accent was quietly Southern, though it veered off on formal occasions into what Geno called neo-Oxfordian, with the *r*'s slightly trilled and a high nasal quality squeezing the vowels.

Chap Baloo, however, was the least of Geno's troubles. The department now sported a specialist in African-American literature (who happened, alas, to be white), a neo-Marxist, three Feminists, a Lacanian, and a deconstructionist (who felt rather defensive about the fact that his particular method had been rudely swept aside in the tidal wave of poststructuralism).

While Geno found all of these approaches to literature interesting in different ways, he found their literal embodiments on this campus unhappily narrow-minded. And they did not like him—mostly because he was a poet, and poets were supposed to be dead.

Geno did not like the old New Critics either, the Sons of Tom (as T. S. Eliot was known to his friends), although they at least seemed willing to grant the existence of contemporary literature. Geno's undergraduate teachers at Dartmouth had all been New Critics. They had studied, almost to a man (and there were only men at Dartmouth), at Yale, where the New Criticism reigned. At Oxford, he had met other kinds of critics—even textual critics who spent years on end in library cubicles with actual manuscripts spread out on the table before them, trying to decide which words James Joyce had actually *meant* to delete from, say, *Finnegans Wake*. It never ceased to amaze Geno that people would spend years and years thinking about such things. At the time, he had been thinking, mostly, about sex.

Sex and poetry. In his mind the two were inseparable. At Oxford, he had written love poems to endless women and, yes, to a few men. Everyone, everything, turned him on: the smell of shampoo on a person's brittle blond hair, the way they laced their boots, the flap of undergraduate gowns in the wind, the slight rustle of paper in a study-hushed library. Almost any tiny disturbance provoked erections, most of which were never eased by the kind of contact he craved.

In fact, the sexual revolution of the sixties and early seventies had rushed by Geno but not through him. It seemed that everyone else at Dartmouth or Oxford was getting it except him. Nowadays, he relived the anxieties of that painful decade in a cushy chair opposite his therapist, Dr. Rose Weintraub, who had studied in Austria with a woman who had met Anna Freud.

Geno had entered therapy some weeks after Susan did, realizing that if he didn't he would quickly lose touch with her. The language of therapy was as distinct—though not as difficult—as Greek or Latin; to keep open the lines of communication with Susan, he knew he must learn to "speak" therapy. At first, his skepticism ran deep. All that slop about projection and introversion, about getting in touch with the inner child. (As far as Susan was concerned, it was time for Geno to slay the inner child and get in touch with the inner adult.) But Rose Weintraub had proven wonderfully benign.

Now he lay awake at night talking to Rose, filling her in on the minutest details of his past, trying to sketch in his history with attention to every shade of feeling, every nuance of self-doubt. He said things to her in these midnight rambles that would never get said in actual sessions, where shyness impeded the utterly frictionless transmission of information that would have been ideal. No matter. He had internalized Rose Weintraub, and he could address her freely within the protective confines of his imagination. He now felt listened to, well heard.

"Professor Genovese?" a voice seemed to be calling. "Are you asleep, Professor?" He startled, seeing before him a blaze of strawberry blond hair. It was the lovely and corruptible Lizzy Nash, with whom he had spent some pleasant time discussing Virginia Woolf. He was her senior thesis supervisor, and he listened for hours to her tales of unrequited and, worse, requited love. He loved Lizzy Nash, with her tight sweat pants and baggy shirts, her Patagonia jackets and hippie-style bandanas, her dark leather hiking boots and minty breath.

She liked to climb mountains, and it showed. Her strong legs and lean body had been up and down countless igneous slabs. She had been to the mountains of Nepal on a month-long expedition with the Barrington Mountaineering Club, and she had spent her junior year in Peru, learning Spanish and fantasizing about the heights of Machu Picchu. Nowadays, she carried a slim volume by Pablo Neruda in her knapsack as if to keep her memories alive.

Geno adored her, though the idea of actually having sex with her had never seemed possible. Their relationship was not like that, though they had smoked dope together, once, at his house; they had gotten high as proverbial kites but ceased, in their flight, to talk about anything more intimate than Virginia Woolf's lesbianism. She had slumped back, suggestively, against the couch in his living room, and Geno half wondered if that was meant as a kind of opening for him. But he did nothing.

Geno and Susan did not have an open marriage. Fidelity seemed to Susan the only plausible way to conduct life, and Geno agreed. He often repeated the word in his head. *Fidelity.* Being faithful to each other. Committed. Living with integrity and contained passion. Affirming limits—like the forms of the sonnet or villanelle—which allowed genuine creativity to flower. "I don't doubt that, in an ideal relationship, one would have other lovers," Susan had said to him on one memorable occasion. "But this is not an ideal relationship."

Not ideal . . . What she meant, he assumed, was that no relationship was ideal. Plato's notion of the ideal was just that: pie in the sky. The Ultimate. Which had nothing to do with the way lives are lived. Geno had decided that wisdom was all on the side of affirming that imperfection, going with rather than against it. He would not, like so many of his colleagues, leap from one despairing relationship to another. Divorce, like smoking and drinking cocktails, struck him as a tacky period thing that smacked of suburban country clubs and the fifties.

More to the point, he loved his wife. And he loved James and Milo. He loved everything about his life, except what he sometimes thought of as *the whole fucking thing*. Maybe it was Barrington College that was driving him bananas. Or Chap Baloo, with his tweedy affectations and painfully unfunny witticisms. Or Agnes Wild, the eco-feminist, who had an office across the hall from him in Milton House. The Anguished Agnes, as he called her. Always suffering. Satisfied by nothing.

"Professor Genovese!"

It was Lizzy calling, the lovely Lizzy.

"Yes?"

"You seem to be kind of . . . spaced out."

"Maybe . . . yeah. Or just a little tired. I didn't sleep

too well last night. Kids, you know . . . bellyaches, that sort of thing."

"I wondered if, like, we could meet for a while. I've got a new idea about *To the Lighthouse*. What I realized, you see, is that it's not really about Mrs. Ramsey at all. It's about the artistic process, and about the feminization of that process. The real hero of the book is Lily Briscoe, the painter. In the end, it's Lily who succeeds in getting her work accomplished. Woolf sees herself, I think, in Lily."

"But Lily is a *failed* artist, an artist *manqué*. No? I mean, it takes her a decade to finish one little painting. Even then, there's no suggestion that the painting is finally any good, is there?"

"Good or bad, it doesn't matter. It's work."

"To an artist, it does matter."

"Not to a real artist."

If you weren't so beautiful, thought Geno, *I would slug you*.

"You may have a point," he said, calmly. He had learned that in the consumer atmosphere of contemporary American education, the customer is always right. "Sure. But I've got a seminar coming up."

"It won't take long."

Geno sighed. "Fine."

He had been going to sit in the library by himself and, perhaps, work on his poems for a while before class. Those little parcels of stolen time were, for him, productive.

"You sure you're okay?"

"Yeah, I'm fine," Geno said. "Come on. We can talk over a cup of tea."

After his seminar Geno planned to attend the monthly department meeting, and this was going to be a blistering one. Agnes Wild's proposal for a course on feminist theories of reading was finally being voted on, and she would need Geno's support to get it through. About ten minutes before the meeting was to begin, Chap Baloo buzzed him in his office.

"Y'all stop by for a sec?"

Where did he get off talking like that? This was Vermont, for God's sake. Robert Frost country. Wearily, he threw some papers and books into his briefcase and shuffled down the hall to Baloo's office.

"Close the door, Geno."

Even though he had tenure, the idea that the chairman of the department was going to speak to him in confidence gave him the willies. Either he or somebody else was in trouble. He found himself flipping a mental Rolodex, trying to imagine what it was he'd done wrong. He blushed slightly, recalling his recent cup of tea with Lizzy Nash. The way she had scrunched her face when he asked her questions about her thesis had driven him nuts. He had wanted to reach for her freckled cheeks with both hands, to cup her face in his palms. For a second, he wondered if he had actually done it.

"Sit down, Geno. You look tired."

"I'm all right." He remained standing.

"What I wanted to say, in private, is that I've had word from Dean Botner about your leave application for next year. I'm afraid the committee has turned you down."

"That's impossible, Chap . . ." His sentence stopped in midflight.

"Your project did not strike them as one that the college ought to support. I think I might say, parenthetically, that I told you so. The committee understands *scholarship*. Your proposal sounds to me like . . . creative writing."

"I'm a poet."

"Yes, yes. But you're also a damned fine scholar. And what the college understands—and is willing to support—is scholarship. You see, Geno, it's almost impossible to judge the quality of a poem or fictional sketch. Criticism, on the other hand, is something one can gauge."

"I don't see any difference. The same kinds of criteria apply. Does the thing make sense? Is it coherent? Does it move the reader?"

"Y'all don't expect an essay on Ben Jonson's prosody or some theory of narrativity to *move the reader*? That strikes me as farfetched."

Geno sighed. "I really need that leave."

"You had a leave only two years ago. Where'd you go—Brazil?"

"The Dominican Republic. But—I paid for that leave myself. It's time the college put up something. I haven't had a real sabbatical in six years."

"I warned you at the time that if you took off a term, even if you paid for it yourself, it would count against you when the time came for your regular leave."

Geno could see that arguing his case would get him nowhere at high speed. He sat down, cracked the joints in his fingers, then stood up. "I believe we have a department meeting," he said matter-of-factly.

"Yes. We're late." Baloo gathered his things. "I just thought I'd let you know about this before you actually got the letter from Botner. And I must say, I'm as disappointed as you are."

Baloo waited for Geno in the hall.

"I have to get something from my office," Geno said. "I'll see you up there."

Baloo nodded and walked away.

But Geno, feeling he couldn't face a department meeting in his current mood, went to the library. Alone, in the privacy of his carrel, nobody could touch him.

Chapter 5

The knights of the order of Saint Iago did not like the idea that their women might easily be seen by other men while they pursued their knightly tasks abroad. So they built a purple limestone fortress called the Convento dos Santos on a steep cliffside in Lisbon. The Convento had long ago ceased to be a preserve of frustrated military wives and was now full of frustrated young women from important Portuguese families. Among these was Dona Felipa, the black-haired daughter of Dom Bartholomew Perestrella and his third wife, Dona Isabel Moniz.

Dona Felipa was getting on a bit. At twenty-five, she was still unmarried, and her parents had begun to wonder if their little scheme would ever pay off. A trusted family counselor had suggested the Convento as the appropriate place for a girl of Dona Felipa's status in society to find the right sort of husband, but it had been several years now since she had moved in and nothing had happened. The theory was that sooner or later a young nobleman or merchant prince would meet her at one of the Convento's well-known Friday masses or the Sunday afternoon tea parties. Failing to find a husband, she could eventually take orders, and thus swell the ranks of the Little Sisters of Mercy.

It was late in the spring of 1478 when Christopher Columbus caught Dona Felipa's eye in the small chapel adjacent to the Convento's hillside garden. The early evening light in the chapel was only enhanced by the altar's dozen blazing candles; the old priest, Father Tomaso, seemed particularly inspired this afternoon as he chirped away in his own incomprehensible Vulgate. His voice echoed off the damp white walls and vaulted ceiling.

Dona Felipa, who had lately grown desperate to leave the Convento, winked at Columbus, who had managed to sit in the pew beside her despite the machinations of Sister Maria Nuncia, an elderly nun who considered Dona Felipa her special charge. Somewhat taken aback by the unexpected wink, Columbus was sufficiently composed to whisper, "Wait for me in the garden."

Sister Maria Nuncia scowled at them both. She was kneeling directly behind them, and nothing escaped her. For three and a half years now, she had been growing closer and closer to Dona Felipa. As her young friend's chances of marriage dwindled, she had become happier and happier. Dona Felipa, she believed, would make an excellent nun. She had more than once observed to Mother Superior that her charge had a particular talent for devotion, that she loved God with a passion rare in these brutal, secular days. As Father Tomaso often said, these were surely the last days of the world. Famine, pestilence, crime, political intrigue and corruption in high places, sexual infidelity: what further signs did one require?

This was no time for a young woman with a religious calling to think about marriage, nevertheless Dona Felipa was determined to find a mate, and here was an unusual young man. A Genoese cartographer who was said to belong to a decent family, he had traveled far and wide by sea. Stories of his adventuring had circulated in the best circles of Lisbon, and some of the wealthiest families considered him an honored guest at their table. Furthermore, he was a devout man who attended daily mass with unfailing regularity. Quite recently, he had begun to attend these Friday afternoon chapel services at the Convento, and no one in the chapel was unaware of his presence. Until today, however, his attention had never dwelled for long on any of the young women whose eyes furtively searched for a connecting gaze.

Columbus wore a green baize cape and high boots of fine black leather. His glorious long hair was red as a foxtail, and it rested neatly on a stiff collar. He had the flinty eyes of a seaman: bright, piercing eyes that could seem green or gray or blue, depending on the light. His tall bearing and powerful shoulders suggested that here was a man who could not be restrained. With the world all before him, he would sail its teeming waters with confidence and ease. That he was obviously not a man of great wealth did not matter especially. Not to Dona Felipa. An unmarried woman of twenty-five cannot be picky.

When the last prayers were said, Columbus walked outside into the garden ahead of her, dawdling beside a large marble sculpture of Our Blessed Lord. He clasped his hands behind his back and fixed his gaze on the sea, which had turned violet in the April dusk.

Dona Felipa passed him slowly, making sure to catch his eye. He followed her along a gravel path into a grove of tall cypress trees. The sun's red ball was fixed in the sights of the narrow path; below them—at the point where the River Tagus bled into the sea—the water seemed to boil.

"I am Christopher Columbus," he said, looking over her shoulder at Sister Maria Nuncia, who quickly stepped behind a large bush.

Dona Felipa introduced herself politely, accentuating the double-barreled load of her inheritance: Perestrella and Moniz. Her father, the son of a noble family of Piacenza, was born in Lisbon; he had some years before been part of a colonizing expedition to the islands of Porto Santo and Madeira, and he had been rewarded by the king with the hereditary governorship of Porto Santo, where he had lived until recently in a quaint seaside house. His wife, Dona Isabel, was the daughter of Gil Ayres Moniz, who belonged to one of the oldest families of the Algarve. Though a relative newcomer to Lisbon, Columbus knew exactly what these surnames signified.

"I've met your father," Columbus said. "He's a splendid man."

She let her eyes drift up from the path to meet his own.

"He is well respected throughout Portugal," he continued. "A remarkable man."

The point had already been made, and she brushed it aside; her father's greatness did not, just now, occupy her thoughts. "Do you come here often?"

She knew perfectly well how often he had been to the Convento for mass, but this was no time for quibbling. She had to keep the conversation in play.

"No, but I shall certainly come in the future, if I can expect to meet you here afterward," he said, reaching out for her hands. It was a bold gesture for a young man in his position. But these were bold times.

"I shall expect you," Dona Felipa said. There was no mistaking her smile, however slight.

They turned their gazes to the west now, drawn by the fiery water. Overhead, a gannet hovered beneath a pearly cloudbank, waiting for a fish to expose itself in the curling surf beneath the cliff. Wiping her eyes, Sister Maria Nuncia crossed herself three times; kneeling in the dark grass, she offered up to God her prayers for the dead.

Chapter 6

Susan worked on her own projects—book reviews, stories, writing in her diary—in the morning soon after James and Milo were bundled into their down-inflated ski jackets and led, often without cheer, to the yellow schoolbus that arrived at 7:40. Geno complained about the way she turned every boarding of the bus into an arctic expedition. "Just shoo them out the goddamn door," he said. "You don't have to lead them. They're not babies."

He seemed to miss the main point: they *weren't* babies. That meant she wanted to baby them all the more, to possess them just a little longer.

Their growing up threw her into despair, though she understood the potential damage of trying to hang on to them too greedily. Her mother had tried to hang on to her, with the result that she now abhorred all transitions. The thought of any child leaving home for college left her in a heap on the floor. She still recalled as if it were yesterday the traumatic day in 1970 when she left for Wellesley from Madison, Wisconsin, taking a cross-country Greyhound. Her father took her to the station in his long white Lincoln. He had tried to convince her to fly, but she had remained firm. She would take the bus. She knew she needed the slow eastward unfolding of the country to smooth her way. She needed the hours and hours of slumping in a fuzzy seat, the bottles of warm Coke, the endless drowsing over *Anna Karenina*. That Greyhound was a chrysalis of sorts, a hard-shelled silver pupa that protected her during the painful transition into independence.

Hers was not an easy family to separate from. Ted Worthington was a strong presence in her life, an American archetype. He had had everything an American mother could have wanted in a son: height, a handsome physique, clear blue eyes, and more energy than was healthy for one man. He was affable, smart (though not intellectual), and sufficiently entrepreneurial to ensure the continued existence of the small family company that he inherited from his father.

The company manufactured a nondescript meat product called Carnex, which looked and smelled a bit like dogfood but had been a breakfast favorite in the Midwest ever since the Depression, when "real" meat became too expensive for many family budgets. The Worthingtons had been making Carnex in Madison since 1929, and Ted was only the second man ever to run the company—the successor to his father, who had started the company from scratch with a loan of two thousand dollars from a benevolent aunt in New Hampshire. Now Susan's elder brother, Charles, was in line for the big job, though rumor had it he wasn't quite right.

"It's drugs, I know it," Susan's mother had said to her on the phone one Sunday afternoon, her traditional time for calling her daughter. "He's acting so . . . unconventional. Your father is beside himself."

Susan had not seen her brother in a year, but she could believe he was acting "unconventional." His years at Choate and Princeton had never sat well. At the Harvard Divinity School he had seemed on the brink of self-discovery and become a practicing Buddhist. But he dropped out, was drafted, and did a tour of duty in Vietnam before returning to Madison, where he married a local girl and became his father's V.P. in charge of everything except money.

Susan liked talking about her family history, and she had been through the whole thing many times with her shrink, Sarah Dillinger. A fiftyish woman with snow-white hair pulled into a bun at the back of her head, Sarah wore brown high-top shoes that tied with black laces, stiff denim shirts that alluded to her radical youth in the Village, and long flowery skirts that aspired to the condition of William Morris wallpaper. She conducted her practice in a light-drenched office that had been added on to her white clapboard farmhouse near Barrington and was known, universally, as the doyenne of therapists in Leicester County.

The initial five sessions with Sarah had been extended indefinitely, and now Susan met with her every Friday afternoon. The weekly sessions were a time of stocktaking and intimate self-revelation, a time when she could let the events of the week settle into an identifiable pattern.

Susan had insisted on meeting in the afternoon in order to keep the morning free for writing. She had gone back to writing after a period of years devoted almost exclusively to small children, and it felt good. She had always known that she could write. Indeed, the *Atlantic* had taken a story of hers in college. And some of the best literary magazines in the country had published her work in the past decade. But a first book of stories still seemed a long way off: mostly because Susan was her own sternest critic, and she had ruthlessly discarded stories that did not strike her as "true." The story that appeared in the *Atlantic*, for instance, she now referred to as "a piece of post-adolescent maundering." Not even Geno's insistence that it was a fine story reassured her.

"You're biased," she would say. "And you're not critical enough."

"I know what I like," he'd respond, partly just to tease.

Susan distrusted people who claimed to know what they liked. They formed a discrete fraternity of critical boobs, "appreciators," as she called them. And their arrogance upset her. If they couldn't formulate a logical response in clear language, they should keep their opinions to themselves.

On the afternoon of the day that Geno almost drowned their youngest son, Susan had an uncomfortable session with Sarah Dillinger.

The session began in the usual way, in silence. For five minutes or so (that always felt like twenty or thirty) she sat tight-lipped on the overstuffed couch with soft pillows holding her up as if on a paisley cloud. Spider plants drooped from hanging pots beside her head, but she focused on a handsome delphinium with blue irregular-shaped flowers that sat on a small cherry table by the window. One of the things she admired about Sarah was her flowers. In or out of season, she managed to lay her hands on the exact flowers to encourage a state of spiritual elevation in her clients.

Susan finally broke the ice. "I don't understand him anymore. He's gotten so inward, kind of . . . edgy. He's no longer trustworthy. He almost killed Milo this morning out on the pond, ice-skating. It's like he isn't even thinking. He's in some kind of daze."

Sarah sat in a big armchair with her legs crossed and her hands folded, and her gaze did not waver. She was paid to make sure that it didn't.

"Geno is a good man, and he loves me. I never doubt that, not for a moment. But sometimes it seems as if love isn't enough." She rubbed her hands together slowly. "I don't mean that, probably. But I wanted to say it."

"It doesn't matter whether you meant it or not. I'm not judging you," Sarah said.

"I know. I just . . . I don't know. I don't understand. I feel empty sometimes. Maybe I should just go out and get a teaching job or something. All I seem to do is make notes for stories that don't get written. The other day I started a short story, but it just stopped after a couple of sentences."

Sarah did not say anything, though Susan looked to her hopefully.

"Geno seems obsessed about this leave," she said, finally. "We're talking about going somewhere exotic . . . maybe the Dominican Republic, for a couple of months. We liked it there a lot the last time." She paused. "He's working on this poem about Columbus—a long poem." She looked out the window, thinking. "He's obsessed with politics these days—God, it gets into everything. But he's confused about that, too. I'm starting to think that politics is an excuse. An excuse for not thinking, for not dealing with things."

"You've spent a lot of time here today talking about Geno," Sarah offered. "Is there something about yourself that you're avoiding?"

Susan bit her lip, twisting her mouth to one side. "I don't know."

"Is Geno still in therapy?"

She nodded. "He really likes Rose Weintraub."

Sarah Dillinger suppressed a shiver. Rose Weintraub was not her favorite person.

"I can't imagine what they talk about," Susan continued.

"If you want to know, you should ask him. There's nothing wrong with asking direct questions." She paused. "Does he ask you anything directly?"

Susan could feel the tears welling up. No. He did not ask her anything directly. Perhaps he used to, but she couldn't recall.

"You're upset, Susan."

"I'm all right."

"You are," Sarah said. "You're fine."

Susan smiled a little, having heard all of this before. She'd heard almost everything Sarah said to her before, but that wasn't the point. The point of therapy was the context of acceptance, the recovery of silence, the opportunity to repeat oneself endlessly if need be, always in search of the exact formulation, a language adequate to the emotions felt. It amazed Susan how tinny and hollow her speech sounded, secondhand and threadbare. Her goal in therapy, as in writing, was to utter a few simple and true sentences. The words would start inside of her, and they would emerge and seem as real to her, as firm and boundary-making, as a dry stone wall.

Susan left this session, however, feeling less than satisfied. And this was unusual, since she commonly felt a sense of release as she pulled down the long dirt driveway from Sarah's farmhouse, a sense of having picked her way toward a clearing in the woods. Perhaps she hadn't been open enough with Sarah? Or perhaps the incident with Milo had simply been too upsetting?

Geno's car was parked in front of the garage, and Susan wondered why he was home so early. Department meetings rarely ended on time, and a baby-sitter had been hired for the late afternoon and evening; Geno was supposed to go directly to Enid Willers' house after the meeting for a dinner party, and she had planned to meet him there.

She found him staring out the front window with his arms crossed.

"You skipped the meeting?"

"Fuck the meeting," he said.

Susan hated it when he talked like that. It set such a bad

example for the children, and they already had a problem with James about swearing. He had called his teacher "a ball buster" to her face only a week before, and she had called to complain.

"You were turned down for the leave, huh?"

Geno looked at her with the kind of fawnlike gaze one more usually sees on adolescent boys. "How did you know that?"

"I'm a good guesser."

Geno nodded grimly.

"So you'll apply for another leave next year. No big deal."

No big deal for you, thought Geno. What he couldn't easily explain was that he felt burned out, as a teacher. As a writer, he felt the hideous pressure of unwritten work building up inside of him. Images, fragments of language, voices: they came to him in the shower, on the way into work, while he was skiing through the woods with James, sometimes in the middle of the night or even when he and Susan were making love. His notebooks had been filling up with undigested and unrevised work for too long. What he needed now was time. Time to prune the tangling vines that had been growing wildly in his head for the past half a dozen years or so. Time to catch the voices, to let the fragments gather into whole sentences, whole paragraphs and pages.

"Enid likes her guests to arrive on time, darling," Susan said, rushing off to the den to separate James and Milo, who were fighting over a TV show.

"What's going on, guy?" she said, seeing that James was sitting on Milo, who had the channel changer stuffed into his underpants. He had his hands on his younger brother's neck.

"He's got the changer!"

"I want to see 'Sesame Street'!"

" 'Sesame Street' is for babies."

Susan sat calmly on the sofa. "Come here, guys. One on either side of me."

James let go of Milo's neck and got up. Milo, whimpering, followed. They sat on either side of their mother, and she hugged them close to her.

"Now, that's better," she said. "Haven't we talked about this business of threatening each other before?"

The boys grunted.

"What did I say, James?"

" 'Don't beat on him.' "

"That's right. Don't do it."

"But he wouldn't give me the changer."

"Is that true, Milo?"

"Yes."

"So what are we going to do about it?" Susan said.

Milo shrugged.

"I'll give you my Nolan Ryan baseball card," James said, "if you let me watch anything I want after school for three weeks."

Milo brightened. "I can have Nolan Ryan? Okay."

"There," said Susan. "That's the way to talk. Isn't that better?"

James reluctantly shook his head, taking the channel changer, flipping on "Transformers."

Geno listened at the door, marveling at the way Susan could deal with them: so calmly, firmly. God, why was he such a fool when it came to James and Milo? As he walked upstairs for a shower, he kept thinking about the way his kids had become so mesmerized by TV. Could it be anything but damaging to a young and developing psyche? If only they could live somewhere—on some planet in outer space, if necessary—where TV was still not known. It sickened him to see James or Milo sitting there with the switcher in hand, channel surfing (though he neglected to remember that he'd dumped them in front of the yawning screen since they were old enough to sit still unattended).

So much noise was accumulating in his head now that he needed the ten minutes of steamy escape provided by a hot shower. Stripped, standing in the white-tiled stall, he turned the water as hot as he could stand it. The stream drilled his face, foamed in his hair. Then he turned and let the needles numb his spine and create a large oval patch of tomato-red skin from his neck to his lower back. Standing erect in the shower, he felt renewed: an American Adam, clean and free of the petty nonsense of the academy, with its medieval hierarchies and covert gradations, this invisible ladder that he—and everyone around him—seemed to be climbing. Up, up, up. Into oblivion.

The road to Enid Willers' house was paved with good intentions. Both Geno and Susan liked her, though she was not easy to like. A divorced woman of sixty, she had pre-dated the feminist revolution by two decades. Ascending the academic ladder had been, for her, a particularly grueling and lonely process. The rungs were slippery, and she had fallen off several times, only to hoist herself to her feet with considerable courage to begin again.

Barrington College had appointed Enid nearly a decade before to its most prestigious chair, rescuing her from the limbo of a big Western state university. For too many years she'd been condemned to endless sections of Freshman Comp, where the rules of grammar and syntax had crowded her imagination, blocking out nearly everything else. When her conventional marriage disintegrated in the conventional ways—her husband, a gynecologist, married a young nurse who shared his love of Monday-night football—she took matters into her own hands. Chaining herself to a desk in the university library, she produced a massive two-volume biography of Emily Dickinson. Every known scrap of information and some tidbits of new stuff were crammed into those volumes, which the *New York Review of Books* described as "exhaustive if not exhausting."

Enid was an old-style feminist of the sort who believed that the only way for a woman to succeed in a man's world was to be Manlier-than-Thou. She drank bourbon on the rocks, cursed like a Boy Scout, and had little sympathy for the plight of her younger female colleagues. As a result, she was much courted and much feared.

The men usually found her acceptable if not exactly a gas. She flattered them broadly, having noticed many decades ago the uses of overpraise. Even Geno found himself mildly titillated by her response to his poems. Indeed, she made a point of teaching Geno's first (and only) book of poems in one of her classes almost every year. And she always invited him to the class as a celebrity guest, where he would merrily submit to a fifty-minute hour of questions and comments. "When did you first begin to think of yourself as a writer, Professor Genovese?" "Where do your poems come from?" "How do you know when a poem is finished?" "What are you working on now?"

Recollections of a recent session with one of her classes absorbed Geno as he drove beside his silent wife along the winding road to Enid's house, a huge contemporary structure made of glass and stone that perched on an isolated hilltop some half a dozen miles outside of Barrington. The more he thought about Enid, the more highly he thought of her as a teacher. She thought of her classes as an art form, and she controlled every phase of each with the meticulousness of Joyce or Flaubert, making sure that no gesture was wasted. By the time the bell was struck, every loose end had been neatly folded into the larger whole. Geno's classes were by comparison picaresque; they tended to veer away from the main stream of argument, to live in little pools and eddies.

This was the mud season in Vermont, a time when everything went soft underfoot, and he was tempted to throw his Jeep—a gorgeous red Cherokee Limited that he'd bought only a few months before—into four-wheel drive. More than once he had been asked to come and help dig Enid out of a snowstorm, so he was familiar with the particular perils of her driveway. Loose gravel sputtered under his tires.

"Your driving is making me sick," Susan said. "Can't you stay in low or something?"

"I am in low, damn it."

"Then put it in high."

Geno grunted. His driving was notorious among his friends. Susan knew that one day he would wrap himself around a tree. She only prayed that he did it without the children in the car—or her.

Enid greeted them at the door in a long black skirt with an elastic waist. A thick cashmere shawl had been wrapped around her shoulders to remind her guests that her house was *cold*. Like many Vermonters, she was ecologically minded, and she kept the thermostat at a level several degrees below what anyone, even a menopausal woman, could find comfortable.

"This house is always so cozy," Geno said.

Susan looked at him starkly. Just how un-cozy Enid's house was struck her as she stood in the windy front hall. The bare oak floors stretched in every direction unrelieved by rugs of any kind. Postmodern furniture was positioned at far intervals around the living room. The walls were painted a sickly lime-green and were devoid of ornament, except for the main wall in the living room, where a mobile of metal strips, leather, and denim patches hung above the couch, which resembled a prehistoric animal stretched out for a nap. The curtains were not "real" but *trompe l'oeil*, painted on the lime-green walls by Enid's daughter, Sylvia, who lived in New York and made a living by painting elegant imitation curtains on the walls of expensive apartments.

Geno and Susan were late, as usual, and the other guests were all assembled in the living room with drinks in hand. Fernando Nachez, who chaired the program in Latin American Studies, was holding forth in one corner; he had recently published a book on the *conquistadores*, and he was full of his own conquests. His wife, Mina, was a tall black woman from the Bahamas; she stood languidly beside him in a colorful striped sweater and jeans. Agnes Wild sat uneasily on a couch beside her friend, Jane Burl—a wide-hipped social worker who had been her companion until recently, when some sort of falling-out occurred. They seemed painfully absorbed in each other at the moment, ignoring everyone else in the room.

At the far end of the same couch was Simon Nest, who was flipping indolently through a coffee table book about the Andes. Nest was English, a Chaucerian by training, and he had been teaching at Barrington since the late sixties; he considered himself an expert on everything from Wagner to Wittgenstein: one of those apolitical British know-it-alls who began to haunt American campuses when, in the midseventies, it became apparent that the United Kingdom had gone into perpetual Decline and Fall.

"She's done it again," Geno whispered to Susan.

They both marveled at Enid's ability to create strange bedfellows. Her dinner parties were among the cultural oddities of the Barrington social scene and, as a result, much envied.

Enid poured a stiff bourbon for Geno, who normally drank white wine. "It won't hurt you," she said. "I heard about your leave." Her white hair stood on her head like a mound of snow, and her pink eyeglasses caught the light and glittered.

"Or my non-leave," he said.

Susan served herself a glass of white Bordeaux, filling half the glass with seltzer. She realized at once that she, not Geno, would be driving home. It annoyed her to see him taking that drink from Enid, since they had talked about this little problem of his before. He was basically a nondrinker, but Enid seemed to enjoy getting him juiced. She liked to get everyone juiced, in fact. Her favorite party was one that whorled out of control, with her sitting at the center like a storm's motionless eye.

The before-dinner conversation centered on Nachez's new book, which opened with a dramatic account of Francisco Pizarro's conquest of the Incas.

"I especially enjoyed the chapter about Pizarro," Enid said.

"He was an incredible man," Nachez responded in thickly accented English. "I could have written a whole book about him."

"What I've never understood," she went on, "is how he managed to conquer—what was it, a nation of twenty million people?—with only two hundred soldiers."

"Plus a few slaves and collaborating Incas," Simon Nest added. "If memory serves me well."

"You'd wonder, wouldn't you, how such a thing was possible?" Enid said.

"The situation has got to be more complex than it sounds," Agnes Wild said, clearing her throat. "These statistics always annoy me. They explain nothing about what really happened." She paused. "History is written by the winners, of course. And so it's slanted."

Jane Burl flipped a wing of hair that had fallen into her

eyes to one side. She was too distracted by whatever was going on between herself and Agnes to focus on the Incas.

Nachez loved being on his own turf and quickly rushed in with a response. "Agnes is right, in fact. The story has its interesting complications. One of them is that the Spaniards had merely to snatch the emperor. Once they got him, the whole society just . . . crumbled." He made a curious sweeping gesture with one hand. "It was very like the Soviet Union under Stalin—a perfectly vertical and totalitarian society. If you get the head man, it's all over."

Nest was thrilled. "The Incas simply stood there and let Pizarro's men kill them. They barely lifted a finger in their own self-defense."

"You're a veritable polymath," Agnes said, and Jane Burl laughed hard.

Nachez grinned a gap-toothed grin. "One of the problems with historical discussions nowadays is that nobody believes that such a thing as *truth* exists. Frankly, I'm sick of all this relativism."

Agnes glared at Nachez. The look in her eye said, *I will nail you tonight.*

"It's a question of interpretation, isn't it?" Enid put in, rather tentatively. As host, she understood that the suffering must be spread evenly around the room.

Susan said, "Nobody is questioning whether or not truth exists. It's how one gets at the truth, isn't it? Every perspective is necessarily different from other perspective, so the truth lies somewhere in the middle."

Geno nodded gratefully to Susan. He was smoldering inside, and it was not just the whisky. He hated it when a doltish fact-mongerer like Nachez got on his high horse and began to ride. For the moment, however, he slumped into the couch.

Enid had employed one of her students to help with the dinner party, a fragile-looking sophomore with long blond hair and high cheekbones; she called them all to the table in a fluting voice. Little name cards directed everyone to his or her proper seat; they all waited in deferential silence as plates of pasta in a foamy pesto sauce were set in front of them. Simon Nest, self-appointed *arbiter bibendi*, poured everyone a glass of towel-dry Frascati. "I hope you all like white wine," he said. "That's all there is."

Nest was what they used to call a "walker," one of those unattached men frequently called upon to make the boy-girl count at dinner parties come out even. He sat in the host's chair at the head of the table, while Enid sat opposite him at the other end. His forte was fanning conversational coals to a fresh flame when they threatened to die out, and tonight was no exception. "We should take care not to underestimate the Incas," he said. "They specialized in human sacrifices, of course. But so did the Aztecs, and the Aztecs were far worse—bloody barbarous, the lot of them. What one admires about the Incas was their organizing ability. In no time at all they organized much of a vast continent. It was very sophisticated, even by our standards."

"You're a Stalinist at heart, aren't you, my dear?" Enid said, twinkling.

"Unlike many of my colleagues, I see nothing wrong with

authority," he said. He cast a vague look of accusation at Geno, who bit his lip.

"Nest, you amaze me," Nachez said, his mouth full of pasta. "How is it that you're so familiar with the Incas? That's not your field at all."

"Your book, dear chap," he said. "I have read your book."

Geno found his hand reaching again and again for the Frascati, and the faces around him soon began to blur; the conversation sounded progressively more absurd to him as the alchohol content of his blood rose. Nest blathered on about the Incas, and Nachez weighed in expertly on the conquest of the Indies. And the whole thing seemed positively silly.

Now something decadently French involving lots of white onions, scallops, and tips of asparagus appeared in front of each guest. Geno, in a blur, dug in, taking several forkfuls of asparagus—one of his favorite tastes. He was beginning to feel a tinge of mellowness when Nachez turned on him unexpectedly, his eyes sparking.

"Cat got your tongue, Genovese?" He said his name in the Italian way, pronouncing the final vowel. "I've heard through the grapevine that you're writing something about Columbus. Is this true?"

"Some poems," Geno said, trying to focus.

"How do you view Columbus, then?" Simon Nest asked, sensing that the conversation had begun to elude him.

Geno looked at him blankly.

"Surely there are two sides on this question," Nest said.

"Surely a dozen sides," Geno said, wondering why it was that so many Brits began their sentences with *surely*.

Susan cut in. "He's basically anti-Columbus," she said, and blushed slightly, sensing that Geno wanted to answer for himself.

"I'd say it's an absurd question. One admires the man's balls, I suppose. But he was a genocidal maniac. The phrase comes from Noam Chomsky, I think, but it's accurate. I mean, he exterminated a million or more Tainos within a dozen years."

Nest shook his jowels. "Fustian man, the imperial quest, and so forth," he said.

Everyone politely ignored him.

But Nachez was not so calm. "You're off the mark, Genovese. First, you underestimate what it took to sail into the dark like that, and to get the Spanish crown *behind* such a project. And this genocidal thing is just silly. The Taino Indians died of diseases, mostly. You aren't going to blame Columbus for diseases, I hope?"

"Some of them died of diseases—*Western* diseases. But a lot more were murdered. Or died in slavery. A fair number actually committed suicide rather than be subjected to Spanish rule."

Agnes Wild smiled broadly. She was relieved to have Geno speaking up for what she considered her side. Enid, too, seemed happier. Geno's awakening would save the evening from what might have been an ordinary time.

Geno's eyes seemed to catch fire but his tongue grew thick. "If you take Hispaniola alone, it's pretty obvious that a pattern was established—a pattern of intervention and domination, of destruction. We're sitting here, right now, on the graves of Indians. America is a country built on genocide."

"I say, that's a bit . . . melodramatic," Nest said.

"Yes, but it's also true. Some of the early chroniclers—Las Casas and the others—report that the Spaniards actually crucified the Tainos on rows of thirteen crosses, which signified Christ and the twelve apostles. These guys were fucking monsters."

Nest appeared mildly shaken. "This may well be true, but you can't stop history, you know."

"I wonder if Geno really cares about history anyway," Nachez said. "Poets don't, do they? They make the world up—any way they like."

"Don't be an ass," Geno said. He noticed that Agnes, who must have been a little angry with him for skipping the department meeting, smiled at him benignly. He had redeemed himself by taking on the Forces of Darkness.

Nachez leaned menacingly across the table. His hands curled into tight little fists.

A splinter of annoyance shot through Enid. "Oh Fernando, please. Geno didn't mean anything."

"I did, too," Geno said. "An ass is an ass."

Nachez rose.

Geno tried to grin him down. "Asshole," he said.

Susan blanched. She envisioned two wolves of the steppes circling each other. The spirit primeval seemed to reign.

"Sit down, Fernando," Enid said. Looking at Geno now, she added, "This is ridiculous. We're adults . . . remember that . . . adults!"

Geno drew himself up conspicuously to his full six feet and said, "I must pee. You will all please excuse me."

In the bathroom, blessedly alone, he pissed into the pink toilet bowl and looked up through a clear skylight at the bright shower of a billion stars. The aromatic smell of pee infused with asparagus filled him with awe. Such an obvious and physical sign of cause-and-effect and this reminded Geno that he was simply one creature among many, part of the vast and delicately interlocking animal kingdom. This kingdom was full of predatory beasts like Nachez and Columbus, full of victims like the Taino Indians. Full of excited onlookers who chirped from the high limbs of trees and relished the kill, full of creatures in heat, desperate to mate, and full of creatures ready to give birth and to mother. The whole of this fit together in a kaleidoscopic whirl of desire that became, in the end, a kind of destiny. It was something Geno only faintly understood, but he loved it, the majesty and anonymity and cruel inevitability of it all.

"You really fucked up," Susan said, more to the ceiling than to Geno.

The lights were out in their bedroom, but neither of them could sleep.

"I did?"

"You're becoming a real fool. Do you mind if I tell you that?"

"I'd prefer if you told me at breakfast. I was hoping to sleep tonight."

"Is there any time when you wouldn't prefer that I let it go?"

"Get off my case, Sue."

"You embarrassed me tonight."

"But Nachez is ridiculous. And he fucks around with his students. I've heard that from more than one source."

"What's that got to do with anything?"

"I despise that man."

"You never hated anyone in the old days."

"The old days?"

"You've become a babbling idiot. I can't believe you picked such a stupid fight. What's the matter with you?"

"I happen to believe in certain things."

"You may hold some abstract notions—we all do. But you're just using politics. That anger I hear. Where's it coming from?"

"You're the one that's angry. Listen to you."

"I should be angry. You almost drowned our son. I'm scared, Geno. I'm really scared."

"Scared of what?"

"Of us."

"Us?"

"Us."

Chapter 7

Columbus waited in the antechamber for three hours, feeling the tight scratch of his collar. His boots smelled of beeswax and camphor, and his pants felt tight. He listened to the remote grumble of his stomach, which flipped inside him like a fresh-caught fish. Grinning in a mirror, he saw that his teeth were brown as figs and licked them to make them sparkle. The king, Dom João, was known as a vain man, and Columbus understood enough about vain men to know that they took into account the appearance of others.

The interview had been scheduled for nine. It was now a little past noon. Was His Majesty playing a little game here, trying to wear down his nerves? There was obviously some real interest in the proposal. Why else would such an interview have been granted? Columbus thought of another Italian explorer, Antonio da Noli, who had already made a number of glorious discoveries in the name of the Portuguese king. If Antonio da

Noli, a mountebank and fraud, could win Dom João's support, surely *he* could! It amused him to think of da Noli's self-important careering through the elegant salons of Lisbon. That's an Italian for you, he thought.

"Columbus!" a man called from the doorway.

The Genoese straightened his spine.

"His Majesty will see you now." The man bowed to the self-confident suitor, who stepped forward proudly.

Dom João sat on a burnished throne upon a slightly raised platform above the cool marble floor. Aides-de-camp, ladies-in-waiting, advisors, courtiers, harlequins, assorted clerics and hangers-on surrounded the young king. Having taken instructions in protocol from a friend of his mother-in-law, Columbus knew exactly how to comport himself in the royal presence.

"I am a busy man," Dom João said to Columbus, waving him to his feet. "But I suppose We should listen to what you have to say."

Columbus cleared his throat. "I think that what I have to say may possibly be of great interest to Your Majesty," he said, looking directly at the king.

"Speak, dear fellow. We are all ears."

"You have read my proposal?"

"Indeed."

Columbus felt mildly at sea now, the wind breaking across his bowsprit. It struck him that the air in Dom João's ornately gilded chamber was curiously salty. "You have read Marco Polo, Your Highness?"

"We have."

"Then Your Majesty will be aware of Cypango, the great

island kingdom that lies northeast of the Kingdom of Cathay, which is ruled by His Majesty the Grand Khan, which means 'King of Kings.' As you will doubtless have heard, even the rooftops of the most ordinary homes in Cypango and Cathay are made of gold. There are gems galore, lovely silks, and every kind of spice. One can hardly imagine the wealth of these faraway lands. The treasure is ours for the taking, Your Excellency."

"Assuming, of course, that one could find Cypango and Cathay. Also assuming that, once found, the natives were generous with their lovely goods. Neither assumption strikes Us as profoundly self-evident."

"The world, Your Majesty, is infinitely smaller than people imagine. It is, as the most learned astonomers inform us, a round object, so it seems perfectly within the bounds of logic to claim that by sailing the Western Ocean one can reach the East—probably much more easily, in fact, than by sailing directly East."

"East is East, and West is West."

"Yes, but surely they are connected? That is, one may cross from one bit to the other bit?"

"A solid point, *signore*. We have no doubt about the roundness of the planet. But We do wonder if there is not a vast and treacherous ocean between here and there. No one has yet, to my knowledge, discovered the limits of the Western Ocean."

Columbus raised his thin forefinger in the air. "I remind you, Your Highness, that the globe is composed of six parts land to one part water, as it is written in the Book of Esdras.

'Six parts hast Thou dried up,' it says. If this be so, and I do not doubt the Word of the Lord, then we have little to fear of the Western Ocean. I suspect that in two or three weeks of steady sailing we should find ourselves happily in Cypango."

"It pleases me that you are familiar with the Word of the Lord."

"I have prayed about this expedition for many years. And the Lord has spoken to me. He has prepared me through decades of careful apprenticeship at sea for this noble expedition."

"Noble?"

"I do not regard this as a mere commercial venture."

"Thank goodness," the king said, catching the eye of one of his chief advisors. A slight rustle of snickers could be heard behind the throne.

"I wish to carry the name of Jesus to the farthest ends of the earth. Why else would there be so much earth? Why the preponderance of land over water, if God did not intend us to use it for His ends?"

"You are eloquent, Christopher Columbus."

"Thank you, sir."

"Indeed, your missionary zeal awakens a kindred spirit within Us. But We notice from your proposal that you are asking for quite a lot in the way of material support: three caravels loaded down with hawk's bells, brass basins, glass beads, red caps, and large rolls of many-colored cloth. You also wish to be knighted, to be appointed an 'Admiral of the Ocean Sea,' and to be named Perpetual Viceroy and Governor of all islands and mainlands discovered by you and your men.

You also expect to retain a tenth of all wealth discovered in those Eastern lands and to retain a percentage of all freight passing between here and there in perpetuity, with these privileges bequeathable to your heirs. That is quite a lot for a missionary of God to ask."

"I am not, Your Majesty, a cleric by profession."

"So We gather."

"But I am sincere. My faith in God has never wavered, and I have understood my mission clearly. One does not embark lightly on such an expedition. Let me only say that the material advantages that would accrue to Your Majesty from such a small outlay of provisions ought to prove considerable. Your glorious name would be sung in the farthest regions of the world."

"We are touched."

Columbus understood that he had been mocked, however slightly. But he was clever enough to realize that it was not to his best advantage to acknowledge anything but utter sincerity. He fixed his eyes, resolutely, on the king's sapphire-studded shoe buckles.

The king continued: "We shall appoint a commission to study the feasibility of the project overall and your proposal in particular."

Columbus bowed respectfully and, sensing an end to the audience, withdrew.

Chapter 8

Susan met Andrew Ridgeway at the A&P. He was standing at the meat counter—a tall, ridiculously thin man in his late twenties. His youth reminded her that hers was dwindling.

Not that she was old. At forty, she was still youngish. Seen from a distance, or in poor light, she could easily be mistaken for a college girl, especially in winter, when she wore a bulky down jacket and a furry hat that left little of the physical person on view.

Andrew was a hippie, one of the latter-day breed who wished they had been old enough in the sixties to have enjoyed them. He drove a VW bus, circa 1969, with a psychedelic mixture of rust and paint on the side doors. An array of bumper stickers on the back window, in fainter and fainter colors, told the whole story. The newest read: "U.S. Out of the Middle East!" A slightly faded one read: "U.S. Out of Central

America!" There was a completely faded one that had once read: "U.S. Out of Vietnam!"

Andrew had inherited the VW from his mentor, a "real" hippie called Banjo Jim, who had moved to Oregon. The bus, he said, wouldn't make it "cross country." He gave it to Andrew as a token of their friendship.

Andrew lived with his dog, Sam, in a log cabin in the woods, what the locals referred to as a "camp." He played a variety of string instruments and during the height of the ski season got gigs at the Barrington Inn.

These gigs did not provide much of a living, but Andrew didn't need much. His grandfather, who had been a surgeon in Connecticut, had left him a small trust fund, and it proved sufficient. Andrew was thus free to play music, read novels, hike in the woods, and keep the VW bus in running order. Once in a while, to splurge, he took a friend to the movies in Burlington.

He had been going out with a plump ex-student called Heather who worked in a pottery shop, but that relationship had been winding down for several months now. He was on the make, and he saw in Susan's eyes a sense of longing; it gathered in the dark hollows of her gaze and thrilled him.

They both grabbed for the same pork tenderloins, and their hands touched.

They stood looking at each other and said nothing, and it struck them both as altogether strange.

"You're obviously not worried about your cholesterol," said Andrew, to break the freeze.

"Are *you*?"

"My philosophy is: You eat, you eat. You die, you die."

Susan was normally skeptical of people who said things like that, but she liked what she saw in front of her: a tender young man with a silky blond beard and long hair parted in the middle. He was a foot taller than she but seemed boylike and fragile. His body smelled faintly of old sweat, but it did not repel her. It was that tinge of earthiness that kept him from floating off the ground.

"I suppose I mistook you for a vegetarian," she said, unable to resist teasing him. As she said that, she felt relieved she hadn't come up with something worse. Having spent so much time around academics, she was used to speaking with a twang of irony.

"It's my thinness," he said. "Everyone assumes that thin people don't eat meat."

Susan had the vague feeling that she had met Andrew somewhere before.

"Haven't I seen you driving out of Sarah Dillinger's house?" he asked.

"Yes," she said.

So that was it. She had seen him in the antechamber of Sarah's office that was used as a waiting room, and she remembered thinking—vaguely thinking—that he seemed oddly attractive. The sort of bohemian adventurer-intellectual one might meet while hiking the Appalachian Trail.

The connection with Sarah turned them into immediate allies. A sense of intimacy informed their conversation now, and they found themselves moving together toward the checkout line, cart by cart.

The parking lot was empty at noon on a weekday. It had been raining all morning, but the clouds had passed, and the sky was immaculately blue. A hint of summer was in the spring air, with sunlight standing in pools of water on the tarmac.

Susan and Andrew stood by his VW van and talked for the sake of talking. Had he ever hiked to the top of Mount Isaac? Had she read the Black Mountain poets? Neither wanted the conversation to end, though they quickly ran out of topics that could warrant their standing like that in a parking lot.

Andrew said, "Why don't you come over to my place for tea?"

"When?"

"Now."

"Now?"

"Yes."

"I'll follow you," she said.

And that was that.

As she drove up the winding country road to the little cabin where he lived, she wondered what in the hell she was doing. If it was hippies she was after, she knew plenty of real ones, friends who had gone back to the land during the Vietnam War and stayed there.

But she was more driven now than driving. A year ago, she would never have dreamed of doing such a thing. What took her by surprise today was that she had no resistance. She was letting the water of feeling seek its own level.

In any case, there was nothing wrong with making a new friend or going back to his place for a cup of tea. That's what she told herself, loudly, in her head. Geno wouldn't mind anyway. Far from being jealous, he encouraged her to make friends of her own. Male or female. He might find it inexplicable that she should have taken a sudden shine to someone she'd met over a meat counter at the A&P. What if he were some kind of pervert? She could hear Geno saying that when she told him about it later.

Indeed, the realization that she would tell Geno everything relaxed her. What she was doing was not, after all, illicit. It was perhaps a bit lunatic, but it was not illicit or covert.

The ruts in the road through a tall stand of Norway pines terrified her. Huge ridges, some of them a foot or two high, had turned this into an obstacle course, while larger holes formed a sequence of mini-lakes along the way. Her steel-gray Audi spun to the left and right, twice almost losing it in a mudhole. The prospect of a tow truck having to rescue her made her squirm.

At last she drew up to the cabin, which had a sloping lawn that retained its greenness from last summer. She looked around. There was a lovely view of the mountains in the distance, and the nearby woods still had patches of snow in the shadowy places. A stream crackled somewhere, perhaps a hundred yards away: the unmistakable sound of water swollen by snowmelt, a tumult of twigs, black branches, ice. It made her feel happy and fresh. Alive.

Andrew was standing on the porch, waiting for her. His arms were full of groceries.

"Hi," he said. "Come on in."

She followed him, taking in every detail. The dark interior suffused with the smell of woodsmoke. The Vermont Castings stove in one corner, squat and blazing. The Oriental rugs, worn threadbare by generations of upper-middle-class New Englanders. The little alcove with a picture of some Indian guru above a makeshift altar, and the residue of incense.

An assortment of string instruments crowded one corner of the cabin, which was a single room. There was a beaten-up couch near the woodstove, and along the south wall floor was a futon, neatly covered by a handmade quilt. A small kitchen lined the north wall, and a tiny breakfast table was pushed against the couch.

"Cozy," said Susan.

"It's cramped," Andrew said. "But I don't mind. In Bangkok, they'd fit six families into a space like this."

She assumed he had been to Bangkok or he'd have picked another, more obviously crowded, city in the Third World, such as Calcutta. Everyone always dumped on Calcutta.

There was a huge poster of a rainbow pinned to the wall behind his couch.

"You like rainbows, huh?" Susan asked, teasing slightly.

"The Rainbows are coming, you know."

"The Rainbows?"

"The Rainbow Family of Light. They're a kind of . . . sect. Not a sect, really. It's very informal." He was struggling now to find the words. "I've got friends in Colorado, in Berkeley, in Idaho. It's like an association of communes. They're hippies. Old-fashioned hippies."

"And they're coming?"

"Every year on July Fourth they meet somewhere different for a celebration. Thousands of them. They're coming here this time. You should plan to go. I went last year out in Oregon. It's like . . . like mind-blowing. You can really feel it—the spirit."

"I see." Her eyes fell on a portrait of an Indian. "Who's the guru?"

"Sri Bhagada Vishnu."

"Ah," she said, not quite ready to reveal her ignorance or, worse, her skepticism.

"I'm not exactly a votary," he said. "But I meditate along certain lines . . . when I get the time."

Fortunately, Andrew was too self-absorbed to question her about her meditative practice.

"Do you like Indian music?"

Susan admitted a lack of familiarity with the subject, but Andrew was unperturbed. Blithely, he put on a scratched old record of sitar music with some kind of percussion instruments in the background. It was oddly seductive.

"Do you smoke?"

Susan almost said no. But she caught herself when she realized he was talking about grass. Grass was okay, though she and Geno rarely indulged. Somewhere, in the eighties, they had lost interest in dope.

Sitting across from Andrew on the floor on a small tribal rug in front of the stove, cross-legged, Susan watched as he meticulously rolled a joint.

"It's Guatemalan," he said.

"Good."

Good? She wondered why she was sitting here like some half-baked Buddha, waiting for a drag of something that would only make her dizzy as hell. Or sick. The last time she smoked hash—in the Dominican Republic two years ago—it had made her throw up.

A lonely feeling overwhelmed her now, and she missed Geno. The gulf between her and Andrew seemed so nakedly apparent as he sat there, fiddling with the joint, moving his head back and forth with the music. Was she really *that* much older than Andrew Ridgeway?

Such was her evenhanded nature that as soon as she had finished trashing Andrew in her mind, she began to note his good points. She was clearly attracted to his slender hips and skinny legs. To the innocence of his gaze, which observed the world with a peculiar mixture of lordly indifference and easy acceptance. To the rough timbre of his voice, so much manlier in its way than Geno's.

She liked the clean sparkle of his hair, too; how it barely grazed his shoulders, and the way he parted it neatly in the middle. The part was a lovely straight white line in the center of his scalp, and she wished she could touch it.

So she did.

She leaned forward, and she ran her forefinger down the part, starting at the back and working her way to the brow.

Andrew, with his head bent forward over the joint, seemed hardly to notice. He did not say anything. He did not even look up in wonderment, as she expected he might.

He simply lit the joint and passed it to her.

She inhaled deeply, feeling the hot smoke bite into her

lungs; then she pressed down and held her breath tightly. Moments later, she let a cloud of smoke explode from her lips.

"God," she said, coughing. "I'm out of practice!"

Andrew smiled serenely, taking the joint from Susan. He sucked in slowly, lovingly, seeming not to strain in the slightest. His expertise was evident in every gesture, in every nuance of expression from the slight grimace to the lowered eyelids.

They said nothing and passed the joint back and forth half a dozen times.

Susan felt wonderful, tingling all over. The music became weirdly palpable, as if the notes could be gathered in a net like fish and studied.

Andrew was talking about the oddness of their meeting and how unusual it was to bump into somebody one could like at once. It was so difficult to find people he could like anymore. The world had grown harder and meaner in spirit since George Bush became president, he said. At least Reagan was dumb. One could forgive dumbness. Meanness was something else.

Susan told Andrew that she liked his directness. Not enough people were direct these days. They didn't have the courage.

Andrew nodded. "Kids have a natural directness," he said. "It's only when they grow up that all the shit happens, and they clam up. They learn from their elders that you can only succeed by going around behind everybody." He paused. "Have you got kids?"

"Two," she said. "Two little boys."

He smiled at her, happy, and when she saw that he was happy for her, she was moved.

"I'm not always a very good mother," she said. After a pause, she added: "I wish I were."

Andrew unexpectedly raised both hands, as if beckoning Susan to cross some mysterious gulf.

She understood, and she pitched forward and let her head fall into his lap.

She let him run his fingers gently through her hair, and it was thrilling.

"I'd like to make love with you, Susan," Andrew said, after a long time. By now the sitar music had stopped, and the needle was grinding in the inside groove.

"I'm afraid I can't," she said.

He nodded slightly, to show that he understood. Then he bent over her and put his lips to hers. She opened herself to him, letting him put his tongue deeply into her mouth. For what seemed like an eternity—a lovely eternity—he kissed her, searching out every crevice of her mouth, going around and beneath her tongue, letting his own teeth clatter against hers.

She did not stop his hand when he reached under her wool sweater, though it frightened her slightly. His palm pressed hard against her left nipple, and it felt good to her.

"Can I make you come?" he asked in his almost childlike way. She noticed that his hand was now on her crotch, ready to unzip her jeans.

She shook her head. It was not okay. She almost said, "I'm sorry," but she stopped herself. She was too old and wise for that kind of thing.

"Would you like some tea?" he said, pulling away from her with considerable determination. "Earl Grey?"

She did not like Earl Grey, but it hardly mattered. "Sure. Thanks."

When she finally stepped outside, into the cool air, it was nearly time for dinner. Geno would be home now, with the boys. And there was almost nothing in the house for dinner. She had all the groceries.

But Susan didn't worry. Remembering what Sarah Dillinger always said about guilt, she stifled that feeling before it had time to root and grow.

Chapter 9

The farm country around Barrington was somber at night, especially in late spring, when the rich fields seemed to cast their darkness upward into the sky. The draughty houses sat on little hilltops in ghostly moonlight, their windows lit up like jack-o'-lantern eyes. The light seemed to protest against the dark, to insist on something human in the inhuman context of these wild surroundings.

Ever since Geno and Susan had moved to the farm, they had paid huge electric bills. Geno loved the light—he was as scared of the dark as he'd been as a child. It frightened him just to go from the driveway across the lawn to the front porch. The sky overhead seemed too vast, and the noises all too real: a tomcat mewling in the distance, an owl descending on a rabbit, or a coy dog baying at the moon. In the hot summer months, the deafening roar of locusts rose in the hayfields—billions of insects that made a high-pitched throb of the kind that must have sent the ancient Israelites into perpetual frenzy.

One heard only a milder version of such things in Meadow Pond, New Jersey, where Geno had grown up in a middle-class suburban house in what his father always called "the development." That is, one heard a domestic dog bark at a domestic cat, the occasional woodpecker fretting a tree trunk, and the rasping coughs of elderly neighbors on their screened-in porches. There were crickets, of course, but their noise was usually drowned by the swirling spray of lawn-watering devices or an ambulance.

Tonight, not long before the end of the spring semester, Geno was heading to the library, where he intended to do some research on the Taino Indians—a gentle race whose fate at the hands of Columbus and his men brought blood to Geno's face. The more he read about these men, the less he could believe they belonged to the human race. Whole villages would kill their children and then slit their own throats when they heard that Columbus or one of his brothers was coming. One famous chieftain, on being put to death, was told that if he repented for his sins, God would welcome him to heaven. He asked his executioner, "Will there be any Spaniards in heaven?" The man nodded his head. "Then I shall go to hell," he said.

Geno wanted to write something about the Tainos, but tonight he would just be taking notes. Susan, meanwhile, was putting the children to bed; aware that he was feeling pressed, and wanting some time alone to absorb her day with Andrew, she told him not to hurry.

Geno thought that one of the worst things about teaching was the loss of certain students. They came into one's life as children needing to be looked after, taught, allowed to run free, encouraged to lash out at one's best arguments and make a case for their own positions, however feeble. And they must finally be let go.

It frightened him to think of how many good friends he had lost in the last fifteen years of teaching, the young faces, attentive minds, and lovely bodies that would grace his life for a few years, then evaporate. A few kept in touch, sporadically, writing from Wall Street or D.C. or Berkeley to say that this higher degree was won, that child born, this spouse added or subtracted, that house or condo bought. For the most part, he never heard from them again.

No wonder he always cried at graduations.

When he got to the library and sat down in his carrel with his books spread out around him, he could think of nothing tonight but the loss of Lizzy Nash.

He didn't love Lizzy Nash. He wasn't even that close to her. But he couldn't stop thinking about her. He enjoyed her silly enthusiasm for Peruvian history (which, to his annoyance, she had studied with Fernando Nachez, who was also her faculty advisor). He even liked her jejune thesis on Virginia Woolf, which he had insisted on advising himself—over the protests of Agnes Wild, who considered Woolf her exclusive property. He even found her foolish attempts at fiction entertaining. The stories were slipped under his door like secret messages, and he felt that more was going on than met the eye whenever she came into his office to discuss them.

Lizzie often wrote about sex. They all did, since it was deeply on their minds. Some were in the process of losing their virginity, although this number dwindled every year. But they seemed to understand nothing about the complexity of sustained sexual relations, such as those involved in marriage.

Geno puzzled over the delicate nature of those relations. His early sexual life had seemed deeply irregular. He had liked men and women alike, and not until he was in his middle twenties had he settled comfortably on the idea of heterosexual monogamy. The notion that a man and woman might find enough to say to each other to sustain a lifetime of intimacy was surely one of humankind's supreme fictions. To his amazement, he had found that Susan did interest him in a way that was sustaining. The original attraction, which had more to do with class than gender, had only matured. He found the difference between them erotic in itself: her otherness, as a mind, as a physical texture and outline, as a way of being in the world, excited him. Their slow dance toward periodic climaxes intrigued him.

When things were going well between them, every minute of the day was part of the process of seduction, and that seduction was as much spiritual as physical, the sense of union amounting to a kind of sensuous like-mindedness. He was deeply committed to what John Milton had called the "daily decencies" of married life, and these decencies were the product of a complete affection, one that incorporated difference, dissonance, and disattraction.

But his relationship with Susan did not mean that other bodies and minds were of no interest. There was a natural oscillation in their marriage between a positive and a negative pole. When they were moving toward the positive pole, he did not think much about other women. He found Susan waxing in his mind like an August moon, enlarged and breathable. During the waning phases, he found his attention scattered. He became alert as a dog, watching other women, and men, attentive to every smell, every turn of phrase. Beautiful joggers, in gym shorts, with long gangly legs, could stop his heart as he drove by them on the road.

At times, a terrible longing overwhelmed him, and he felt homesick for something he could not even imagine—something like death, which struck him as blissful in a Keatsian way, a kind of ultimate reconciliation of body and spirit in the moment of extinction. He longed for that Buddhist ideal, the point of extraction from the great wheel of desire, the endless cycle of birth, copulation, and death.

Death was not something he was afraid of. It was no more frightening than birth, when the spirit "came down" to earth. Mortal Life, he thought, was just a brief interlude that interrupted his Eternal Life. The actual nature of his Eternal Life did not concern him. It was the great mystery at the center of all religions. He was, if anything, glad not to know. The mental space opened up by this mystery gave the imagination a place to root, and there was no telling what might grow there, what terrible beauty might be born.

These thoughts coursed, like hot blood, through Geno's brain as he sat before his books, nibbling on the end of a

No. 2 pencil. The lush smell of spring air filled his nostrils. And before long Geno found himself crossing the quad, following his own zigzag way to Lizzie Nash's dorm.

Professors do not normally go into student dorms without an invitation to some tediously formal wine-and-cheese party intended to drum up support for the Mountaineering Club or the Ballroom Dancing Society. Once, to Geno's chagrin, he had been asked to speak to the Young Republicans. They assumed that because he alluded to politics in so many lectures, he was interested in the next presidential election. It did not go over well when he told them that American democracy was only *somewhat* democratic. It went over even less well when he said that there was really only one party, the Party of Business, with two branches. He told them that no particular politician could change anything, that these guys were all bought by G.E. or I.B.M., and that their function was to see that fat contracts went to the people who funded them. "The system has to change," was about all Geno said in the direction of finding a solution, and this upset everyone. "You're all good Americans," he told them, "and that means you believe there's a solution to all problems. Well, there's no solution. The only thing we can do is try to ease the suffering wherever we find it. And to complain like hell about what's happening every day of the week." He felt proud of having said that. It offered a note of optimism where one could not easily be found. People can't tolerate too much bad news at once.

Now he stood in the lobby off Newhouse, a co-ed dorm on the edge of the campus overlooking a small forest of white pine and drooping tamarack.

Exams were approaching, and students everywhere looked strung out, their eyes bulging, their fingers trembling from excessive cups of coffee. Those enamored of their own seediness—always a sizable group on every campus in late spring—smoked cigarettes by the dozen and avoided showers. They memorized theorems all night, read Mann or Rimbaud, watched old movies, or had sex with as many different people as they could manage.

Geno vaguely recognized the two students sitting in the lounge, though—to his relief—neither looked up as he passed. He slipped into the dark stairwell and climbed, two steps at a time, coming out onto the third floor with a bound, breathless, still afraid of running into someone he would know.

The floor was deserted, although light fell on the otherwise dark hallway from a few open doors.

Geno stole past these doors, seeing that the rooms were empty.

Where was everyone?

He came to Lizzie's door and knocked softly, and heard, he thought, a slight shuffling sound within. The door opened.

"Geno!"

He shushed her.

"What's wrong?" she asked, letting him in.

"People are studying."

"Hardly anyone's here," she said. "They're showing that *Rocky Horror* movie."

Geno nodded, relieved. "Were you asleep already?"

Lizzie shook her head. "I was up all night, working on you-know-what."

"*Ms.* Woolf . . ."

Lizzie grimaced slightly, and Geno felt stupid.

"I was working in the library and got bored," Geno went on.

"Would you like some tea?"

"Got any wine?"

Lizzy smiled, producing a bottle of lukewarm plonk from Chile.

"I always feel bad drinking Chilean wine," Geno said. "I keep thinking about Allende. There he was, a democratically elected Marxist, and there was so much hope in that country."

Lizzy's face wrinkled.

"You know, Allende. He was overthrown by the CIA. We stuck in Pinochet, a real bastard."

Lizzie poured the wine. "Fernando says that Allende was potentially a dictator himself."

"Fernando?"

"Professor Nachez."

"Ah . . . your advisor."

Lizzy leaned closer to him, and he could smell the garlic on her breath. Her breath always seemed to smell of garlic, and it excited him—a sense of Mediterranean earthiness.

"He tends to be very right-wing, of course," Lizzie said.

"He's an asshole."

Lizzie looked terribly uncomfortable now, and Geno backtracked quickly.

"I actually like Fernando a lot, when he stays away from politics. He's a very productive scholar."

This seemed to reassure her, and she sipped the wine freely. Before long, she was quoting Neruda by the yard.

They were halfway through their third glass when Geno realized that Lizzie was naked beneath a thin cotton nightdress. It was obviously another of her Peruvian souvenirs, and it contrasted nicely with her red hair, so frizzy and unkempt, like tangled dreams.

Her chest was rather flat, like Susan's, with the breasts showing slightly through the soft material. She sat with her legs crossed, Indian style, and the nightdress rode up to midthigh. Were there freckles on her thighs, or was he seeing things?

They sat on the floor, on a small blue rug, leaning against her narrow bed.

The room was lit by a small bed lamp that hung from the cinderblock wall, casting a whitish pool of light on the rumpled sheets. Geno felt his palms growing wet and cold. What he wanted, so badly he could taste it, was to bury his face in Lizzy's stomach, to lick her thighs, to open her sweetly with his tongue. He wanted to lie beside her with that bed lamp glowing on their bare arms and backs. He wanted to hold her, hold her, hold her.

Rose Weintraub showed no expression as Geno talked. It occurred to him that he could have said that he had torn Lizzie apart with his bare fingers or slit her throat and Rose would have simply nodded or said, "How does that make you feel?"

A full moon of silence hung in the air between them.

Geno settled into the sofa, aware of the two potted plants at either side, their waxy leaves catching the morning light in odd ways. The white walls of the room had a wonderful freshness about them. He liked it here, except when the silences came, as they always did when Geno approached some difficult aspect of "his material."

The silences did not trouble Rose. Successful clients worked through them, finding a language adequate to their experience. But Geno did not want to front his experience boldly at the moment. He wanted to sidestep the details of his affair with Lizzie Nash, having stopped his narrative at the point where he wanted to bury his face in Lizzie's pubic hair.

One of his problems in therapy was becoming clear to him. He felt hesitant to approach the truth; indeed, he was prone to lie, if that felt more comfortable.

And it did. Geno had become used to what he called his "little fictions," telling himself that life was built on these fictions, that it was nearly impossible to tell the truth anyway. What would "telling the truth" mean? In most cases there was nothing but interpretation. The literal events mattered less than one's impression.

"Did you have sex with her?" Rose asked.

Geno hesitated, then nodded his head.

"You actually had intercourse?"

"Yes," Geno said.

That was the literal and unexamined truth. It stunned him that she had dared to ask, and that he had admitted it so bluntly. Some secrets one keeps even from oneself.

The incident with Lizzie Nash had occurred only a week before, but it had almost fallen from his conscious mind. He had fucked Lizzie Nash in her dorm room, and he had forgotten it.

That night, after "it" had happened, he had gone back to his library carrel, where he opened his poetry notebook with an overwhelming desire to write something eternal. And the lines had come with a rush, stopping only because a custodian had knocked on his door to say the place was closing.

He took the newly minted poem home to Susan, waking her from a sound sleep to read it, slowly and sonorously.

Susan was annoyed, but she listened, struggling through her exhaustion to make sense of the lines. When he finished, in about ten minutes, she told him that the metaphors seemed, to her, a bit "overripe." He should go to bed and sleep on it.

This response frustrated Geno, but he thanked her. She was usually right about these things. Slipping out of his sweaty clothes, he took a long hot shower, getting every bit of Lizzy Nash that still clung to him off his skin. Before getting into bed, he took a Valium and fell into a deep but dreamless sleep.

When he woke, about seven, he looked at Susan in the strong yellow light that pillared through a narrow band where the window shade had not been pulled down all the way. She was entirely beautiful to him, her dark hair shot through with a few strands of silver and spilling over the fresh white pillowcase. Her chest rose and fell, ever so gently. Geno propped himself on one elbow, hovering beside her as if reading her face. He noticed that tiny wrinkles had begun spidering out from her eyes and the sides of her lips, although this was not unattractive to him in the slightest. Unlike Lizzy's face, which still boasted the rather undefined puffiness of adolescence, Susan's was sharp and settled; she had found the lines of her existence, and she wore them well.

Geno woke her gently, lolling his tongue along her inner thighs, enjoying the slightly saline tinge of the sleep-warm skin. Responding almost instinctively, Susan spread her legs wide, letting him work along the soft furrows, putting a finger into her as he licked. Before she had even wakened fully or opened her eyes, she rocked violently in a spasm of love.

Geno realized that his whole face was wet now, salty with tears.

"Are you okay, Geno?"

He opened his eyes. It was Rose Weintraub, her face leaning forward. Had he been dreaming?

"You seemed to have gone to sleep," she said. "And now—you're crying."

"I'm fine."

"You've had a hard time, haven't you?"

"Me?"

"Yes." She paused. "You should take care of yourself."

Geno let out a long sigh. " 'My own heart let me more have pity on,' " he said.

"Excuse me?"

"It's a line from a poem. Hopkins."

"I don't know that poem."

Geno stood to leave, even though his fifty-minute hour was far from up. "I'm tired, Rose," he said. "I'm going home."

Chapter 10

Columbus liked to fish off Porto Santo, where he and Dona Felipa lived in a house that had belonged to her father, Dom Bartholomew, who had been governor of the island. The stone cottage perched on a promontory looking out to Capo Blanco; the invisible coast of Africa loomed in the distance.

A fisherman's daughter, Maria Caterina, helped him each morning with the boat. She was unlike the other islanders, with her green eyes and blond hair. Her father, who once sailed to Norway with the Portuguese navy, had brought her back when she was a child, without her mother, who was said to have died en route.

Maria Caterina was seventeen now, and she was beautiful.

Columbus thought about her often, and he had no doubt that he would seduce her when the time was ripe.

He had become increasingly bored with Dona Felipa,

who'd grown testy in the past few months. She longed for her mother, Dona Isabel, and her family's witty table in Lisbon. The happiest years of her life were those spent shortly after her marriage to Columbus, when they both lived with her mother. It had seemed to her then that Columbus was terribly happy. He loved the important visitors who dined at their table: successful merchants, eminent clerics, courtiers, men of leisure, learned scholars. Although it embarrassed her that he so obviously *used* everyone he met.

Sometimes, in the middle of the night, Columbus wondered how it could be that the daughter of Dona Isabel—the most brazenly charming hostess in Lisbon—was so dull. Even on Porto Santo, she did not stand out.

He had never imagined she would be dull. But then, he had never thought about it. Her rank in Portuguese society was enough to make her interesting. And she was, in fact, physically appealing, though it had recently occurred to him that her nose was too long, that her ears stuck out indiscreetly, and that her huge bosom was, perhaps, not what he had imagined in the dreamy days before his wedding night. It had also never occurred to him before that she was so terribly loud, that her voice tended to squawk rather than purr. In all, there was something *excessive* about Dona Felipa.

What he liked about Maria Caterina was her simplicity. Her nose was straight, as was her hair. Her lips were elegantly thin. Her bosom was barely perceptible under a muslin blouse. And she did not put powdery substances on her face or add coloring to her cheeks, as did Dona Felipa, who continued to make herself up daily as if she were expecting a baroness for lunch. Maria Caterina let the sun color her cheeks and bleach her hair. She let the salt spray of the sea freshen her skin.

It did not trouble Columbus that Maria Caterina's hands were coarse, like a man's. Or that her breath reeked of garlic—he actually loved to inhale a woman's garlicky breath. Her rude, simple language—the speech she had learned from her father and his friends—appealed to him. Moreover, she worshiped Columbus, who flattered her and told her crazy stories about his madcap adventures at sea. Most of them were untrue, but this hardly mattered. He knew enough to make them plausible, and that was the point of storytelling, after all.

Columbus took Maria Caterina fishing with him today. She had been begging to go along, and he was only going out for a little while, so he consented.

They dropped nets over the side of the small boat and trawled, letting the current take them a long way down the coastline, which glistened in the morning light. As they worked, Columbus told her about his wife's amazing family. His father-in-law, recently deceased, had arrived on Porto Santo in 1425 with a colonizing expedition sent by the great Infante, Dom Henrique. Having conquered the island merely by stepping ashore with a handful of soldiers, he decided to stay for a while. "The only way you can be sure that a piece of geography is yours," he used to say, "is to live on it."

Live on it he did. His favorite dish was rabbit stew, which he simmered over an open fire with lots of onions. He had brought a she-rabbit with a new litter with him on the ship, and he set them up in royal style in a little pen. Alas, they escaped, dashing about the rocky island and reproducing themselves as rabbits will. Before long the island was infested, with long ears poking out of every nook and cranny and white bunnytails bobbing over each hillcrest.

This wasn't so bad, thought Dom Bartholomew at first; he had his fill of rabbit stew every single night of the week. The problem was the vegetable course. Within a year, the rabbits had managed to whittle away at every bit of greenness that had formerly sprouted from this paradisal island. Soon Porto Santo was a brown rock in the middle of this glistening sea, a barren outcrop.

The island was so damaged by the rabbits that the Portuguese conquerors decided to pull up their shallow roots and move to neighboring Madeira, thirty miles to the north. They would stay away until the balance of nature was restored.

Now it was. The rabbits had been killed off by the natives or died of starvation or disease. And Dona Felipa's brother was now governor of the island, which had gradually turned green again.

Maria Caterina was thrilled by this story, which she had heard many times from her father and his friends; but Columbus was a better storyteller. He made everything seem so dramatic!

When he kissed her, suddenly, at sea, she did not know what to do. *But he's a married man . . . a father!* she thought to herself. On the other hand, she liked his kisses, which were the first she had ever known. The idea of resisting him did not occur to her. A man's will is the wind's will.

That night, lying beside his soundly sleeping wife, listening to the rough breathing of his two-year-old son, Columbus wondered about the strangeness of life. What separated one man from another? Were all women interchangeable?

She slept intensely now, snoring lightly. And Columbus could not resist her, lifting the hem of her satiny nightdress. She surprised him by raising her hips a little, puckering for entry. If she was asleep, she was soon to have a wondrous dream, Columbus thought as he leaned over her. He rode her into the hard deep night, feeling a deep love—not for his wife—but for the whole world. It was the world he loved, its taste and texture, the way it presented itself boldly at its moment of ripeness.

Chapter 11

Geno did not respond to the pathetic notes and frustrated stories from Lizzy Nash that began to pile up in his box. He figured that with only four weeks till graduation, he was home free. Her plans for the summer, and grad school, were set now: she had signed up for a ten-week stint in the woods of Montana with Outward Bound. After that, she would head straight to Los Angeles for an MFA in screenwriting at the University of Southern California. By mid-September, Barrington College would be a faint shimmer in her mind, and she would think of Geno—and talk about him—in the years to come as a crucial mentor.

He could not avoid meeting with her about her thesis, however. It was finished, and he had read it. There was really not much more to be said about it, but he could hardly avoid a brief final conference. The truth was that Lizzy Nash would not set the world of Woolf studies ablaze with her insights about "the artistic process." Her work was respectable, not zinging; she had applied herself energetically, she was intelligent enough, and the writing had moments of grace. This was B work, he guessed, which meant he would give her a B+.

One day, not minutes before Geno planned to take off for home (he had promised James and Milo that they could go out to Lake Orion for a picnic that afternoon), someone knocked at his office door in Milton House. The rest of the floor was empty, except for Agnes Wild, who sat in her office reading with her door open.

"Hello?"

"Geno?"

Lizzie Nash stood in the doorway in jeans and tee shirt, a Guatamalan handbag thrown over her shoulder.

"Come in, Lizzie."

He took off his reading glasses and saw that her freckled face was redder than usual; her lip quivered slightly, and her blue eyes stung when he caught them directly.

"You haven't been answering my notes," she said, the almost undetectable slur of a lisp betraying her anxiety.

He folded his hands in his lap, but this felt awkward, so he unfolded them. During embarrassing conversations, he never quite knew where to put his hands.

"I'm sorry," he said. "I was just about to . . . to call you. This has been . . . crazy. You know, end of term. I'm up to the ass in papers and exams."

"Am I making you nervous or something?"

He blushed. "No, of course not. I was concentrating." He held up a student exam as if to prove it.

"Am I interrupting you?"

"It's good to see you," he said firmly. "It really is."

Lizzie took that as an invitation to sit down in the rumpled armchair beside the desk. Her red hair was pulled back tightly, though countless loose strands dangled or soared.

Geno got up to close the door, remembering that Agnes Wild had very large ears.

"What happened between us last week," Geno said. "That was nice, Lizzie."

"It was three weeks ago."

Geno looked at his hands. "Time flies."

"I thought you'd call . . . or come by. Something."

Geno knew he'd blown it. "I should have. What you've got to understand . . . Well, you don't have to, but I wish you would." He stumbled for words. "What I mean, or think I mean, is that I wish I hadn't let that happen."

Lizzy Nash looked at him coldly as he fumbled through his shrunken lexicon of emotions. She did not respond.

Geno let a genuine silence grow between them, one not unlike those he had learned to absorb in his sessions with Rose Weintraub. It surprised him that Lizzy was so good at this. She showed no sign of saying anything.

"I'm fond of you. You know that," he said.

Lizzy shook her head in wonderment.

"I'll never forget that night."

"Bullshit," she said.

"I'm serious."

"Bullshit."

Geno had somehow not counted on this. How do you respond to someone who says either nothing or "Bullshit"?

"What did you expect, Liz? That I should leave my wife and run off to Colorado with you? Or take up screenwriting?"

Lizzy Nash shook her head. "You're un-fucking-believable," she said.

Geno wished this ridiculous nightmare would go away.

"Have you read my thesis?" she asked. "That's what I came to talk about."

Finally. The solid ground of intellectual repartee. They could proceed to a careful discussion of Virginia Woolf's obviously failed attempt to portray the artistic process in the character of Lily Briscoe and, more to the point, to Lizzy Nash's flawed but occasionally perceptive attempt to describe this failed attempt.

Geno opened a manila folder that contained her thesis and passed it to Lizzy. The B+ was boldly marked on the top lefthand corner and circled.

"I'm a little surprised by the grade," she said quickly.

"B-plus is solid work."

"You said last month that I was really on to something. I sort of . . . guessed you meant I was doing A work."

"I don't like to talk about grades during the term. I think it sets up an artificial barrier. The grade doesn't mean anything."

"If it doesn't mean anything, why bother? Let's call it a 'Pass' or something."

"I'd prefer to grade along those lines. Not to grade at all, in fact. But Barrington College is a fairly traditional place, as you may have noticed."

"The sort of place where professors seduce their students and the students like it. Is that what you mean?"

Geno couldn't believe his ears.

"Maybe *you* seduced me. I happen to recall some of the notes and stories you popped into my box." He didn't like the tone he'd fallen into. "Anyway, it's pointless to talk about 'seduction.' I did something I felt like doing at the time, something I should probably not have done. You are twenty-two years old, Lizzie. You probably made a mistake, too."

Her blue eyes turned blear. She wiped them with the edge of her tee shirt, exposing a bare stretch of stomach. "I'm upset about this grade. I really thought I'd written an amazing fucking thesis."

"It's got some great stuff in it. I'm only quarreling with the shape of the whole. And I'm not quarreling very hard. A B-plus is a fine grade." He saw she was unconvinced. "In any case, you've already been accepted at U.S.C.—that's an achievement."

Lizzie said nothing, and Geno watched her carefully.

"Let's talk about the specifics," he said. "I've made some notes on the text itself, and there's a letter to you at the back. I go into my objections to certain lines of argument and say what I like about it, too."

"Goodbye, Geno."

He looked at her pleadingly. "Sit down, Liz."

She bit her lip, sighed, then left, shutting the door firmly behind her.

Geno sat there for some time, staring ahead at the floor-to-ceiling bookcase that lined the wall opposite his desk. Those books contained story upon story of wickedness, love, folly, and heroic passion. He felt sordid, thinking about those stories. His petty crime was small as crimes go. Had he taken advantage of his position, his "power" over Lizzie? Probably. There was just no point in what he'd done. He was not desperate or crazed. He could understand what he'd done in sympathetic terms had he been either, but he was a man of sound mind in love with his own wife who had succumbed to a stupid desire for gratification. The guilt of this act weighed on him now, quite literally, and he could hardly move.

The children adored Lake Orion, and so did Geno. It was situated near the top of a pass through the Green Mountains, perhaps two miles off the road. One parked in a clearing, then hiked up- and downhill for about half an hour—just enough exercise to raise a mild sweat.

The path through the woods embodied everything that Geno liked about living in New England. There was so much a sense of the wild natural world here, the wilderness that underlies everything.

The wilderness—except in darkness—appealed to Geno. It had become, in fact, something of a religion. As a child, he'd wanted to believe in the traditional God of Christianity, whom his parents offered on a platter. *Believe, and ye shall be saved*, their message ran, and the point remained a good one. But the conventional language of religion had ceased to move him after early adolescence, and the hard shell of dogma crumbled permanently in his freshman year at Dartmouth, when he read Paul Tillich and Martin Buber. Now he saw organized religion as something that pulled him away from the quiet center discoverable in these woods.

The path through the woods was itself rich in metaphor, and it was—after all—only through metaphor that the mind made connections. Robert Frost had written beautifully about two roads diverging "in a yellow wood," and those two roads offered the purest, simplest emblem of moral choice. But it was too simple. More than two roads usually diverged. Path led to path, and one easily—too easily—got lost amid the branching tines.

Today a light wind blew off the lake, and Geno felt his scalp prickle with anticipation. He carried a notebook with him for writing poems in, just in case. His knapsack was full of cookies and a Thermos full of white grape juice—white because it would not stain if spilled. The children had raced ahead of him.

He rounded a bend and saw the lake shimmer in the woods. It was a pond, really. A piece of the late spring sky fallen to earth and rippling incessantly from a point below the surface and toward the center, probably the point where an underground stream welled up.

The icy temperature of the water—even in August—was

a sign that Lake Orion was spring-fed. How cold it would be now, in May, was something only a polar bear would want to know.

There was a sloping flat rock, immense in size, where bathers and picnickers sat. They had the whole place to themselves today, as Geno expected. He sat down in a warm little crevice—a point in the rock that formed a natural seat; from there he'd watch the boys throw stones, catch salamanders, or fence with makeshift swords. The ritual was familiar: they'd start off playing, then Milo would tease James, and James would respond unvaliantly. Blows would lead to shrieks, perhaps a mild trickle of blood from somebody's nose or a scraped wrist or kneecap. After one of them had been duly wounded, they would subside into genial play again.

The boys had disappeared into the woods in search of kindling and wood, hoping that if they found enough Geno would consent to light a fire. This was just the age for pyromania, and Geno had remembered to bring matches. Having been himself thwarted by his parents when it came to fires, he wanted his boys to have the freedom to make a hugely satisfying campfire.

He walked to the edge of the water and bent low, seeing himself big-eyed Narcissus: a lean-faced man in early middle age. A handsome man with wild red hair and a long straight nose. He smiled, and the face smiled back. He made a weirdo grimace, and the image grimaced weirdly. His big, thin hands fluttered over the water at the wrists like giant aspen leaves, and Geno wished, suddenly, that he were Picasso.

He stepped out onto a long wooden raft that lived permanently here at Lake Orion. It had been built, he imagined, by some eager-beaver Boy Scouts, the planks having been nailed crudely and strapped with wire to a couple of sturdy logs. Geno had been coming here for a decade and passed many a fine hour on this raft. He thought of paddling out to the middle today, but a slight updraft chilled this intention, and he retreated to his rocky niche.

The kids' voices drifted indistinctly over the treetops: hollow chirping voices that carried across the water, then echoed back to where Geno slumped. As long as he could hear them, he knew they were not too far away.

He began to scribble in his notebook, and soon he found himself writing a poem about walking through the woods, returning to the metaphor of the two roads diverging. The poem was addressed to Susan, and it gathered quickly on the page, with few glitches:

Love, I am I, but you are you.
Two things in nature never were the same;
we know that somehow, but we still assume
that one thing is another blesséd thing
or, if not so, then near enough to count
as something kin.
Today, for instance,
on a hike toward this ice-blue water
cupped among the pines, I found myself
comparing this to that and that to this.
The path I came by was a mental trace
through fuzzy thoughts—an opening to follow

foot by foot, the branches giving way
to further sightings of another stretch.
Proverbially, forks appeared to tempt
my resolution, and I deigned to choose
a single way, since doubling back is never
any good and mostly I will nudge
ahead no matter, willy-nilly, and believe
my choice was deft if not inspired.

The objects on my path—bright things
like blackbirds, bluets, stones—fell into place
to form a picture of the world I'd find
if I were only dreaming, hardly real.
I don't believe the half of what I see,
since other worlds exist beyond it:
worlds where nothing is itself alone
but part of something I can only scry
in inklings on the trail, unlikely omens,
accidental glimpses, sleights of mind,
as when the wind becomes a sign,
a metaphor of motion not my own.

Two things in nature never were the same,
The world keeps doubling on itself and leads
away. But somehow in the highest, farthest
realms of separation, we must come
together, me and you. Love, let's
embrace our frail conceits and know
that one thing is another thing,

that you and I are parcel of a whole
we only half believe is really there.

Geno reread the poem slowly. He liked working in a fluid, essayistic form. The cadence—a loose blank verse—was the fundamental line of English poetry, and Geno liked to imagine that his own version of the meter echoed poets from Shakespeare through Wallace Stevens. He had been trying to bring to poetry the sinewy, larruping voice of discursive prose. But he didn't want to sacrifice anything: the bite of poetry, the compactness, the aphoristic high.

"Daddy! Daddy!"

Behind him, somewhere in the brush, he heard the shriek.

Geno pushed through the thick undergrowth to get to James, whose voice it was.

"Where are you?" he called.

"Over here, Daddy."

James hovered over Milo, who sat on the ground with his cheeks tear-smudged. He held his arm up like a broken wing.

"Milo, sweetie," Geno said, bending. "Does it hurt bad?"

Milo said nothing.

"So what happened, fellas?"

James eagerly put in his version of events before Milo could speak. "He wanted to climb that tree over there, but it was my tree."

"How could it be *your* tree?"

"I claimed it. *That* was his tree." He pointed to another.

"It doesn't matter whose tree it was anyway. How did he fall?"

Milo brightened with anger. "He pushed me."

"You pushed him, James?"

"He was right behind me! I might have fallen!"

"He kicked me in the face," Milo said.

Geno sighed. "I'm very disappointed in you, James."

"It's not my fault! I didn't do anything!"

"Knocking somebody out of a tree is something, James." He could feel the hollowness in his voice, and it upset him. Why couldn't he speak firmly?

Milo slobbered into his good hand. "He tried to kill me."

"I want to kill him," James added.

"This is no way to talk, guys. I don't want to hear this kind of talk!"

"I mean it," James said. "I wish he was dead."

Milo screamed, "I wish you were dead, too!"

Geno, briefly, wished they were both dead.

"My arm is hurt," said Milo.

Geno examined it gently. "You may have broken it, Milo. But it's no big deal. The doctor can fix it."

"No needles!" Milo said.

"There's no needles. They'll just put a cast on it." He held up his hand. "See this hand?"

The boys gaped.

"I broke a bone right here, behind my thumb, when I was ten. I had a cast that started at the fingers and went right up to my elbow. My friends in school all put their names on it. I hated to see that cast go."

"They saw them off—with a big saw," James told Milo, gleefully.

"The saws have no teeth," Geno added. "The blade just kind of . . . vibrates. It can't cut you."

He felt good now, seeing that he had their attention. But he wished he could find easier ways to make a connection, and that someone didn't always have to get hurt for it to happen.

That night, after the boys had been put to sleep with long bedtime stories (and endless special favors for Milo), Geno and Susan sat in the living room with a bottle of wine between them.

"So where the fuck were you?" Susan asked.

"What?"

"Today. Weren't you paying attention?" She looked at him hard. "Milo could have broken his neck."

Geno was on trial, again, and it made him angry. On the one hand, he deserved it. For whatever reason, his mind did wander. He was famous for it. Students described him as a "space cadet," and one of his colleagues had recently said that to get his attention one had to set off a bomb in his face. He blamed this habit on his work, but this satisfied no one, not even himself. The Romantic figure of the artist as genius, self-absorbed and heedless of the world around him, didn't wash anymore. Geno, in any case, knew better. A writer may well be inward, self-reflective, and meditative. He should be, perhaps. But he must also attend to the world.

"You can't have been watching them," Susan said.

"I was writing a poem. I'll show it to you."

Susan frowned. "And you wonder why I get upset with you, Geno? I'm not unreasonable. You take a six-year-old and a nine-year-old into the middle of the woods, and what do you do? You write poetry."

"I like to write poetry."

"It's ridiculous, the way these kids hurt each other."

"I read in the paper last week about some kids in New York who tried to hang somebody—a grown man."

Susan was not impressed. "You always change the subject."

"This is the same subject—kids doing stupid things."

"Let's talk about *our* kids, dammit. Or about you."

"I don't like to talk about myself. It makes me feel . . . soiled."

Susan raised her eyebrows.

"I especially don't like talking about my shortcomings as a father."

"You're a good father—when you try. You hardly even have to try. All you have to do is *care*."

"Care? Jesus Christ, I care. I care too much. I love those boys."

"It's not just a question of love, Geno. It's you. You've got to wake up. You're a goddamn . . . somnambulant!"

"I gotta look that up."

"You're hard to live with, did you know that? You're so . . . frustrating. I know you love me and all that. But I can't feel you. I can't feel your presence."

"I'm here."

"Then fucking *be* here!"

"Jesus."

"I can't find you, Geno. I know you're angry with me sometimes, but you don't show it. I need you to show it. Let me know where you are, who you are. It's like I'm living with some ghost."

"You wanna fight, is that it?"

Susan's lips quivered.

"You know I hate to fight," Geno said.

"There's a lot to fight about. I wish we *would* fight."

"So let's fight."

"I don't go in for shadowboxing," she said. "Where the fuck are you, Geno?"

"I'm here."

"I see you, but I don't feel you."

Geno began crawling toward Susan on his knees.

"Please, honey. I'm trying to talk to you seriously."

"I want to fuck," he said.

"Then go fuck yourself." She stood to avoid him.

Geno reached out for her ankle.

"Please," she said, pulling away from him. "This isn't funny. I can't talk to you. I feel like I'm . . . alone."

He let go of her, and she left the room.

Frustrated, he stepped outside onto the front porch and looked out over the Green Mountains, barely visible against a grape-colored sky. The stars had come out, little chinks in the armor of heaven. A nearly full moon tilted on one side, like a damaged soccer ball. The air had the frosty tinge of late spring in Vermont—and it made the skin on his arms prickle slightly. He liked that. It reminded him that he was here, at least in body. What he had to do was get his mind and body into the same emotional sphere. But how, he wondered? How?

Chapter 12

Dona Isabel Moniz was startled one evening in late spring when her daughter, Dona Felipa, appeared in the narrow doorway of her Lisbon house with Diego—now four—in her arms. It was not only that she had appeared without warning. She looked dreadful: her eyes sunken into shadowy caves, her cheekbones like blades of rock threatening to poke through a thin crust of dirt.

"Where is Christopher?"

"I'm not sure," she said. "Somewhere in Italy, I think."

"What do you mean, you're not sure?"

Dona Felipa burst into sobs that frightened little Diego so thoroughly that he began to shake and sob, too. After a few angry snaps of Dona Isabel's mighty finger, servants descended on the hapless mother and child and helped them with their bags.

Diego was fed and put to bed by an elderly kitchen maid who had always adored Dona Felipa, while Dona Felipa and her mother sat in the dark drawing room over a glass of Madeira. The terrible tales of what had happened on Porto Santo during the past few years trickled out slowly at first, then gathered to a torrent as Dona Isabel sat there, wide-eyed, listening to her obviously unwell daughter.

Columbus, as Dona Isabel knew, always insisted that Dona Felipa remain there while he took various short-term commissions on merchant ships sailing to North Africa or around the Mediterranean. He adored the sea. Another way of looking at it was, of course, that family life did not satisfy him. Dona Isabel found none of this surprising, but she was startled to learn that he had fathered another child on Porto Santo. The child had died, fortunately, or God knows what responsibilities they might have been compelled to assume.

Suddenly Dona Felipa began coughing—uncontrollably. She doubled over.

"What on earth is this?" her mother said, rushing to pat her daughter's back.

Her response sputtered out between coughing fits. "I'm not well."

"Has this been going on for a long time, dear?"

Her daughter nodded, trying to control the spasms.

Dona Isabel asked a servant to bring the bottle of brown liquid for stifling coughs that she kept in a medicine chest in her bedroom. It was an obscure mixture of herbs and spices soaked in a heavy syrup of honey and port, and it had served the family well for many decades.

Dona Felipa smiled, refusing her mother's treatment. "I'd rather die, Mama. I really would!"

Dona Isabel insisted that her daughter go straight to bed. "And sleep in tomorrow. Don't even think about getting up."

It was May, and the leaves had finally appeared on the plane trees in the walled garden of the Perestrella y Moniz townhouse; one could dream for hours among the forsythia (whose yellow flowers had already fallen) and bougainvillea. Diego, beneath his flame-red hair, seemed horribly subdued. He sat alone in the garden and drew pictures of a round world in the dirt.

Dona Isabel, meanwhile, summoned a handful of Lisbon's most celebrated doctors, each of whom examined her daughter in turn. They believed that Dona Felipa's problems were temporary—the natural result of her adventures on Porto Santo. The fact that she had been coughing blood did not worry them, since they had tested the blood and found it "throat" blood instead of "lung" blood. One of them, a Dr. Manuelo, had bled her thoroughly, while another, a Dr. Ruiz, had put leaches from the Algarve on her breasts—an almost certain cure for a racking cough. A famous visiting professor of medicine from the University of Bologna had been called in for consultation, and he recommended a diet of mustard greens and garlic cloves soaked in pine oil. Dona Isabel discounted the part about the garlic cloves because of the man's country of origin, but she did manage to find a small portion of mustard greens, which did nothing for Dona Felipa but loosen her bowels.

Dona Felipa seemed resistant to all ministrations and grew thinner by the day. Her eyes grew saucerlike as the face that held them seemed to wither. Her wrist bones and shoulder blades stuck out, and her mind wandered like a fish astray in waters too deep for its imagination—crashing into rocks, getting tangled in languorous blue weeds, swimming inexorably toward the open mouth of a giant prehistoric beast.

Columbus arrived in Lisbon at the house of Dona Isabel in midsummer, carrying a huge sack of maps and miscellaneous manuscripts salvaged from the study of Dr. Paolo Toscanelli, whose widow he had just visited in Florence. These documents confirmed everything he had previously suspected about the shape of the earth and possible routes across the Atlantic to Cypango and the Indies. He felt certain, now, that the sovereigns of Castile would support him in his venture. For such a tiny investment they would acquire nothing less than an exclusive hold on the vast wealth of the East. And he, for his part, would be rich and powerful. Nobody would slander him again, calling him a "filthy Genoese dog," as one friend of the Perestrella family had put it at his wedding. He would show the arrogant bastards—all of them.

"Please, Christopher, come in," Dona Isabel said coolly as she led her son-in-law into the darkened drawing room.

He sniffed the air. It seemed unusually musty and dank, as if the room were a million years old. A bleak portrait of

Dom Bartholomew—who in real life had been a jovial and kindly man—glowered from the wall.

"Sit down, Christopher. I'm afraid there is bad news."

Columbus frowned. "Why is it that something always comes up when I'm away?" He was about to launch into a comic description of Dr. Toscanelli's wife for the benefit of Dona Isabel when she put a withered hand on his shoulder.

"Your wife died six weeks ago," she said. "We had to bury her without you, of course. There was no way of getting in touch."

"Dead?" He scratched his head, as if trying to dig something from the long curls.

"She suffered an apoplexy, brought on—I suspect—by the cough. A fever occurred . . . a week or so before. She lost consciousness several days before the end, so it was not difficult." She moved through this sentence with a glacial slowness. "Not difficult for her."

"Felipa is dead?"

Dona Isabel nodded.

"And where's Diego?"

"In the garden, I think. He'll be glad to see you."

Columbus sighed. *Isn't that just like her?* he thought. *To die when I have such good news, so many wonderful stories.* He walked to the window and opened the heavy curtain. His beautiful son was there, drawing circles in the dirt. The boy's face was smudged, his hair a mass of fiery curls. "He will make a fine sailor," Columbus said.

A week later, having settled everything with Dona Felipa's family, Columbus took off from Lisbon with Diego aboard a creaking merchant vessel headed for Andalusia. They sailed for a week, rounding Cape St. Vincent in a windstorm, crossing the bar of Saltes, then laying anchor off the melancholy town of Palos on the Río Tinto. From there, Columbus would pursue his great project, offering himself and his services to the king and queen of Castile.

Chapter 13

"You're an asshole, Milo."

"I'm telling Mommy you said that. She told you not to curse, didn't she?"

"You're a tattletale. Always were, always will be."

"You kicked me out of that tree."

"You deserved it."

"I didn't."

"Yes, you did. You're always telling lies about me. You're a fucking liar, that's what you are."

"You said 'fuck.' "

"So what?"

"Daddy said don't say 'fuck' anymore. You heard him, too."

"Shut up, Milo."

"No, you."

"I'd like to shut you up for good."

"Let's watch TV, huh? It's Saturday. The good cartoons come on today."

"I don't like TV. You're the one who likes TV. TV is boring."

"There's cartoons."

"I hate cartoons. They're for idiot kids. Like you."

"Jaaames."

"Milooooo."

"James."

"Milo."

"You like 'Ninja Turtles.' "

"It's violent. I don't like violent shows. I like to *be* violent."

"My arm is killing me."

"Wait till they have to inject your elbow."

"What's that?"

"In a week or so, they'll put a big long needle into your elbow. It brings down the swelling. Mommy will take you to the hospital, but she won't tell you what they're gonna do. She thinks it'll scare you. It's like . . . ten inches. This long!"

"Who told you that?"

"Ronald Beemer."

"He's a turkey."

"It happened to him last summer. He had a cast on his arm and his leg. He was in a car crash."

"And they put a needle into the cast?"

"A big one. First they stuck it into his elbow, then into his knee. The knee hurts a lot worse. You're lucky."

"I don't believe any of this."

"You can believe it or not. See if I care."

"I hate you, James."

"If you had any idea—*any* idea—how I felt about you, you'd kill yourself right now. Hang yourself or something."

"I'd kill you first."

"Oh, yeah?"

"Here's my butt, James. Kiss my butt."

"Damn you!"

"Go ahead. Kiss my butt."

Geno had just come inside Susan—a burst of feeling that began in his heels and rocked all the way through his groin to the base of his skull. "That was wonderful," he said, his voice barely audible through his quick panting.

Susan nodded, folding both hands around the back of his neck, kissing his forehead.

"Did you like it, too?"

She looked up at him searchingly, wondering why he still felt so uncertain about these things. Hadn't she registered her pleasure? She stroked his longish red hair, lit now from behind by the morning sun.

"Did you?" he insisted.

"I did. Yes." She sat up now and kissed the hairs of his chest, letting him stroke her back with his large, rough hands.

It was Saturday morning, a time when they commonly made love. In the evenings they were too tired for sex, and in the mornings—weekday mornings—there was no time. After their recent cooling in the wake of Milo's accident, and because he felt so guilty about his affair with Lizzie Nash, it was important to Geno that their lovemaking be good today.

"The kids are fighting again," Susan said with a sigh.

Geno pretended not to have heard. But Milo's wailing increased to a point where only the dead could have ignored it. "Fucking kids," Geno said, throwing on a pair of jeans.

In the kitchen, as expected, he found Milo lying on the floor, his wail rising in pitiful undulation. And James was nowhere to be found.

"Hello?"

"Hi!"

"Who's this?"

"What? It's your mother, Susan."

"Oh, hi."

"Were you sleeping? It's what, ten o'clock out there?"

"I was reading in bed."

"Where's Geno?"

"Downstairs, I think. With the boys."

"Were they fighting?"

"Not really."

"You've got to get control of those children. A little discipline goes a long way, you know."

"You're the expert, of course."

"Why are you always sarcastic with me, Susan? You're not like that with your father."

"Is Dad there?"

"He's on the other phone."

"Hello, Susan."

"Hi, Dad."

"Did Geno get that fellowship he was hoping for?"

"His leave? No. He didn't get it."

"So he'll have to teach next year."

"Yes."

"I don't know why he complains about teaching. What's he teach, a few hours a week?"

"Mother, you don't know anything about it."

"She's right, Helen."

"Be quiet, Ted."

"Listen, dear. Something has happened. Are you there, Susan?"

"I'm here, Mother."

"It's your brother, Charles. He's left Cicely."

"And the girls?"

"He left everyone."

"And Carnex?"

"Tell her, Ted."

"He told me to shove Carnex up my ass."

"Ted!"

"You said to tell her."

"This is awful, Dad."

"Can you imagine your brother saying such a thing, Susan? Your father is a mess."

"I'm hardly a mess, Helen. Don't overstate everything."

"How do you feel about this, Dad?"

"I wish Charles had come to me first."

"So what's all this mean?"

"Darling, I don't want to upset you or anything, but Charles is on drugs."

"We think he's on drugs is what your mother means."

"Face it, Ted. Your son is a druggie."

"Is this true, Dad?"

"He's taking marijuana."

"Are you laughing, Susan? I thought I heard you laughing. Susan, are you there?"

"I'm here, Mother. No, I was just coughing. I have a cold."

"It might be your allergies. It's almost summer. You always start to cough in summer."

"I'm worried about Charles. Where is he?"

"We wondered if maybe you knew something. He just . . . left."

"Hasn't he left word with Cicely?"

"Nothing. He told your father to shove Carnex up his ass, and he left."

"This is bad."

"It's not good."

"He was having problems at work. I should have sensed that something was up."

"Ted, I don't know where your head is."

"I don't understand that boy. I never did."

"Listen, Susan. We won't take up all your time. But let

us know the minute you hear anything. He's bound to call you. You and he were always so close."

"I'll let you know if I hear anything."

"Bye, darling."

"Bye, Mother."

"Bye, Susan."

"Bye, Dad."

Chapter 14

After his weekly meeting with Rose Weintraub, Geno wandered across the campus to Milton House. He was feeling better now, light-headed, even happy. Therapy was cleansing for him, an expurgation. And, unless he was deeply mistaken, he was moving closer to his emotional center.

Life was so baffling, the kaleidoscope of selves he had to inhabit daily—each requiring a change of mental costume. Rose had helped him to sift through those selves, had urged him to accept the artificiality—and truth-value—of different but not mutually exclusive roles. He was a husband, a teacher, a poet, a father, a lover. Each was a mask, and each brought out a different aspect of some adamant core, a piece of the eternal Geno.

Classes were over, and most of the exams were given and graded. Graduation would happen in about a week. And there was a blessed aura of pause at Barrington—a halo of ease. The campus felt light, buoyant. A sigh of relief seemed to exude from the pavement, the lawns and verdant pathways, even the granite buildings themselves.

Geno found a pink slip in his box, however, that mildly upset him. "Call Dean Botner's office," it said. The English Department secretary had written the note in her looping cursive—the kind of handwriting one expected of a grade school teacher making a demonstration for her pupils.

What did Botner want with him? To warn him about getting his grades in on time? He hoped not. It had made him furious when, a couple of years ago, some assistant dean had inquired about his grades four days before they were actually due! Maybe something had changed about the leave? If the college had suddenly gotten a windfall grant from somewhere, they might well add a few leaves.

"Dean Botner." The man said that as if unconvinced.

"Larry, it's Chris Genovese."

"Geno!" Botner was unusually friendly.

"You wanted to see me?"

"I did. Are you free? I've got a staff meeting in an hour, but I'll be here till then."

"Sure. I'll be right over."

"Good." Botner hung up with peculiar abruptness.

Geno knew that something was up, something terrible. He had been around academics long enough to know their ways, and Botner's friendliness meant bad news.

The administration of Barrington College kept to itself in a small clapboard building in the northeast corner of the campus, not far from the gym. It was called Stone House, though it was the only building on Barrington's granitic campus *not* made of stone. It had been named for a generous graduate, Genevieve Stone '28, who had built it in 1973 to honor her late husband, Gene Stone '27. Her only stipulation had been that the building be made of "anything but stone."

Botner's secretary waved Geno in. "He's waiting, Professor Genovese," she said, cheerily. That cheeriness froze Geno's heart. She was not a warm woman, and her smile was like a crack in a block of dry ice.

"Hello, Geno."

"Larry."

Geno took up the only obvious chair, which was opposite the dean's.

"I won't beat around the bush, Geno."

"Please, don't."

"There's been a formal complaint. A student of yours—Ms. Elizabeth Nash. You know her?"

"Of course."

"Yes. Well, she has charged you with sexual harassment."

"What?"

"You know, this sort of thing is in the air now."

"This is crazy."

"I quite agree."

"It's crap. I'll swear to that on a stack of Bibles."

"I believe you, Geno, but we've got to approach this seriously. She's filed a complaint with the Committee on Human Relations, and they will offer you a hearing next week."

"*Offer* me a hearing?"

"Next Monday. At ten, in the conference room upstairs."

"I see."

"We've been through this kind of thing before. I suggest you take it easy."

"Nice, Larry. Take it easy. I can see why they made you a dean."

Botner shifted in his chair. The tiny blue veins near the surface of his alcoholic's face threatened to pop.

"Should I hire a lawyer or anything?"

"Not yet. If this thing goes further, which I don't think it will, well, maybe. The college would provide you with legal counsel, if that became necessary. This is all very preliminary."

"I don't like the sound of that . . . preliminary. It suggests that something will follow. Like prison."

"Let's not worry about this until the time comes."

"Ah, yes. Back-burner it for a week."

"Try to."

"Well, thanks, Larry." He stood. "It's been nice talking to you, as always."

"I know you're upset, Geno. I want you to know I understand."

"Thanks, Larry."

He actually meant that. Thanks. It surprised him how gently and offhandedly Larry Botner had managed that little interview. He was professional, but he had shown sympathy. He had not overstated anything. Indeed, the whole thing had been neatly downplayed.

Maybe he wasn't really in bad trouble. Maybe he only imagined he would lose his job, be blackballed from academic employment for the rest of his life, be lambasted in the national press, and so forth. The possibilities for disaster were limitless. This was just what Barrington needed now: a sacrificial lamb. Well, he was *Christ*-opher, wasn't he? (He could feel Susan wincing at the pun.) Jesus Fucking Genovese.

Susan was sitting on the porch when he drove up, watching Milo and James, who seemed preoccupied with a kite that she had bought for them a few days before. Milo, with his arm in a cast, was standing beside his older brother, hurling instructions. James had a tolerant look on his face. The kite soared above the trees. It was brilliant yellow, full and fluttering.

Geno sat beside Susan on the side steps.

"Hi," she said.

"Hi, honey."

"They love that kite. James has finally got the hang of it."

"I see."

"Milo can't wait for the cast to come off."

"I bet."

"How was your therapy?"

"Okay. And yours?"

"It went okay. Sometimes I think I'm actually getting somewhere."

"Good."

Geno wasn't sure exactly how he would say what he had to say. But now seemed like as good a time as any.

"There's something I've got to tell you. It's not going to be easy. But I want you to know."

Susan put on her detached look, and Geno was grateful for that.

"To begin with, I had sex with a student a few weeks ago. Lizzy Nash. I don't know what came over me. It was stupid. Fucking stupid."

Susan did not move. She did not even blink. Was he really saying what he seemed to be saying?

"And today, this afternoon, Botner called me into his office. Lizzy Nash has complained about me to the Human Relations committee. There's going to be a hearing next Monday."

After a longish pause, Susan said, "Anything else? I mean, have you shot anyone lately?"

Geno offered a rueful smile. The fact that Susan had reacted with a touch of humor made everything possible.

"I thought you'd want to know."

"I don't *want* to know. I *have* to know."

"Yeah."

"Sometimes I think I don't know you very well, Geno."

"Really?"

"You're like . . . unfathomable."

"I'm trying to be honest with you."

"I believe that, but it doesn't help very much. I don't know what to say to you."

Geno shrugged. He was trembling inside. He felt so alone, so confused. He wanted to ditch everything, to get the hell out of there. To fly to Alaska. Or Patagonia. That was it. He could become a sheep farmer in Patagonia.

"I'm going to get the dinner on the table."

"What is it?"

"Pasta."

"Good."

"And fish."

"I like fish."

Geno stood up, face to face with Susan. "Can I kiss you, honey?"

"No."

"No?"

"I don't want to kiss you now." She turned away from him and went into the kitchen.

Geno felt his shoulders pull forward into his chest, his spine curling into the letter *C*. Sitting on the steps, exhausted, he noticed a white-tailed rabbit scampering through the nearby brush. It darted out into the big field near the pond, zigzagging as it ran. Looking up, he saw a red-tailed hawk hanging in the wind, hovering. It was all so obvious and cruel, he thought. So fucking obvious and cruel.

Chapter 15

Columbus took it as a good sign that Diego never mentioned his mother. Instead, he sat on the foredeck throughout the voyage to Castile without complaining, without referring to anything except "the black birds, the black birds everywhere."

"The birds are white," Columbus said. "I don't know what you mean."

"I saw black ones."

"Maybe."

Cormorants, thought Columbus. The boy must have seen cormorants: black satanic birds whose long necks unfurled ominously from their sooty bodies. They gathered like specks of dust on the cobalt water, fishing. He considered them very bad luck.

Looking at Diego, Columbus found himself thinking about his long-deceased father, Domenico, who had caused him so much grief. It comforted him to realize that Diego would never think of him in the same light. What troubled him had been his father's incompetence. He knew his trade well enough. As a master clothier, he bought the wool himself, had it dyed, and employed journeymen weavers to turn it into cloth, which he then sold to tailors and dressmakers in Genoa and Savona. Had he stopped there, all would have been well. But Domenico was ambitious beyond his talents, and he suffered from dreams of grandeur. He wanted more of what he already had: money, friends, and respect in the community.

What he got, finally, was less of each—especially after he decided to become a wine and cheese merchant. Everyone knew that huge profits were made in these luxurious products of the Italian genius for food, but only the shrewdest of men knew which strings to pull. Domenico invested every extra penny he made as a clothier, and then some, in wine and cheese, establishing contacts with an array of spurious dealers and retailers. He set himself up royally in an old warehouse near the Porta di Sta. Andrea.

"Do you know about the Medicis?" he would ask Christopher, his eldest son. "One day the name of Columbus will be just as famous. Our wines and cheeses will be devoured from London to Athens!"

Domenico was soon bankrupt, and were it not for a beneficent uncle, Christopher and his brothers and their sister, the voluptuous Bianchinetta, would have starved.

Despite his lack of business acumen, Domenico was popular in Genoa and, later, Savona. Everyone forgave him easily for his mistakes. Throughout his long life, he enjoyed the company of loud and friendly Genoese merchants; like most of them, he drank too much. Christopher remembered with distaste the evenings when Domenico staggered home past midnight to wake his long-suffering wife, Susanna. She questioned him, over breakfast, about his nocturnal pastimes, always worried that he had been roaming the dockside brothels with Pietro Bombaloso, a wayward friend who was like an uncle to the Columbus children. Domenico would grow stern. "Shut thy mouth, wife," he would say.

The town of Palos, where they anchored in the mouth of the Río Tinto, was moribund; indeed, the contrast with Lisbon weighed on Columbus as he loaded his and his son's few belongings into an oxcart. He had never been here before, but he'd heard a lot about this region. These marshy coastal waters owned a dreadful history, having been the site of Castile's slave trade until just a few years before, when the African trade was banned in Castile. Shiploads of naked men, women, and children would arrive in crowded caravels to be sold for huge profits at public auction in Huelva, a nearby town. Columbus had never understood the point of banning slavery. These Africans were not, after all, Christians.

Although his family had not been religious except in a perfunctory way, Columbus loved God. He had always loved God. Every morning at sunrise he said his rosaries and every night before falling asleep he prayed to three different saints. He attended mass whenever the opportunity arose. And he fantasized about life in a monastery. Had he not been a seaman, he'd have surely been a monk. That's what he told himself.

And that's what he told the Franciscans at La Rábida, the old monastary situated on a pale bluff overlooking the Río

Tinto. It had caught his eye as soon as they rounded the point where the Río Tinto met the Río Odiel: a pink cluster of stone buildings with a huge bell tower from which (he imagined) one got a splendid view of the sandy dunes, the marshy headlands, the marram grass, and limestone slopes below.

Columbus was squinting at La Rábida in the distance when a rainbow appeared around the bell tower. At last, a good omen! "That will be your new home, Diego," he had told his dumbfounded son. "You will board with the good fathers, but I'll send for you as soon as I can."

"I want to go with you," Diego said, in a weak voice.

"That's not possible, son."

"Why?"

The leathery face of Columbus tightened. "You must not question your elders. Your elders know better."

The boy did not respond.

They were met at the dusty gates of La Rábida by an elderly and deeply bored friar, Fray Juan Pérez, who recognized instinctively that Columbus was a man full of stories. Fray Juan adored good stories, so he eagerly welcomed these visitors to the monastery. He set them down at a long plank table, fed them a bowl of soup with fresh-baked bread, and called for his superior, Fray Antonio de Marchena—a spunky man of fifty-six who fancied himself an *astrólogo*, adept at reading and intrepreting the starry skies.

Fray Antonio listened avidly to Columbus, who told him about his great enterprise, for which he hoped to gain support from the king and queen of Spain. "I shall introduce you to my friend, Don Enrique," he announced rather unexpectedly, referring to Don Enrique de Guzmán, Duke of Medina Sidonia.

"You are most kind, Fray Antonio."

Columbus realized at once that a path might lead directly through Don Enrique to Isabella and Ferdinand. He guessed that these aristocrats all knew each other, therefore it hardly mattered which duke or duchess he chose for a starting point.

"Don Enrique is rich. *Very* rich," Fray Juan added, his eyes glistening.

"That's splendid," Columbus said. "I, on the other hand, am a man with a large future but not much present. My dear son, Diego, is a motherless child, and I can't help but wonder if, perhaps, I might board Diego at La Rábida for a certain period of time."

Diego bit his lip and suppressed a tear.

"By all means!" Fray Juan said, putting an arm around the boy's shoulders. "We'll take very good care of him!"

"I would consider that a great favor."

Fray Antonio smiled. He invited Columbus to his study for a glass of port, suggesting to Fray Juan that, perhaps, it was past the child's bedtime.

Columbus kissed Diego on the forehead. "Everything will be all right," he whispered in the child's small ear. "I swear!"

The boy nodded.

He did not look back as he was led by the elderly Fray Juan to a bed of straw in the loft over the refectory.

Chapter 16

Geno woke in a sanguine mood on the morning of his inquisition. Getting to his library carrel early, he wrote forty-three lines of his Columbus poem in a blaze of composition. He'd been thinking about the death of Dona Felipa in Lisbon for some weeks. His thoughts also turned to the painful journey to Castile that Columbus took with little Diego. It must have hurt him to board his small son at La Rábida. The coincidence that Fray Antonio de Marchena happened to be staying at La Rábida when Columbus arrived seemed miraculous.

The idea that one's fate is woven into the stars had always seemed foolish to Geno, the stuff of supermarket tabloids and New Age freaks. Vermont overflowed with palm readers, astrologers, and assorted wide-eyed prophets and opinionated mountebanks, and Geno disparaged them. But he did not discount the possibility that mysterious forces were at work in the universe. History brimmed with unexplainable coincidences; indeed, his own life was teeming with them.

It did not seem "coincidental," for instance, that he and Susan were together. They'd met in a grocery store in Boston called Erewhon at exactly the same time both were reading the novel *Erewhon*, by Samuel Bulter (a fact they discovered over dinner that same night). Susan had been standing at the vitamin section when he first saw her, her bare legs bronzed with sun; she was reaching to pick a bottle of lecithin off the top shelf. Geno had been taking lecithin at the time, and he said to her, "That's powerful stuff! Be careful!" They began talking about its potency, and one thing led to another.

Susan's first impression was that he must be some kind of quack. But she liked him immediately. She was living at the time with a man named Ben who played bass guitar with a hard rock band in Cambridge called Sewage. Susan knew that Sewage came first in his life, and she was not happy. In any case the relationship had never been "serious," but she felt strange about leaving him so quickly for Geno. It took only three days. Geno was spending the summer in Concord and writing his book on modern poetry—a souped-up version of his doctoral thesis. He chose Concord as a place to pass the idyllic summer days because Thoreau and Emerson had lived there, and Emerson was the fountainhead, as he always said. Susan agreed. In fact, Geno seduced Susan (the night following their initial date) by reading aloud to her the essay "On Friendship." She did not actually decide to marry him till some months later, when he insisted on reading aloud the whole of "Nature." She figured you could trust a man who loved "Nature."

They were married in Madison at a big white Presbyterian church, with three bridesmaids who all dressed in the same memorable shade of peach with big floppy hats like English royalty wear. In keeping with a shared streak of not-so-latent Anglophilia, they took their honeymoon in the English Lake District, near Windermere, where they spent two weeks wandering along sheep-strewn byways that Wordsworth and his sister, Dorothy, might have walked. They even passed a long afternoon in the cottage at Grasmere where many of Wordsworth's best poems were written and where he entertained his melancholy friend, Coleridge.

Susan spent much of the trip reading Dorothy's *Journals*, which she considered a notch above Wordsworth's poems. "His work is so thin," she said. "Dorothy had guts."

What Geno needed today was Dorothy's guts. Lots of them. He couldn't imagine what would happen at Stone House this afternoon. What did Lizzy Nash think she was doing? He should probably have gotten her side of the story personally—even though Chap Baloo had advised against it. Lizzy wasn't crazy or, as far as he could tell, malicious. She might have been put up to this by someone. But who?

He stepped out of the carrel to stretch his legs, pausing to stare through one of the library's huge glass walls at the luxuriantly green campus, all perfectly manicured by armies of men on mowers. Trees lined the walks: slim-necked elms (spared the ravages of Dutch elm disease at great expense to the college) and lacy willows, imposing oaks and chalk-white birches. In a little copse were maples, poplars, and white pines. This was indeed a parcel of Eden, snakes and all.

With a flutter in his gut, Geno packed his leather briefcase and set off for Stone House. He waited until the chapel bell gonged twice before knocking at the conference room door.

"Come in," called Botner.

An ex officio member of the Human Relations committee, Botner sat in on all important meetings. The others were Agnes Wild, who loved to get on committees with gossip potential; Ralph Mendelson, a philosopher; and Maria Martinez, who had just been hired by Fernando Nachez to teach Central American politics. A prim-looking student called Bill Reid was also there in a button-down oxford shirt; he sat next to Lizzy, who avoided Geno's gaze.

"Please, sit down," Botner said.

"Thank you."

"You know why we're here, of course." The dean used his most deanly voice.

"I do," Geno said gravely, as if committing himself to Holy Matrimony. "But I can't say I understand the issue."

"Perhaps I'll ask Professor Wild, who is chairperson of this committee, to explain."

Agnes Wild opened a manila folder. "This isn't a trial or tribunal," she said. "It's an informal inquiry. Ms. Nash has registered a complaint with us. She maintains—in essence—that you gave her a lower grade than she deserved on her senior thesis for reasons that are not entirely academic."

"Such as?" Geno knew Agnes well, and he was surprised to see her acting as if she hardly knew him.

"She believes that sexual harassment was involved, and this is what concerns us."

"Does she claim I harassed her?"

"Yes, in fact."

Geno decided that he must speak directly to Lizzy. "Is this what you claim, Lizzy?"

Lizzy looked down. "Yes," she said.

"I see."

Botner grimaced, then spoke. "I suppose we should consider the nature of this alleged harassment."

"Let's," said Geno. "I'm eager to hear about it myself."

"Lizzy, would you like to tell us what happened?" Agnes asked, casting a peculiarly knowing look at the flustered student.

It swept into Geno's mind that Agnes had instigated this, and he cursed himself for not figuring it out before. She and Geno had never really hit it off. The fact that she was openly lesbian didn't bother him in the slightest; on the contrary, he liked that about her. Gay people understood the duplicitous nature of all public discourse, and he admired that. Nor did he object to her feminism; he appreciated that side of her, and he stood by her there. It was her tone and methods. She could be snide and conniving.

Agnes sat there today drumming her thin fingers on the wooden table; her black hair seemed to be turning white on the spot, her nostrils quivering. When she spoke, she never looked at Geno directly; rather, she seemed to talk over him or around him. He wanted to shake her by the collarbone, to say, "It's me, Agnes! Are you in there, darling?"

But what could have motivated her to stoop so low? Was it merely that he had insisted on directing Lizzy's thesis on Virginia Woolf instead of her? Hadn't Lizzie, in any case, been writing on Woolf with him and on Neruda with Nachez? Why were academics so goddamned petty anyway?

Lizzie Nash said, "Professor Genovese gave me no indication throughout the term that my thesis was going badly. Unless I read him completely wrong, I'd say that he liked it—or claimed to like it. That's what I thought. It was . . . my impression."

Geno couldn't stand it. "I *did* like it, damn it! I gave you a B-plus. A B-plus is a *good grade*! 'B' means good. The 'plus' means *very* good."

"This is not the appropriate place for a discussion of the relative value of grades," Agnes said. "The point is that Ms. Nash felt misled."

Botner intervened. "I don't think we'll get anywhere along these lines. It's not good teaching to give a student the wrong impression, that's for sure. But neither can it be called immoral. Let's turn to the sexual harassment part." He looked straight at Lizzy: "Elizabeth?"

Geno's stomach tightened.

"Professor Genovese said various things that I would consider . . . seductive. If I'm not mistaken, sexual harassment occurs when there is sexual pressure applied to a student."

The committee stared, ad hoc, at Geno.

"I fucked her," Geno said. "Or, conversely, she fucked me."

Lizzy's normally ruddy face paled. Even her freckles, like

stars in the dawn sky, faded into the broader pigment of her skin, appalled.

"You needn't all look so shocked," Geno said. "It happens all the time. Boy meets girl. Boy sleeps with girl."

Larry Botner glared at him. "This is absurd, Geno. You're making things worse for yourself."

"I don't consider what I did a sin against Barrington College. It wasn't nice, I'll say that much. I've already apologized to Susan, my wife. If she can forgive me, surely Barrington can." He stood up, raised his arms to the ceiling. "Have a heart, Barrington," he bellowed. "Have a fucking heart!"

Agnes Wild spoke up quietly. "A professor has certain advantages—powerful ones, in fact. We're talking about abuse of power here."

"Even if the student consents?" Geno asked. "I mean, it's not rape that I'm being charged with, is it? Lizzy wanted me to have sex with her."

Agnes looked askance.

Geno said, "I've got a stack of interesting letters—even some short stories—from Ms. Nash. She put them into my mailbox in the course of the semester." He dipped into his briefcase and took out a thick manila envelope marked *Nash* and tossed it on the table. "Read to your heart's content, honorable friends. I think you'll get a better idea of what may have happened between myself and Ms. Nash."

Botner snatched up the envelope. "The committee will consider this material sometime before its next meeting," he said.

Agnes Wild maintained an expressionless face, but her ears—her very large ears—went pink at the edges.

"Good," Geno said.

Lizzy Nash had never regained her freckles; indeed, her eyes were full of tears. And Geno was full of sorrow now. The poor girl had been misled.

"I'm sorry, Lizzy," he said.

She did not look at him.

"Well, if you'll all excuse me, I'm afraid I have another appointment," he said, zipping his briefcase shut. He felt like a businessman now: precise, straight-edged, methodical, direct. "I'll be happy to meet with you again, if that's required." With a brief nod to the committee, he left the room.

Susan bent over a long strip of earth with a trowel, putting in a row of basil plants for summer pesto. Their sweet smell filled her nostrils. The sun sloped toward the western horizon, bathing the distant Adirondacks in a peculiar, buttery glow. Hummingbirds stitched the air, more like outsized insects than birds, approaching one at a time the feeder that swung from the porch rafters.

The kids had gone off to play and have dinner with friends, and Susan had been alone all afternoon. Her mind turned inevitably to Geno. She pitied him for his lack of judgment in the affair with Lizzy Nash, but she hated his stupidity and callowness. Men should by their fourth decade have left adolescence *behind* them, but she knew that few of them did, recalling how her mother had indulged Charles.

Charles, in her mother's mind, was the brilliant one, the promising one, the heir apparent, while Susan was—well, the girl. And girls didn't catch the limelight. They assisted men, nurtured, aided and abetted them. They provided a genially bemused audience for male antics. They clapped and cheered, wept and cautioned, while their privileged boy-men behaved as they always had from early childhood on through dotage.

Andrew Ridgeway was hardly exempt from this critique. She could see him sitting in the woods, burning his incense, and reciting his mantra in forty years. His Bob Dylan records would spin through eternity—a spiral of music liberated from time's claustrophobic circle.

Since her initial meeting with Andrew at the A&P, and her subsequent visit to his "camp" in the hills, she'd met him twice for afternoon tea: once again at his place, once at a hip little café. Andrew had called her several times at home, though she had asked him not to do this. It wasn't so much that there was anything between them: Susan had not crossed any visible lines. But she understood perfectly well that sex—like a sword—flashed in the air between them. It would be only too easy to fall on that blade and get hurt.

Susan wished she had mentioned Andrew to Geno, but she hadn't. For reasons obscure to herself, she wanted to hoard the eroticism of this contact, however oblique it might be. The fantasy would evaporate upon exposure, and she needed it now. Her life with Geno seemed oddly de-eroticized in the wake of his anxiety over Lizzy Nash. She knew there was no attachment between him and Lizzy, nothing that could threaten their marriage, but the whole thing hurt her terribly. It was so unthoughtful and impulsive. What she needed was time to reconstruct her relations with Geno, to let her anger subside.

Geno's tires sputtered on the driveway, kicking up pebbles, and Susan waited nervously as he parked.

"So what happened?" she asked, as he approached.

"I don't really know, but I felt good about it. And bad, too. I guess . . ."

"You look happy enough."

"Repression. I've repressed all the lousy parts. What you see is not what you get."

"Was Agnes in charge?"

"Was she ever. It's all her doing."

"No."

"I think so. You know how she thinks she owns Virginia Woolf. It bugged her that I wanted to direct Lizzy's thesis. She's just getting back at me. It's demonic. The woman is gonzo."

"She's been miserable, you know. This thing with Jane is getting under her skin."

"Jane Burl is a menace. Agnes is better off without her."

"That's not how she sees it. In any case, you're dead wrong about Agnes. She's not mean-spirited."

"Okay, she's just sour."

"She's hurt."

Geno was exasperated, but he admired Susan for her rigor. She let nothing pass.

Inside, they sat down to a quiet dinner without the children: a plate of fettucine tossed in a pesto sauce, followed by grilled salmon and a salad of mixed greens—arugula, Boston lettuce, endive. They shared an icy bottle of Orvieto.

"I think there's been a lot of plotting about this thing," Geno said, sipping Green Mountain vanilla roast decaf.

"You're quite mad," Susan said. "Paranoid."

"Mad as a hatter?"

"How mad are hatters?"

"I don't know. I think the expression has something to do with the glue that hatmakers in London used to fix the bands inside the hats. It drove them all bananas."

"How come your head is so filled with things like that?"

"I ignore the important things."

"How do you feel about me? Do you like me still?"

"I love you, don't I?"

"Is that a question?"

Susan reached across the table for his hand, and he reached out to meet her halfway.

Chapter 17

Like most aristocrats, Don Enrique de Guzmán, Duke of Medina Sidonia, had money in excess of brains. But he liked Columbus, who told long and amusing stories, and he promised to send him across the Western Ocean with two or three ships. "The boy will drop off into space, I suspect," he told his wife, Florencia. "But there's a chance that he may be right."

Unfortunately, the duke was having dinner in Seville with the king and queen one night when the choleric Duke of Cádiz was also present. When Don Enrique told everyone about the impending voyage of Columbus, Cádiz called Don Enrique a "bloody fool."

Don Enrique subsequently broke the duke's aquiline nose, and blood gushed over the tablecloth, ruining a lovely dinner. King Ferdinand ordered Don Enrique out of Seville at once.

One positive result of the ducal battle at the royal table was that everybody who was anybody in Andalusía heard about

Columbus and his project. Soon the goddess Fortuna favored Columbus by sending his way a wealthy count by the name of Luis de la Cerda, who owned a large fleet of merchant ships; he was willing to take a chance on this headstrong Genoese. Don Luis wrote to his sovereigns, who immediately wrote back to say that Columbus ought to present himself in Cordova, where the king and queen occupied the Alcazar—a fortress owned by the sultans in the days of Moorish power. So Columbus set off for Cordova.

The royal couple were not there when he arrived, but the courtier in charge knew exactly who Columbus was and sent him to a small apartment with a view of the distant hills and told him to wait. He would be summoned in due course.

Columbus waited happily. He liked to walk, and he soon knew every alley and close in Cordova by heart. And he quickly met the town's leading citizens, including Leonardo de Esbarraya—a fellow Genoese who ran an apothecary shop.

It so happened that Leonardo's shop had become an informal gathering spot for local surgeons, astrologers, and amateur scientists. He and his friends admired Columbus as a man who'd apparently been everywhere and done everything. They readily agreed with him that the world was round, though estimates of its size varied. Leonardo himself believed that it would take a biblical seven years to sail westward to Cypango.

The apothecary talked loudly and ate hugely. His great belly shook when he laughed, and he laughed a lot. He was famous in Cordova for his medicinal potions, which had cured everything from gout and apoplectic neuralgia to bubonic plague. His best friend was a jolly wine-maker called

Rodrigo de Harana, who had a strong interest in all things maritime.

Rodrigo invited Columbus to his home for dinner one evening, where he met the wine-maker's niece, Beatriz. Columbus found her fresh and beautiful. Her russet hair was shot through with gold, and she exuded a kind of informal sexiness that he'd not seen before except among the peasant women of Liguria. She poured wine into his pewter goblet with a slantwise grin and didn't hesitate to tease him. "Be careful, sailor. It's strong stuff," she said, winking. Leaning over him as she poured, she exposed the freckled cleft between her breasts.

Columbus called on Rodrigo and his family often, largely because of Beatriz. Soon they became friends, and before long she was sleeping with him at his apartment.

He would make love to her in the late afternoons, when the honey-colored Andalusian light flushed his bedroom. They would continue, with many climaxes, through the early evening. He adored her flinty green eyes, her silken skin, and the way she smelled like rain. It often struck him he was crazy to leave Spain for Cypango. Even the immense wealth of the Orient did not compare with Beatriz. "I'll stay with you forever," he whispered, letting his tongue follow his words into the innermost caverns of her ear.

When the king and queen finally summoned him, he changed his tune. Sexual activity occludes the visionary mind, he told himself. And what his situation required now was vision. He simply had to make Ferdinand and Isabella see what he could see: the speckled rooftops and gilded minarets of the East, the ships laden with spices, gold, and precious gems.

Once, when Beatriz came knocking on his apartment door in the late afternoon (her hair and feet were freshly washed, her fingernails were painted, and her breath was tinged with garlic—just the way he liked it), Columbus was thinking about his upcoming presentation at the royal court. "Go away! I'm thinking!" he shouted.

"It's Beatriz!" She put her ear to the door and waited.

"I'm thinking! Go away!"

Beatriz felt deeply wounded. She was pregnant with his child, though he had yet to find out about it. Walking alone over the cobbled streets back to her uncle's house, she wondered what sort of man this was, who could turn her away because—of all things—he was thinking!

Chapter 18

Geno could feel the great wheel turning. His relations with Susan had taken on a fresh coloration, the tinge of experience. Years ago he would never have guessed that marriage could be so hard; that it required something like daily revision, reinvention, to make it work.

With the change of weather, Geno and Susan had taken to going on little hikes with the boys in the afternoons—usually late in the day, when the sun cut slantwise through the trees. They would hunt for Indian arrowheads, for rabbit holes, for deer and bear tracks. Susan had recently bought a tape of birdcalls, and Geno offered each boy a quarter who could identify one call properly (though he wasn't sure what he'd do if they tried, since the red-winged blackbird was the only one he remembered).

As they returned home on this particular afternoon they

saw that a man was sitting on their lawn in the lotus position with a rainbow-colored beret tipped sideways on his head; a gold earring glittered in his left earlobe. For a long time, approaching the house, they could not tell who it was.

"Is he a robber?" Milo asked.

"Maybe," said Geno. He liked teasing the kids about robbers.

"It's your Uncle Charles," said Susan, shielding her eyes from the sun's glare. "Good grief."

"What's he doing?" asked James.

"Is he like sleeping or what?" Milo wondered as they came closer. They approached him tentatively, walking up to him on tiptoe; James cupped his hands to his uncle's ear. "Uncle Charles!" The man's eyelids fluttered. He looked at James with mild surprise.

"You in there, Uncle Charles?" James asked, waving a hand in front of the man's eyes.

"Hello, nephew," Charles said.

"Welcome to Vermont, Charles," Susan said. "Does Mother know your whereabouts? Or Cicely?"

"Nope," he said. "And I trust you won't tell them."

Susan frowned; she hated it when he involved her in his little games.

That night, after the children had been put to bed, Geno and Susan sat with Charles in the living room.

"God, it's so beautiful here," Charles said, looking out

the window at the fiery tip of Mount Isaac. "It's like . . . a postcard. A nice postcard."

"What's going on, Charles? You should know that Mother is very upset with you."

"I couldn't take it any longer," he said. "Or them."

"Cicely and the girls?"

"Everyone in Madison. And Carnex was stifling."

Susan understood only too well. The family circle was nothing less than strangulating, and the community looked to anyone called Worthington for something akin to moral leadership. It was all a bore.

"So where are you going?" Geno asked.

"Here."

"Ah."

"Don't worry. I won't stay in your house for long. I plan to build a cabin in the woods."

"Like Thoreau," Geno said.

Charles began to laugh weirdly, his eyes twitching.

Susan went into the kitchen to make herbal tea. It was just too difficult to be around Charles when he was manic. The bizarre laugh and facial twitching were familiar to her as signs of trouble. From the kitchen she could hear her brother rambling on. He'd had it with "industry," with living life in a straitjacket. His spiritual values had been almost extinguished. He wanted to get back in touch with the natural world and himself. He sought a "new relationship with God."

"That's a tall order," Geno said.

Susan heard the slight twang of irony in his voice, and it embarrassed her. If Charles detected it, he would be upset. But she knew that Geno was also serious. He had a way of saying a thing like that and having it—even *meaning* it—both ways.

"It's what I need," Charles said. "I feel bad about the girls. But they're Cicely's girls. I should have acted earlier. Maybe they'd be my girls, too, if I had."

Geno said nothing. He couldn't imagine a father saying such a thing about his children. Milo and James were as much his boys as Susan's.

"Red Zinger all around," Susan said, entering with a tray.

"I got here in time for the Rainbow Celebration," Charles said, taking the mug of tea.

"What?" asked Geno.

"The Rainbow Family of Light," he explained. "Twenty thousand of them will be here next weekend for July Fourth."

Susan could feel her entire body blush at the mention of the Rainbow thing. She could see that poster hanging over Andrew's couch.

"Here?" Geno asked. He looked worried.

"In Vermont. They meet every year on the Fourth. Haven't you read about them?"

"Who are they?"

"Hippies. *Real* hippies."

"I didn't think anyone used that word anymore," Susan said. "Not seriously."

"The counterculture—the green revolution. Whatever you want to call it," Charles said. "It never died. That's just what the media want you to believe. It went underground." He folded his legs under him like a Buddha. "The Rainbow people are dedicated to the environment. Their basic idea is that we should not disturb the natural world. The earth is our mother."

"I agree with that," Geno said.

"Maybe the earth is our father," Susan said, holding the mug of tea in both hands. "Or maybe we shouldn't think of nature as something that needs a gender."

"You're right, Susie," said Charles. "I hadn't thought of that."

Susan inwardly shuddered, remembering how her brother's perfunctory responses always irritated her, even when she was a small girl. She wondered if his reactions had something to do with her or if he was just like that . . .

"Are you a member of this group, Charles?" Geno asked.

"There's no membership. Anyone who admires a rainbow belongs."

"Ah."

"There's a Rainbow commune near Madison. I lived with them for a couple weeks when I left Cicely, and they told me about this tribal gathering. I thought, gee, my sister lives there."

"So here you are," Susan said.

"Somewhere over the rainbow," Geno added.

"It's crazy," said Susan, who did not want to attend the Rainbow Celebration.

"It's not crazy. I want the boys to see what the sixties were like."

"This is the nineties, Geno. You can't bring back the sixties by wearing a rainbow tee shirt and bellbottoms. What the boys will see up there is a bunch of burnt-out cases pretending that two decades haven't happened."

"Think of it as an outing. A hike. A party." He could not fathom her resistance. What did it matter anyway?

"We don't belong there," Susan continued. "We'll feel like . . . like tourists."

"Voyeurs?" Geno liked the sound of that word.

"Something like that."

"Baloney." He began mass-producing peanut-butter-and-jelly sandwiches as he talked. "You don't have to come if you don't want, honey. Charles and I can handle the boys."

Susan took a spoonful of peanut butter for herself and leaned against the counter, thinking. How likely was it that she'd run into Andrew in the midst of a crowd of twenty thousand? "I'll come," she said.

"Good. We'll have a good time." He finished slapping the sandwiches together, poured iced tea into a large Thermos, and put two cans of root beer in his knapsack for the kids. He was happy today. Anything that reminded him of the sixties attracted him, even though he'd never been a "hippie," per se. He doubted, in fact, that many people had ever thought of themselves in those terms.

For him, the sixties was about Vietnam. He had genuinely despised that war, not only because he was afraid to die in a remote swamp himself (though he was); it had as much, or more, to do with what America was doing to the Vietnamese. It still infuriated him when people talked about American wars and only took into account American casualties. How many millions of people suffered death or injury or grievous loss because of American power in that war? Or in subsequent wars, such as the Persian Gulf War? Geno believed that, somehow, for a very brief period, young people in the sixties had caught a glimpse of something eternal and good. They had mustered the will to resist the powers above and beyond them. The real spirit of the America that he loved had been animated, set free, in that moment of conflict.

Susan sympathized with most of this, although it often frightened her that Geno responded so emotionally, so hysterically, to the subject of American power. Her agenda was much more concrete than his. She liked working with citizens' groups to clean up the environment, to oppose nuclear power plants, to try to get the public's consciousness raised on specific issues. She and several friends had pushed a recycling program through the Barrington town council, and she was currently working on a proposal designed to keep toxic waste dumps out of Vermont altogether. It annoyed her that Geno, for all his political feelings, didn't seem to want to engage in these grassroots efforts. It was the legacy of the sixties that mattered—the feminist movement, the ecological movement, the ongoing peace movement—not the sixties themselves.

The boys, who had never heard of the sixties, sensed that a real adventure lay ahead of them.

"What *are* hippies?" Milo asked.

"Hippies are normal people," Geno said. "They prefer

not to work, I guess. But they're good people." He didn't like how that came out. "When I said they don't like to work, what I meant was that they believe in play. In real play. They make things, they do things—they even earn money. But whatever they do is done, well . . . playfully."

Susan, who stood behind him, rolled her eyes at Geno's half-assed attempt to control the way James and Milo perceived the world. Why couldn't he let the boys discover and interpret the world without having to take his spin into account?

They drove the Jeep up into the mountains, feeling the temperature of the air drop as they climbed. The "main circle," which was the focal point of the Rainbow gathering, would be held at noon deep in the Texas Falls National Forest. Decades began to fall away as they approached the parking area; hundreds of VW buses, spray-painted with peace symbols and plastered over with bumper stickers protesting everything from apartheid to the destruction of the Brazilian rain forests, parked hip to hip in a huge weedy field. Geno parked as close to the trail as he could.

"This is a pretty fancy machine for a hippie," Susan said. "I mean, how many hippies have leather seats and electric windows? And air-conditioning!"

"Air-conditioning is bad," Charles said. "It depletes the ozone layer."

Geno resolutely ignored them. He would not be teased about his Cherokee, which he loved.

They set off in a small platoon of Rainbow people. Milo and James quickly found some hippie kids to walk with, and Charles attached himself to a Buddhist monk from Ohio called

Brother Mort. Geno listened in nervously as Charles explained to Brother Mort that he was hoping to set up a Buddhist retreat in the Vermont hills, a place where people could "find an inner space to live in."

Susan chatted with the boys about the Indians who used to live in these woods, and Geno eavesdropped with admiration. He loved the way she could talk to them in their language, at their level of humor and understanding. It was often difficult for him to meet them where they were.

The hike in lasted nearly two hours, with a steep ascent in places. About half a mile from the main circle the path crossed a plank bridge that overlooked a bright waterfall where a dozen bathers, most of them naked, were scrubbing one another's backs in the shallows below.

Milo cried, "Can we swim, Mama?"

"You can wade," she said. "That cast shouldn't get wet."

"I'm not swimming here," said James.

"You can keep your underwear on, honey," Susan said.

Charles and Brother Mort parked themselves happily on a huge boulder to discuss the universe, while Geno, Susan, and the boys lowered themselves down the steep slope to the base of the falls.

"God, I never knew about this place," Geno said, following the boys down the embankment. He stopped to admire the gurgling stream, which cut between sharp boulders at the top and tumbled in a misty din over the rocky ledge. A thick branch was suddenly swept over the top, and Geno winced as it fell into the pool below. "Jesus! Did you see that?"

"What?" asked James.

"That branch—like a tree trunk? I'm glad nobody was swimming below it."

"Waterfalls are scary," Milo said. "Let's skip it."

"Don't be stupid," James said. "It's only water."

Geno said, "Just stay in the shallow part, guys. Like your mother said, we don't have very long."

Milo and James stripped to their underpants and paddled around for ten or fifteen minutes in the shallows, tossing clumps of mud at each other in a way that annoyed the other bathers, one of whom shouted, "Cut it out!"

Geno turned a look of displeasure on the man. "Come on, fellas," he said to Milo and James.

As they approached the main circle, encampments began to crop up on either side of the path: small tent villages with dining and medical tents. The strumming of guitars was omnipresent, and classic folk tunes shifted among the foliage like a familiar wind. It seemed that nobody in these woods was going to work on Maggie's farm no more.

The final climb lasted for ten minutes, and one could hear tribal drums beating in the distance. At the crest of the path the whole gathering was now visible: twenty thousand hippies and hangers-on in concentric circles. Geno studied the faces, most of which were totally unfamiliar, though it surprised him that, here and there, a familiar face mingled with the rest. It occurred to him that Lizzie Nash would attend such an event: she was always pining after the sixties, which had passed their peak before she was even born.

"Wow," said James, surveying the broad scene.

The Rainbow scouts had somehow found this remote and

lovely clearing: a field cradled in the hills like a dry mountain lake; from where Geno stood one could see range after range of mountains, each a slightly deeper shade of green. And the effect was dazzling, especially with the sun high overhead, hot and white.

"We should visit the Kiddie Village," Brother Mort said. "All the Rainbow people with children camp together. It's fun."

"Let's go, Daddy!" Milo begged.

They circled the crowd till they found an encampment where about thirty teepees were pitched in a vague circle. Makeshift swings and teeter-totters were in use by a small army of smudgy-faced hippie kids—miniature versions of their parents. They wore berets and odd hats, jeans, psychedelic tee shirts, bandanas—the works. A few were naked, or near naked, their bodies striped with war paint.

"I don't like it here," Milo said.

A small boy with yellow smiling suns painted on his belly approached Milo. "Wanna play cowboys and Indians? You can be a cowboy."

"I don't want to play."

"Why not?"

"I don't want to!" Milo sheltered behind Susan.

James said, "They're weirdos. They're all weirdos."

Geno bent down to eye level with James. "You'll hurt their feelings, James. Is that what you want?"

"I don't like them."

"We'll talk about this later. But behave yourself. You're embarrassing me."

A heavyset mother with stringy blond hair and bare breasts walked up to Susan. "I'm Running Water," she said. "Would you like to join the earth circle, sister?"

"Not just now, thanks," Susan said.

They watched closely as Running Water with a dozen or so mothers and children formed a circle and began their dance, chanting a song they all seemed to know: "The earth is our mother. We must take good care of it." The refrain was repeated over and over to an Indian beat as a fat, black-bearded man kept the rhythm on a bongo drum.

A bald and muscular man with red stripes on his cheeks and a gray goatee was standing on a nearby rock, addressing a small group of men. He radiated strength. "Are you going to sit back and watch them destroy our planet? Are you?" He was angry now, pointing and shouting. "Are you?"

A younger man raised his hand. "I hope you're not suggesting violence, Brother Ed?"

"Violence sometimes demands violence!" the man cried. "We should have stopped them in Iraq! We should have blown up the fucking bombers before they blew up the Iraqi people!"

"Bullshit!" another man yelled. "Violence creates violence!"

There was a murmur of agreement, but the bald man ignored it and continued his harangue.

Brother Mort touched Geno's elbow. "Let's go back to the main circle. It's almost time."

At noon exactly a man in a Viking helmet blew into a conch: a long mournful sound. A wing of silence covered the crowd, while at the center of the circle a man with a frizzy white beard and painted face raised a feather in the air. He cried, "Oooom!" The long vowel opened across the field. First a few, then a thousand, then several thousand voices joined in as the haunting primeval sound blew over the tops of trees. The field seemed to swirl.

"This is too weird," James said. "Let's go home."

Geno shushed him.

The group chant was finally broken by a rollicking band of children pouring into the main circle from the Kiddie Village. A wild cheer went up from the crowd. A man on tall stilts who was dressed up like Uncle Sam waved an American flag.

"Look up, Daddy!" Milo called.

Susan was already pointing to the sun.

"A rainbow!"

Geno's first thought was: group hallucination. He squinted. "My God," he said. "It's really a rainbow, isn't it?"

"It's freaky," Charles said. "Who would believe this?"

"It's a sunbow," Susan explained. "You can't have a rainbow when there's no rain."

Indian drums began to beat in unison, and soon thousands of people were dancing. Geno pushed into the crowd with James and Milo on either hand, enjoying the surge of emotion, the smell of sweat, the noise, the group vibration. He wanted now, more than anything, to feel a part of this place. To connect. He was not, after all, a "tourist" here. He was really here. He was part of the Rainbow himself.

"Dance, guys!" he said to the boys, who seemed terrified by what they saw. "You're Indians, both of you!"

"Maybe *you're* an Indian," James said. "I'm a cowboy."

The boys watched in disbelief as their father lifted his legs and waved his arms, imitating the motion of those around him. A war cry rose in his throat.

A toothless woman with black marks on her face and tangled red hair not unlike his own began to circle him. She tore her shirt off, and her large breasts flopped. On her stomach was a tattoo: a black snake that slithered when she rippled her stomach. James and Milo stared at the snake with eyes as big as silver dollars.

Milo seemed to be enjoying himself now until a muscular black man, naked except for a peaked Robin Hood hat, tried to lift him into his arms. "Don't, mister!" he cried, squirming free. The black man chirped like a tropical bird, sticking out his tongue as Milo backed away holding his cast high in the air as if to protect it.

A small group of children in loincloths with painted faces called to Milo from the edge of the crowd, and Milo, thinking he recognized one of them, ran through the crowd in their direction.

"Milo?" Geno called, seeing his son rush off. He couldn't imagine where the boy was going and went after him. The path, however, was blocked by a tall man in a cowboy hat and Western vest; his dark glasses seemed to rest on a fluffy mustache.

"Geno, howdy boy!"

Geno couldn't believe it. "Fernando!"

"What are you doing here with all these Indians?"

"What are *you* doing here?" Geno looked around him, hoping to catch a glimpse of Milo.

"Your friend Miss Nash is here," Nachez said. "Have you seen her?"

"Lizzie is here?" His heart tumbled like a floor through a burning building as his eyes darted from side to side. Somehow the thought of seeing Lizzie Nash here ruined the whole thing.

With a wave, Nachez disappeared into the crowd with a woman who was not his wife. "Asshole!" Geno called after him, but Nachez did not look back.

"O Captain, My Captain!" a voice cried, tugging at his arm. Geno was being led through the crowd by a lovely semi-naked woman masquerading as Pocahontas. Her skin was a deep ruddy brown, and she had long black hair braided into a long tail that fell along her spine. Her firm buttocks rose and fell as she walked, pulling him along. It wasn't that she was pulling hard, but Geno couldn't seem to resist her.

At the edge of the woods, she stopped. Turning to Geno, she held up what looked like a chocolate brownie. "Eat this!"

"What is it?"

"It's Columbian," she said.

"No, thank you."

She lifted it to Geno's lips. "Eat!"

Her eyes were among the loveliest eyes he'd ever seen. He took the brownie and nibbled at one corner.

"Eat it all!" she said.

He nodded, gobbling it down. He could never resist a

woman with a definite idea, and he was not about to begin here. It tasted like an ordinary chocolate brownie, but he could hardly imagine what the effects might be. "Thank you," he said, licking his fingers. His eyes kept drifting to her small, upturned breasts. He guessed that she was about twenty.

A boy dressed like a turkey did a dance around them now, and Geno shouted, "Bang! Bang!" The turkey-boy fell to the ground, and Pocahontas began to wail. "You killed my turkey!" she cried. "Come along! You must pay for your transgressions!" Her breath was hot and close to him, and—unless he was imagining things—it smelled of garlic.

Geno could feel his cock swelling in his pants. He followed her helplessly through a thicket of hackberry and thistle, coming into a bright clearing on the other side. *What are you doing, you asshole?* he said to himself. *Go back, go back, go back . . .*

"This way!" she called.

A few teepees had been pitched near the farthest edge of the clearing, and a dozen Indians sat cross-legged around a fire. When they saw Geno, they jumped to attention. With his peripheral vision, he could see another group of Indians emerging from the woods. It was all very realistic, he thought. Was this, indeed, some kind of historical reenactment?

He was seized from behind in a kind of bear hug.

"Let go of me, damn it!"

"White man, where do you come from?"

"Fuck off!" Geno shouted, shaking himself free. He began walking away when he was struck hard on the back of the head. He fell into the rough grass, face forward. Perfectly conscious, though shocked, he could hear them talking in what was unquestionably a Native American language. Near the teepees a war party seemed to be gathering in the shape of young men with spears, tomahawks, and bows.

A handful of Indians conferred beside Geno, who became increasingly aware that nobody was playing. Whipping around, thus barely avoiding a tomahawk's fierce swing, Geno leaped to his feet. Without looking back, he dashed across the field toward the hackberry and thistle patch and burst through the thicket. The branches stung his face, but nothing was going to stop him now. He tumbled into a picnic that consisted of two teenage girls and a young man in a sailor suit. They were passing a bong.

"Hey, man!" the sailor said. "You need a hit or something?"

"Indians!" he cried, panting. "There's Indians through the bushes there!"

"We're all Indians," one of the girls said. She did not seem more than fifteen, and her bandana had a yellow feather stuck in the back.

Geno sighed. The girl was so innocent and tender, her breasts still developing. Had her parents just let her come up here like this? Without supervision?

"Daddy!"

Geno swung around. It was James.

"Honey!"

"Mama wants you!"

Susan stood nearby and did not seem happy. "Where the hell have you been?" she said as Geno approached her.

"I'm not sure."

Susan reached her hand to the back of Geno's head. "Christ, you're bleeding! What happened?"

"I guess I fell . . . or something," he said. He simply could not think what else to say about what had happened in the other clearing. Perhaps he'd really fainted or something. Maybe he'd reacted badly to that brownie and fallen and hit his head. Yes, that's what must have happened . . .

"Where is Milo?"

"He was with *you*," Susan said.

"He was with both of us!" An undertow of panic washed through his voice as he began to scan the crowd. "He can't have gone far."

They began working systematically through the dithyrambic throng.

"Got a lid, brother?" a man with straggly blond hair asked Geno, grabbing his elbow hard.

Geno shook him off, fighting his way through the labyrinth of dope, of rising dust, body sweat, and (was it possible?) excrement. In his peripheral vision a naked couple fell upon each other in the woods. The line from Yeats about love pitching its tent "in the place of excrement" resounded in his head.

"Milo!" he called, and—miraculously—saw him. The boy was sitting under a tree with Brother Mort. Geno rushed over.

"You mustn't dash off like that," Geno said, panting. "Mama and I were scared."

"He's quite the little entertainer," Brother Mort said.

"Children are wiser than adults." The Buddhist sparkled in the intense sunlight. "I should be writing down all the lovely things he has said!"

Susan caught up to them, relieved.

"Let's go home, Daddy!"

The drumming continued, loudly, behind them.

"Are you ready, Susan?"

"Is the Pope a you-know-what?"

"Where's Charles?"

"He's found a soul mate, I believe. He said he will hitch a ride home later."

"A woman?"

"Something like that."

Geno imagined Charles flopping about in the high grass with the big toothless woman and shrugged.

"Light is God," said Brother Mort. "Your son told me that! Isn't it marvelous?"

"Did you say that, honey?" Susan asked.

Milo grinned.

Brother Mort looked at him, awestruck. "I'm so glad I met you all." He bowed to them, his hands folded before him as if praying.

"Likewise," Geno said, bowing.

They began the hike to the parking lot without enthusiasm. It was a long way down.

Later, in the Jeep, Susan turned to Geno with a worried look.

"Are you okay, honey? You really hurt yourself up there."

Geno grunted and felt the wound at the back of his head; blood was still seeping through his makeshift bandage, but there was little in the way of pain. What on earth had happened up there? Should he even bother to tell Susan about the Indians he had met, and how they had tried to kill him with a tomahawk? Had the whole thing been some kind of hallucination?

"Susie," he said, "the world is divided into two kinds of people—cowboys and Indians."

James liked this and issued a war cry.

"And what are you, dear?" Susan asked, with mild amusement. "Are you an Indian or a cowboy?"

He bit his lip, thinking. But he didn't answer.

That night, after the children were tucked in, Susan and Geno made love, but the lovemaking wasn't terribly satisfying to either party. An invisible plane seemed to have come between them, and their deepest, truest feelings could not pass through it. But even mediocre sex is better than nothing, thought Geno, as he fondled Susan's ear with his tongue.

She lay naked on her stomach, virtually passed out though it was only ten. The hike up to Texas Falls had exhausted her.

For some time Geno ran his fingers down the length of her back, letting his palm glide into the lovely depression at the base of her spine. He kept thinking about the ass on Pocahontas, and how it had moved up and down when she walked. And he could not get his mind off those Indians, if they were Indians, who'd attacked him.

A cool breeze startled him, and he sat up to close the

window. It was odd here in Vermont how, in midsummer, a breeze could feel so cold. As he slid down the pane, he noticed a mysterious car parked at the bottom of the driveway. Geno strained to see who was there, and he began to worry. He'd often read in the papers about the new "sophisticated" thieves who cased a house for months before descending, usually when the owners were out of town. They took only the good stuff: silver, vintage wines, paintings, genuine orientals. TVs they avoided. They wouldn't even take jewelry unless it was special—like a string of real pearls.

"I'll be right back, honey," he said, his voice quaking slightly.

Susan, who was almost asleep, could hear the panic in his voice. "What's the matter?"

"You stay here—and don't move."

Susan sat up and watched as Geno threw on his jeans and sweatshirt. He didn't keep a gun in the house like many Vermonters, but he shoved Milo's plastic water pistol in his pocket and slipped out the back door. It was very dark tonight, and Geno hated it: the oppressive sense of black, smothering infinity. But he pressed on. Moving breathlessly over the field, he circled in a way that would not attract the attention of the person in the unidentified car, which still sat there in the driveway.

This is weird, he thought. *Very weird.*

Geno felt surprisingly in control of the situation as he approached the car from behind, keeping low so as not to attract the driver's attention. As he got closer, he could see a man leaning forward in the driver's seat with binoculars to his face and could hardly believe it. The idea that this guy would be spying on his house—his life!—at this time of night unfastened the bonds of common sense.

Walking straight up to the window, which happened to be rolled down, he put the pistol right into the man's left ear.

"It's loaded," Geno said.

"Don't shoot!" the man cried.

"Don't even think about reaching for a gun," Geno said, wondering what to say next. It had been a while since he'd seen a good police movie. "Get out—slowly. Very slowly. And don't let your hands get out of sight!"

The man obeyed, stumbling as he stepped from the car.

"Hands up!" Geno shouted.

The man thrust his hands into the air.

"Now march. Into the house!"

He followed closely behind the intruder, occasionally nudging his backbone with the plastic gun. "Go straight into the house, using the side porch," he said. His own knees were so weak he could barely walk, but his voice held firm.

The man entered through the side door, and Geno—right behind him—flicked on the light. He directed the man into the kitchen, where he flicked on another light.

"Now sit down—and don't even think of moving!" Geno said, far too loudly, his voice an octave higher than usual.

He took the cordless phone off the hook and dialed the operator, who connected him to the police. Hastily, he explained to the dispatcher that he was holding an intruder captive. She said a police car would come immediately.

Meanwhile, there were footsteps on the stairs. Susan

stepped into the kitchen in her terry cloth robe. Her eyes were full of sleep.

"Over here, Susan!" Geno shouted. "Get behind me. The police are coming!"

Susan's eyes widened, and Geno took a good look at his prisoner for the first time. The young man must be about thirty, he guessed, and he wore a rainbow-colored beret, tie-dyed jeans, and red basketball sneakers. A necklace of white pukka beads glistened around his throat. His tee shirt read: "Down with CIA terrorism!"

"Andrew!" Susan said with a gasp. "What are you doing here, Andrew?"

Chapter 19

"I don't see why you insist on going through the whole thing again," Ferdinand said, stepping into his pantaloons. "I don't trust this Genoese. I never did, frankly."

Isabella sat in her nightdress in a high-backed Venetian chair with silver brocading on the backrest and gilded claws. Her feet stretched out on a sandalwood stool. Marianetta, her favorite lady-in-waiting, fanned her with a delicate paper crescent sent home by a loyal subject from the East.

"He keeps coming back at us. He's mad, I suspect."

"He's not."

"We've discussed this so many times, dear."

Isabella said nothing, but Marianetta looked terribly uncomfortable. She hated it when her sovereigns squabbled like this.

"Why do we have to do it *again*, that's what I don't understand."

The queen yawned. Her husband, dear as he was, did not appreciate her intuitive genius.

"Fray Juan insists," she said.

"And who is Fray Juan?"

"Some Franciscan, I believe. Isn't he Bishop Benvenuto's cousin?"

The king had no idea. All he knew was that his wife adored this pushy Genoese upstart, who had been following them around Spain for several years now, begging for attention. During the siege of Baza, Columbus had been boringly prominent, performing unnecessary heroics. On top of which, he had a knack for getting to know everybody who was anybody, so there was always some third-rate courtier whispering in his ear, "Columbus would like a word with you, Your Majesty."

Isabella had formed a commission to study this Enterprise of the Indies, as Columbus called it. Hernando de Talavera, the queen's confessor, had been charged with studying the Enterprise and writing a report on the likelihood of its successful prosecution. In his conclusion, delivered in Seville, he listed five main objections to the project:

1 It would take three years to get to Cypango—at best.
2 The Western Ocean is probably unnavigable.
3 Even if Columbus reached the other side of the

world, he would have difficulty making it back.

4 Saint Augustine says explicitly that there is nothing but limitless ocean to the west of Europe.

5 So many years after the Creation, it is unlikely that anything of interest could be found.

The commission had soundly rejected the Great Enterprise once and for all, and Ferdinand applauded their decision. "The matter is closed," he said. For her part, the queen moped around the castle, but she quickly agreed that Columbus had best return to Genoa—or wherever.

Now here he was, ready with more arguments and "visual exhibitions." The man did not know when to quit.

"I really don't think we have anything to gain by going through it again," Ferdinand said.

"It doesn't hurt to listen," Isabella replied. "I still think it's a good idea."

"You recall what Talavera said."

"Talavera is a toady. He guessed—correctly, I must say—what you wanted to hear. Well, it's not what *I* wanted to hear."

Ferdinand suspected that his wife had found this man attractive. He'd seen them strolling together in the cloisters in Granada, chatting like old friends. What other explanation could there be? Then again, if she really liked him, why would she want to send him so gaily over the edge of the world?

Isabella knew exactly what Ferdinand was thinking. "He's

asking for little in the way of money, darling. A few ships and supplies. If he succeeds, all the wealth of Cypango and the Indies will be ours. The Great Khan will pay us homage. We'll be able to finance a vast crusade in Palestine."

Ferdinand looked at her sternly: *"Duda Sant' Augustin,"* he said, in Latin, repeating the phrase that Talavera's commission had cited: "Saint Augustine doubts."

"Saint Augustine lived a long time ago," the queen said. "Nor have I ever liked his books."

"That doesn't mean he was wrong."

"Nor does it mean he was right."

Marianetta bit her painted nails.

"You like him, don't you?" Ferdinand asked.

"Who?"

"Columbus!"

"Of course not. I neither like nor dislike him. I find his project intriguing, and I suspect he is right about the size of the Western Ocean. I'm also aware of the fact that we require money—huge sums of money—to prosecute our plans for Spain."

Her green eyes glittered as she tilted her head back slightly. She looked like what she was: a great and glorious queen.

"I hope this interview won't last too long," Ferdinand said.

The queen smiled, feeling triumphant.

Marianetta fanned wildly.

The king squinted into a large gilt-edged mirror given to them as a wedding present by a wealthy Bavarian prince.

"You admire yourself overmuch, Ferdinand," the queen said.

"I shall take that as a compliment."

"You take everything I say as a compliment."

Ferdinand smiled at her. "That way, my dear, I am never disappointed."

Chapter 20

Susan and Geno huddled in a plastic booth in the nonsmoking section of the local Burger King. Muzak swirled in the room like smoke.

"Noise pollution," Geno said. "This place is fucking awful."

Susan, sipping her milkshake, looked out the window at a passing tractor-trailer. "I like the spring," she said. "The light is wonderful this time of year. More horizontal."

"The country is being ruined by these franchises," Geno continued, as if she hadn't spoken. "McDonald's, Burger King, Wendy's, Howard Johnson—you name it—crap. These towns had diners in the old days that served real food. They had *character*, for God's sake!"

"Stop fulminating," Susan said. "It's so boring."

A fat woman of sixty in curlers wedged herself into a tiny booth beside them and lit a cigarillo, and Geno scowled at her. He was paranoid about people listening in when he had important things to say. Even when he had nothing especially private to say, he didn't like the feeling that someone could overhear him.

"I can't believe you got that thing going with Andrew behind my back," Geno said. "It floored me, it really did."

Susan seemed unperturbed.

"Where did you meet that guy?" he continued.

"In a grocery store."

"You met *me* in a grocery store!"

"I guess I find groceries erotic or something." She bit into her cheeseburger. "You know, meat counters."

"He's a lunatic . . . creeping around our house at night like that, spying on us, for Chrissake. If I had any balls, I'd have strangled him."

"Have you been reading Robert Bly or something? Hemingway? This macho shit is amazing."

"This guy lurks outside our bedroom window with binoculars, and you call it normal? He's a Peeping Tom. We could press charges, you know. We should."

"He's just a lonely fellow," she said, taking the pickle off her cheeseburger. "Anyway, he apologized. I don't know what else you expected him to do."

"So did you sleep with him?"

"That's not your business." She recovered her burger and looked at him hard.

"What the hell do you mean?"

Ever so slightly, her voice rose. "I didn't raise a fuss about who you happened to fuck, did I?"

"That's not fair."

"It's damn fair!"

"Susan, please . . . you're shouting."

"I'll shout if I want to shout. I'm pissed off at you, Geno. You go around fucking students, and you expect me to take it? Am I supposed to be some goddamn little doormat?" She put down her cheeseburger definitively, too upset to eat.

"It's not something I care to talk about."

"That's too bad, then, because I'd like to talk about it. I'd like to know what you thought you were doing."

"I made a mistake."

She pressed down her anger. "I want to understand you, Geno. I realize that, lately, we've been . . . disconnected."

"It's been going on for quite a while."

"We should have got a handle on it sooner. This is fucking dangerous stuff."

"I know that."

"I didn't sleep with Andrew Ridgeway. We had a few friendly meetings."

Geno raised his eyebrows.

"Tea, cupcakes. A little hash. A veggie roll at Maude's Place."

"I was sure he was a vegetarian."

"You should know that I never intended to sleep with him."

"Sex isn't the point. You never even mentioned him."

"I would have."

"And I would have mentioned Lizzie."

"You're lying."

"I am, aren't I?" He snickered, but the laugh was hollow.

Susan had tears in her eyes now. "Geno . . . you're so goddamn self-satisfied. It's repugnant. You know, we edge up to serious conversation—real conversation—and you back away. What are you afraid of?"

"Can we talk about something else?"

"Like what?"

"This fucking Burger King. How about that? Do you realize where the meat for these hamburgers comes from? From Argentina and Brazil. From countries where they chop down rain forests, where the governments make the peasants stop growing food for themselves so they can produce cheap protein for us." He paused for dramatic effect, taking a sip of coffee. "And look at this building—a cheap excrescence on the landscape. We're a nation without values, without even a sense of aesthetics. God, I hate this place more and more every day."

Susan let his peroration sink in, then she said, "I wouldn't mind it if you were really talking about politics, but this is all projection."

"Projection—I hate that fucking word! Give me a break, Susie."

"Give *me* a break!"

"You're shouting at me."

"I'll shout at anybody I want to shout at!"

Susan stood up. "I don't like talking to you when you're in a belligerent mood."

Geno stood, eyeball to eyeball. "Sit down, Susan."

"Stop ordering me around!"

"I get it. You pretended to forgive me for what happened between me and Lizzie, and now look at you. You're mad as hell, aren't you?"

"You're an asshole!"

The fat woman beside them belched and grinned, and Geno glared at the woman, who looked away, taking a long drag on her cigarillo.

Susan, meanwhile, rushed from the Burger King.

"Come on, Susan," he said, hustling after her into the parking lot. He shouted into the back of her neck as they walked. "This is crazy. I don't understand why we're acting like this. Me *or* you. We didn't used to."

Susan stopped a couple of feet from her car.

"Fuck off," she said.

"Why don't *you* fuck off?"

Susan stepped quickly into the driver's seat and sped off, leaving Geno by himself in the parking lot of the Burger King.

He looked around him, dismayed. The sun beat down on the pavement, which smelled of tar. A large trash can beside him spilled over with plastic wrappers, cups, and cardboard boxes. Down the road he could see what looked from where he was like an endless string of gas stations, used-car lots, and assorted convenience stores.

"Fuck all of you!" he said, hurling what remained of his cheeseburger at the shiny Burger King.

Scavenging gulls, who'd found a new home at the hamburger joint, swooped down on the food at once.

Geno called B&B taxi, which took him to the Barrington campus along Route 9 in a rusty blue '84 Chevy. This road had been nothing but a slice of macadam through a cornfield when Geno arrived in Barrington seventeen years ago, but for him it was ruined now. Neon signs had arrived a decade ago, advertising a pizza shop and a bowling alley. Gas stations went up quickly, followed by an A&P, a Super Drug, and a Miracle Mart.

Soon after their wedding, Geno and Susan had moved into a redbrick apartment building two blocks off campus on a leafy elm-shaded street. First the elms died, then a Pizza Hut opened up across the street, and the traffic worsened. Frustrated, they began hunting for a farmhouse outside of town.

Geno loved the remoter parts of Vermont, places where one could imagine the twentieth century had barely begun. The farmhouse he and Susan found, with a long view of Mount Isaac, was perfect. Sitting in an Adirondack chair on the front lawn, one could believe the year was 1911.

The main thing about Vermont, for Geno, was that it wasn't New Jersey. His home state embodied the worst aspects of this catastrophic century. At one time its small towns were full of gingerbreaded wood-frame houses, redbrick Federals, neoclassical granite banks, and shimmering limestone courthouses. These had given way to "developments" of split-level eyesores with aluminum siding and screened-in patios.

Geno had grown up in the standard prefab with a two-car garage beneath a master bedroom. His father put a basketball hoop over the garage doors when he was eight, making his son instantly popular in the neighborhood. A gang of boys filled the driveway every afternoon in summer, and a running pick-up game continued until Geno's father, who sold wall-to-wall carpeting for a building supply company in Meadow Pond, arrived home at five-thirty sharp for supper.

Mr. Genovese always came home frazzled, and he gulped a double Manhattan to calm his nerves. Mrs. Genovese made sure the boys abandoned the hoop just before her husband's black Buick nosed into the driveway.

An only child, Geno was raised to believe the universe revolved around him, although he'd been conscious of his father's business troubles from an early age. Mr. Genovese began in sales after the war, working first in automotive supplies. He moved, briefly, to a feed supply store. His cousin, Nick Giacometti, hired him at the building supply company in 1957, and Mr. Genovese gravitated to industrial carpeting. He wore a suit to work every day with a starched shirt and a flowery tie, and it meant a great deal to him that he had a "white collar" job. It upset him that business was never very good.

Mr. Genovese wanted Geno to pursue a career in sales, but his son's academic bent scratched that idea. The scholarship to Dartmouth sealed Geno's fate. From then on, he was never not in school, as student or teacher. And never in New Jersey.

The disturbing thing was that Barrington had come to resemble his hometown more than ever, with condos and tracts of prefab houses spreading like cancer cells on the town's periphery. The village green, with its churches and banks and nineteenth-century storefronts, was—thank God—preserved by tourism. Kitsch had its up side, too. But Geno hadn't quite noticed, until now, how terrifyingly ugly the place was becoming.

The college remained pristine, but its unreality hit Geno hard as the taxi passed through its stone gates. What was he doing here anyway? He must call his father-in-law soon about that loan. If only he could buy, say, twenty thousand dollars of penny stocks in gold mining companies in Peru, his future would be assured. If his calculations were correct, in five years that stock would appreciate tenfold, and he could quit his teaching job, move to the Caribbean, and write poetry till the world turned cold.

Geno walked into Milton House with a heavy heart, trying not to breathe in the smell of institutional floorwax. The corridor was dark.

"Hi, Geno," a voice cried, rather pleasantly.

Geno startled, turning to face Agnes Wild.

"Did I frighten you?"

"You always frighten me."

"I'm glad I ran into you," she said.

"Ditto."

"Really?"

"You really fucked me this time, Agnes."

Agnes looked at him. "You think I put Lizzie up to this, don't you?" She seemed hurt.

"I do."

"Well, I didn't. I had nothing to do with it."

Geno stared at her, uncertain.

"I'd tell you if I did. You know that. Nothing is gained by going behind people's backs."

Geno sighed. She was probably telling the truth. Indeed, he often told Susan that Agnes was too unimaginative to lie. "I assumed you were pissed off about that Virginia Woolf thing."

"I thought that I was more interested in Woolf than you were."

"You are."

"So it was natural that I should want to supervise Lizzie."

"It was." He looked down like a small boy. "I'm sorry. I shouldn't have jumped to conclusions."

"I accept your apology. But you've got a lot of work to do with Lizzie Nash."

"And the Committee on Human Relations."

"I don't know what's going to happen there."

"You're the chairperson!"

"The materials you presented are . . . well . . . hard to digest. We're not legal experts, you know. I don't think we're looking at a legal situation in any case. But there's a point of morality here."

"Ah . . . morality. Yes."

Geno went into his office, closed the door, and drew the blinds. He sat back in his desk chair, his feet on the desk, and closed his eyes, feeling a sharp throb in each temple. His head was killing him now. It seemed that his life—his teaching life, his writing life, his family life—had hit its nadir. It was difficult to imagine how he could regain his wife's trust or find a way to relate to the boys that felt solid and real. The idea of divorce appalled him. A marriage was a mystical unit, consecrated by human and divine love. And he was determined to act responsibly and well—and to earn the union he desired—even if it meant uprooting, moving to a new country, burning his house to the ground to begin again, with bricks and mortar. The time had come, he decided, to rebuild.

A knock came to the door, and he shuddered. Not Lizzie Nash, he hoped. Or Agnes.

"Hello?" he called weakly.

"Excuse me?" said Chap Baloo, pushing the door wide. "That you, old boy?"

"Nobody here but us chickens."

Baloo made himself comfortable in the chair by the bookcase. "I had a call from Botner this morning," Baloo said. "They apparently don't have a decision on your case. Not yet."

"Fuck them," Geno said.

Baloo shifted uncomfortably, twisting his mouth to one side unconsciously. "That's not a good attitude, Geno," he said.

"Frankly, I don't care anymore."

Baloo said, "I don't mean to frighten you, but they could suspend you for a term. Maybe dock your salary."

"Can they fire me?"

"You've got tenure, but I reckon anything's possible." His Southern accent seemed to thicken. "It's a dark mood this country's in."

"I didn't do anything wrong."

Baloo took a pipe from his jacket pocket, though he didn't intend to light it. Pipes were conversation props for him—a residue of Southern gentility. "I'm sorry if this seems to be ruining your summer," he said.

"My summer is fine."

"I saw Susan at the post office just a while ago. She looked awful."

"She's had a bad year," Geno said. "And I guess I haven't made life easy for her."

"Women," said Baloo. "You know the old saying, 'Can't live with them, can't live without them.' " With this, he winked and left, closing the door behind him.

On the way home in the taxi, Geno thought about Baloo's silly old saw. He'd heard it many times, and it typified a familiar male way of regarding women as a kind of foreign country. As an only child, he hadn't really known a woman close up until quite late in adolescence, unless you counted his mother. Susan was the first woman he'd lived with intimately, and he recalled the strangeness of their first months together. Everything about her intrigued him: her smells, her daily habits, the way she stood in front of the mirror and looked into her own eyes. He could never look into his own eyes so intensely.

Susan was bending over a row of flowers when he arrived. She wore a big straw sombrero and jeans, and even though she must have heard the taxi grinding over the pebbles as it climbed the driveway, she didn't look around.

Geno paid the driver and walked to where she was clawing up weeds, and he stood quietly behind her. "We could use some rain, huh?" he said, at last.

She continued with her claw, piling the granular leaves of dandelions in a clump beside her.

"I guess you're not talking, is that it?"

Susan sighed, rocking back on her thighs. Then she started crying. She put her head in her gloved hands, and her shoulders shook.

He knelt beside her. It was so hard to think of anything to say to someone so obviously in pain. What was worse, he felt responsible for that pain.

"I'm sorry, Susie," he said.

She rose slowly, wiping her eyes on a flannel shirtsleeve.

"I guess I'm out of control these days." He was looking at the ground as he talked. "Sometimes I wish we could just get out of here, you know. Start again somewhere else. I might quit teaching."

"You're broke," she said, laughing through the tears now—like sun tearing through a scrim of rain.

"So what?"

"Like hippies, huh?"

He became excited now as a green floating image—an island—appeared in his mind. He closed his eyes to see it more clearly. It was the Dominican Republic, he was sure.

"We could house-sit in Maine," Susan said.

"Maine?"

"Help on a lobster boat or something."

"How about the Dominican Republic? Maine is too cold," he said. "The D.R. is perfect—never too cold or hot."

Susan studied his face like a math problem, saying nothing.

Geno said, "I'm serious."

"I know you are," she said.

Geno came close to her now, wiping the wetness from her eyes with his thumbs. Then he didn't kiss her exactly. He just stood with his lips pressed to hers, slowly breathing her in—the smell of dirt and sweat, tears and sun. She was earth and air, he thought. She was fire and water.

"I love you," he said. "I like you. And I never hate you."

"I'm glad you never hate me," she said.

She put her head on his shoulder, and he let his fingers cup her gourdlike head, feeling her skull beneath the scalp. And he knew he loved her, loved her.

Chapter 21

Charles had spent five days in the mountains with Yellow Moon, a mud-spattered woman in her midtwenties. She was from Arkansas, with an accent thick as kudzu, though she had most recently lived in Boulder. Her name made sense if you looked at her without preconceptions: the whites of her eyes were indeed yellow, while her head was moonlike; even her scalp—visible beneath her bleached-out hair—glowed with a yellowy tint.

She and Charles pitched a tent in the north field adjacent to Geno and Susan's house, and it was established that they could either use the kitchen to cook for themselves or, if they preferred, eat with the family.

"I'm certainly a cook," Yellow Moon volunteered on the first night, her words like mismatched beads on a string. "I do a rice and beans dish much like the Caribbeans."

Geno wondered how was it possible that Charles, who

was so intelligent, could have stuck himself with such a woman.

"The Cubans eat rice and beans, don't they?" Susan asked.

"And the Puerto Ricans," Charles said. "We used to sell a lot of Carnex to the Puerto Ricans—they'd mix it with the rice and beans. Jumped up the protein count by a huge margin."

"That's most disgusting," said Yellow Moon.

"I don't eat meat any longer," Charles said. "I gave it up over two years ago. Even though I was still working for Carnex."

"Milo and James won't eat Carnex," Susan said. "Who would?"

"I'm going to the office," Geno said, lifting the keys to his Jeep from a basket. Milton House was at its best, he thought, when nobody was there, and now that Charles and Yellow Moon had joined the family, it was even better. He would pack a peanut butter sandwich and spend the day there, reading Yeats, listening to tapes on his Walkman, writing poems.

Susan was left behind to attend to Charles, who seemed euphoric in the wake of the Rainbow celebration. Yellow Moon was, she decided, a mistake. But the boys seemed to like her, and she spent hours playing with them, which left Susan with time for herself. She went upstairs into her study, where she hoped to put the finishing touches on her proposal to the Barrington town council about toxic waste dumps.

Her study was her own little world, a tiny room adjacent to their bedroom. It was a place where Susan felt more in touch with the rest of the world than she did with Geno and the boys. When an old story of hers—the one she'd published in the *Atlantic* years ago—got anthologized, she had taken the check for three hundred dollars and bought a Grundig short-wave radio: a neat little thing in a black leather case that pulled in broadcasts from every corner of the globe on thirteen different bands. Once or twice a day, she would steal away to her study and listen to the BBC or one of the broadcasts in English from Berlin, Moscow, or wherever. It quickly became obvious to her that listening to the American media was just not good enough. The truth, as always, was radically subjective; it lived in the interstices between words, in margins, in the blank spaces between paragraphs. One needed many points of view, and she had come to rely on the triangulation of broadcasts from far and wide.

Now the phone was ringing in the bedroom.

"Hello."

"Susan, you're out of breath."

"Hi."

"It's your mother."

"I thought that was your ring."

"Listen, dear. Have you heard from Charles?"

Susan did not answer.

"Are you there, Susan? Listen, darling, I need to know whatever you know. Cicely is hysterical!"

"Ah."

"Are you hiding anything from me, Susan? I can always tell when you're hiding things, you know."

"I'm always hiding things. We all are."

"Susan, please, I'm serious. Where is your brother?"

"I don't want to get into this."

"You're already into it. He's your brother."

"I'm sure he'll contact you when he's ready to talk."

"I can't believe I'm hearing this."

"I suppose you'll have to."

"I will not let you talk to me like that!"

"You can always hang up."

"Darling, what's got into you? Charles is there. Now I know he's there. You might as well have said so. It's so damned obvious when you've been around that boy."

"He's a middle-aged man, Mother."

"He's a boy in his head, believe me. Your father is livid."

"How's Dad?"

"Didn't you hear me? He's livid."

"Tell him I said hello, huh?"

"Susan, tell me the truth about Charles."

"I will not be drawn into this."

"Cicely is one thing, but the girls are another. The girls are crying day and night."

The thought of the girls crying did it. How could her brother be so cruel? "If I see him, I'll tell him. Okay?"

"All right, dear."

"Goodbye, Mother."

"Goodbye."

Susan went back into her study and opened her diary. She felt she had to put something into words, anything: "The summer has already reached its peak—the solstice has come and gone. I find it sad to think of that peak having been reached. The long slope into winter is nerve-wracking. It's the other cycle I prefer: the build to summer."

She scrunched her face up and reread what she had written. The line about the summer solstice embarrassed her. Why rely on tired metaphors? Why be so abstract? The detachment implied by abstractness upset her. It was the thing that bothered her most about Geno. He was so disconnected. And it had gotten worse since the accident on the pond with Milo, which he refused to talk about even though he'd had several nightmares about it. And now, this crazy thing up at the Rainbow gathering. Last night he told her that he thought he'd actually been hit on the head by a real Indian!

Her mother's voice kept ringing in her ears, and it sickened her. Her whole adulthood had been a quiet protest against her mother's kind of life, although she knew that, to the outside, she often looked like a fifties-style housewife, the victim of a male chauvinistic husband. And to some extent, there was truth there: she often felt consumed by Geno. But it was not the same fatal pattern she had seen in her parents' marriage, with Ted in firm control, with Helen tagging along behind. Thank goodness, it was not that.

She used to long to be with her father, who was rarely home. She remembered one time when she was home alone, a girl of about twelve, practicing the piano. She had been trying to get some little musical phrase right without luck, and—on the verge of tears—she had slammed her fist down on the keys, making a weird dischord. Suddenly her father appeared from nowhere, sat down with her, and patiently led her through the notes. Until that moment, she had never realized that he could play. And the way he did it, so methodically and patiently, still moved her deeply.

Her mother, by contrast, seemed hassled and vague, impatient. The poor woman bore full responsibility for her and Charles, and she was so often alone, deserted by her husband. It had only recently dawned on Susan that her father might have been having an affair in those years: he worked so late, and her mother was so fragile, perpetually on the verge of tears.

She looked out the window at the grassy north field, which needed mowing. The maple underneath her window fluttered in a light breeze, while clouds in the distance charged across a windbreak of cedars. Charles was flying a kite that he had made himself only that day, and Yellow Moon stood beside him. Milo and James were chirping like small birds, thrilled by the attention of their uncle and his friend.

"It's my turn! I'm next!" Milo was crying.

A flush of good feeling coursed through Susan's body. And she was grateful for what she had, however flawed it might be.

Geno stepped into the cool bay of the English Department office. The secretary was gone for the rest of July, and the lights were out. Even the shades were drawn.

The only open door in the department belonged to Chap Baloo, who pretty much lived throughout the year in Milton House. He arrived promptly at eight every morning, and he left at six. Often he came back after dinner and worked into the wee hours: nobody knew at what, though students had recently spread a rumor about his connections with the CIA. (Baloo had in fact been an intelligence officer during the Korean War, giving this rumor the slight attachment to reality necessary for it, like all rumors, to thrive.)

The smell of floorwax summoned a knot in Geno's stomach now as it had done when he first attended kindergarten in Meadow Pond. He recalled perfectly the fear he'd felt at Buchanan Elementary in its cavernous pea-green lavatory, where the urinals stood vertically against one wall like upended bathtubs. Bully-boys from the fifth and sixth grades hung out there and smoked cigarettes and drew filthy pictures in the toilet stalls and called the younger boys names like "cocksucker" and "shithead."

He flicked on the light and stood before his dark mailbox, expecting the usual circulars from academic publishing companies. Somebody was always trying to convince him that he should switch to this or that new textbook. It was sickening. The education "industry." His lips moved as he talked to himself and flipped through the junk mail without expectation.

He turned over a letter from something called the MacAlastair Foundation. A request for a letter of recommendation? A polemical broadside? An invitation to subscribe to a newsletter or attend some horrendously dull conference on The World of Tomorrow?

He didn't open the letter but turned to the latest issue of the *New York Review of Books*, which he adored only because of the personal columns at the back. The country overflowed with cranks and kooks looking for soul mates, and these columns attracted *la crème*. Their ads were among the few things that brought tears of joy to his eyes these days. Walking back to his office, he noticed an ad taken out by a "Lover of dachsund flesh and the music of Elgar" who sought a "suitable companion for odd weekends in Rhode Island." There was a definite warning in italics: *"Nothing (or practically nothing) kinky!"* What was Rhode Island coming to?

He continued reading in his office, where the only sound was the heavy tick of an electric clock that had been dying on the wall for ages. Somehow, the letter from the MacAlastair Foundation kept attracting his eye, as if some mystical energy beckoned from its folds. He yawned, reached for it, and split the envelope lengthwise with a pencil. The letter, which branded itself in his memory, read as follows:

Dear Mr. Genovese,

The MacAlastair Foundation was recently established in memory of Frank P. and Fiona R. MacAlastair. As you may know, the MacAlastairs have long been patrons of the arts in America and, of course, their native Scotland. This new foundation has been created to foster creativity in individuals of exceptional promise at an early stage in their careers. You have been identified and selected as such an individual. Congratulations!

We enclose a check for $542,000—a tax-exempt gift (the foundation refers you to IRS ruling #36-447-53211). Our idea is that you should use this money in any way you see fit to further your creativity.

I shall be calling soon to congratulate you personally and to answer any questions you may have. I would also like to find out from you soon if we may use your name in our publicity releases.

Good luck with your prospective projects.

The letter was signed by somebody called Malcolm S. Macready, III—Executive Director of the MacAlastair Foundation. The return address was in Cedar Rapids, Iowa.

Geno stared at the bookcase ahead of him for twenty minutes without seeing the books. He was looking through the wall, in fact, into the future. Money spun the world, and it had begun to spin Geno's with an unexpected velocity.

He found himself scribbling figures on a pad with a trembling pencil, calculating with more zeroes than he was used to. With $542,000 to invest in a solid trust, he could reap at least $45,000 per year. Maybe more. If he could manage to live on less, he could invest all surplus gains in Peruvian gold mining, and his capital would increase exponentially.

He leaped from his chair and circled the desk, suppressing a cheer. Twice his energy rose to such a pitch that he slammed a closed fist into the opposite hand, making a loud smacking noise that briefly relieved the tension.

He began dialing home, to tell Susan, then hung up. He would tell her about it face-to-face, perhaps dropping the letter onto her dinner plate before piling on the pasta.

Drawing a sheet of paper from his desk, he began typing a letter to the dean:

Dear Larry,

I quit. Effective immediately.

He signed his name in a confident, looping scrawl.

And there it was—short but sweet—four little words that severed the cord.

He arrived at the foot of his driveway and braked to look around. The late afternoon sunlight had described its usual semicircle, and the house's crisp mid-nineteenth-century facade was bathed in shadows. The north field caught the light wonderfully, its stubble luminously gold. A few red-streaked clouds drifted on the northwest horizon: a sign that the weather would hold. The purple shadow of the house pulled itself together and fell over the front garden, while a barn cat—one of many that had attached themselves to this property over the years—teetered on a fencepost and meowed.

Geno inhaled deeply. The world had never seemed lovelier or stranger.

When he drove up to the house, Charles and Yellow Moon were chatting with Susan on the lawn. The children were chasing each other around the barn.

Geno strode toward the three adults, feeling in his shirt pocket for the folded check.

"Hi, guys," he said. "Tomatoes coming up?"

Susan was absorbed in trimming the zucchini plants and said nothing.

"Will nobody say hello?"

Susan looked up. "Oh, hi."

"Hi, hi, hi," Geno said. He bounced oddly from foot to foot, his eyebrows lifting with each word.

They looked at him as if he'd acquired a rare disease.

"Anything the matter, honey?" Susan asked.

"Maybe. I've got this little problem, you see."

"Yes?" Charles said, his arms folded at his chest. He leaned forward to listen as if he'd actually graduated from the Harvard Divinity School.

Susan's stomach clenched, thinking it was something to do with Lizzy Nash and the Committee on Human Relations.

"What's the best way to invest half a million or so dollars to ensure a yearly dividend of, say, ten percent?"

Susan panicked.

"That's high," Charles said in a bankerly voice. "But with half a million dollars, you'd find a money manager who could bring it off. Dad gets anywhere from eleven to sixteen percent return on his portfolio."

Yellow Moon closed her eyes. Was this the Rainbow guy she knew and loved?

Charles continued: "There's an investment firm in New York called Beaker, Bench, and Farley. They're absolutely tops."

"Don't tell me they've moved you to the Economics Department," Susan said. "That would be too cruel."

"To me or the Economics Department?" Geno asked, reaching for the check. "There you go, honey. Half a million U.S. dollars."

She took the check and wiped the sweat from her brow. "Is this real?"

"It's a check for 542,000 bucks, sent to me—tax free—courtesy of the MacAlastair Foundation of Cedar Rapids."

Yellow Moon began to leap up and down. "We're rich! We're rich!"

Charles looked at her and frowned.

"I don't get it," Susan said.

Geno handed her the official letter.

"My God," she said, with Charles reading over her shoulder.

"Hooray for you, old boy!" Charles cried. "And well earned, too."

"It's not well earned," Geno said. "It's completely crazy. But I don't care."

The full heft of what had occurred settled only gradually on Susan. She felt dizzy, walking toward the kitchen, where she remembered that a bottle of champagne was hiding in the fridge behind the pineapple juice.

They soon gathered on the front lawn in Adirondack chairs to celebrate.

"There's another interesting wrinkle," Geno said. "I quit my job this afternoon."

"You *what?*" Charles said.

Susan's lower jaw loosened. Her eyes stared blankly ahead.

"You can't just quit a job," Charles said. "You've got a family, and responsibilities."

Nobody commented on this.

"Are you positive it's real, honey?" Susan asked.

Geno grinned slightly and said, "It does feel like I'm dreaming. Then again, it always feels like I'm dreaming."

"That's not what I meant. It must be some joke. Nachez likes to play practical jokes like this, doesn't he?"

Suddenly Geno's cheeks drained of blood, and he had a vision of Fernando Nachez in the mail room surrounded by a group of snickering professors.

"I'll kill the bastard," Geno said.

"Let me see that check," said Charles, coolly.

Geno handed it over, and Charles held it up to the light. He studied it carefully for several minutes as Susan peeked over his shoulder, wondering what her brother could possibly be looking for.

"It's real," Charles said, at last. "No doubt about it."

"I knew it was! This is fabulous!" cried Yellow Moon. "Tell us, Geno—what's your sign?"

"My sign?"

"The zodiac, you know."

"Oh, yes . . . Aries."

She leaped to her feet. "I knew it! I knew it!"

Susan was clearly unhappy. "We should have talked it over before you just quit, Geno." Her voice trembled slightly.

"I had to do it, Susie," he said. "It couldn't wait."

Once again, the situation had slipped out of control. "So what exactly do you plan to *do*, if you don't mind my asking?"

"I've got a plan," he said, his eyes flickering with a weird inward light. "We'll go to the Domincan Republic. I've got it all worked out. We'll buy a little piece of land there, build a house. It'll be fabulous."

"I prefer the Azores," Charles said. "They're totally undiscovered."

Susan was by now distracted by distraction, gazing across the distance to the blue-gray peak of Mount Isaac. This marriage was totally in Geno's hands now, and she felt helpless in the face of his manic resolution. He was like a huge hot wind, blowing across the landscape of her life. And it was all she could do, sometimes, to shelter herself from him, to find a place where the delicate shoots and tendrils of her imagination could take root and stir.

"Columbus," Geno said, more to himself than anybody else. "I've got this feeling about Columbus."

Chapter 22

The great Islamic fortress at Granada fell almost too suddenly. For so many years, those illustrious barriers had seemed insurmountable: high stone walls reflecting amber light. The sultan himself never took the threat seriously. "God will protect us from the barbarians," he always said, contradicting his advisors.

Columbus arrived a day after the main battle. He had seen many terrible things in his life, but this was the worst.

Men lay strewn in the dust in bloodied caftans. A fair number were still alive, crawling through the sanguine dirt on all fours. Some hardly moved. The smell of shit and fester was intense.

A crew of good-hearted Christian souls moved among the vanquished with weary swords, decapitating them one by one.

Many called from a distance for this assistance, exposing the tender flesh of their necks as if to plead.

"Let the beggars die slowly," Columbus said to his companion, a junior officer from Salamanca. "They must understand why God will not be abused."

The junior officer stepped nervously away from the hard-hearted Genoese.

That day Columbus was summoned into the presence of Isabella and Ferdinand. The prospect thrilled him. Triumph, he guessed, was surely at hand. His closest friend at court, Luis de Santangel, had been quite certain that the royal commission's advice to the sovereigns would be dismissed. How could they deny Columbus such a meager outlay of ships and provisions? As for men, there were plenty of prisoners willing to trade a jail cell for a ship's hold. In prison they would certainly die of scurvy, cholera, or dysentery. At sea, well, there was always hope. Or the prospect of mutiny.

It had troubled Ferdinand that Columbus wanted so many personal rewards for his expedition: grand titles and commissions, tithes and revenues. They had never known an explorer whose mind centered so openly on earthly rewards. Wasn't the journey itself the reward?

"Should you succeed," the king had said to Columbus, "God will see that you are handsomely rewarded in heaven."

But Columbus demurred. "*You* shall reward me, Your Majesty," he said. "And it's a small price to pay for what the crown shall gain."

Despite his greed, Isabella found him interesting. But

Ferdinand considered him a bore. "Let's deal with this thing once and for all," he told his wife. "Either ship him back to wherever he came from, or send him to oblivion by sea. I, for one, think the whole business is foolish. I don't know why We consented to meet with him in the first place."

Columbus stood before the king and queen in a lavender suit with shiny black boots and silver buckles. The queen lowered her eyes: it was the buckles that upset her. The king read his proclamation in a tinny voice: "Our Royal Commission has considered your project and decided to reject it. But We do thank you for your assistance in the defeat of the infidels, and We wish you well on your travels. Adieu." The king bowed, and Columbus reciprocated.

To hell with the lot of you, Columbus thought as he packed his bags, saddled a mule, and set off for Cordova, where Beatriz would certainly welcome him in the usual pleasant ways. He had already met a young man from Cádiz who said he could involve him in the African slave trade, and there was surely money there. He would one day finance his expedition to the Indies himself, and all the profits would be his!

Fray Juan rode beside him, in a disagreeably chatty mood. "The best part of all this is that you've saved a bit of money, haven't you?"

Columbus said, "For God's sake, shut up."

Fray Juan took the hint, and they rode in silence through the dusty gates of Granada.

They had not managed ten miles when a messenger on horseback overtook them at the village of Pinos-Puente. Columbus was so lost in reflection, he barely noticed that a young man was addressing him in the most excited manner.

"The queen has asked me personally to beg you to return. She wishes to speak with you."

"Who?"

"Isabella, our sovereign queen."

"Ah . . . the queen."

"The queen, my lord!" said Fray Juan, who was quite beside himself now. "We must return at once!"

Columbus understood everything in a moment of miraculous recognition. He raised both hands to the heavens and cried, "Thank you, Lord God Almighty!" Leaping from the mule, he dropped in the red dust to praise God, Jesus, and the Virgin Mary. He also thanked Saint Andrea, the patron saint of mariners, who had been good to him in the past.

"Hurry, my lord!" Fray Juan said.

But Columbus would not be hurried. He had prayed so many times for a miracle, with poor results. Now that God had finally answered his prayers, this was no time to stint on praise.

Luis de Santangel smiled knowingly at Columbus, who entered the royal chamber with his head proudly erect. Ferdinand was not present.

Columbus knelt before Isabella, bowing his head.

"My dear Columbus," the queen said. "Rise."

"Your Royal Highness," he said, expectantly.

"We have changed Our mind about your Enterprise of the Indies," she said.

Columbus looked her in the eye directly, showing no emotion. In his heart of hearts, he felt nothing but contempt for royalty. By accident of birth, they held all the cards in their delicate fingers. Columbus, by virtue of courage and imagination, faith and hope, knew that he deserved whatever honors the world could bestow upon him.

"We shall do everything we can to see that your project is accomplished," the queen continued.

Columbus sighed inwardly.

"God will assist you, We know. You are setting forth to accomplish great things on His behalf."

Columbus nodded and grinned, sensing that the queen required something in the way of an immediate response. He listened as she outlined possible sources of financing for the expedition. Columbus would sail directly under Spanish commission, bearing a letter of introduction to the Great Khan or any sovereign head of state he might encounter. The terms of his reward, which had so concerned him, would be negotiated in due course.

"Thank you, Your Majesty," Columbus said. "I shall not fail, I assure you."

The queen bowed her head.

Had she winked? Columbus wondered. *My God, the queen has winked at me!* he said to himself.

He winked back, boldly.

The queen stared at him hard. "Go thy way," she said, making the sign of the cross.

Everyone around her made the sign of the cross.

Columbus, kneeling again, also made the sign of the

cross. With his head bowed, he heard a flurry of footsteps and shuffling of silk. The queen had taken herself away.

Luis de Santangel kissed him. "I spoke to her personally after you left," he told him. "I said, 'For such a small investment—think of the potential reward!' I told her I'd happily put up the money myself, if she didn't have it."

"Did she have it?"

"Does the Queen of Spain have a couple of million maravedis?"

He left Luis de Santangel laughing and stepped into the brilliant adjoining courtyard. The delicate Moorish arches seemed to lift his heart. The news of his good fortune had not, to his amazement, buoyed him; rather, he now felt a sinking feeling, a sense of vistas opening before him that would almost certainly be as strange and difficult as the ones through which he'd already passed.

PART TWO

Chapter 23

The brown wasteland of Haiti gave way sharply to the miraculous green of the Dominican Republic as the Boeing 727 banked sharply to the south.

Geno leaned over Susan's lap to look down. "Fucking Haitians," he said. "They've ruined that place!"

"Don't blame the Haitians," Susan said. "It's Papa Doc and Baby Doc—they were brutal."

"Okay, then it's the fault of their leaders. They should have outlawed that kind of desecration." He paused. "But the people themselves—they just let it happen."

A look of annoyance crossed Susan's face. "Stop being simpleminded, Geno."

"I'm not," he said, hollowly. How could he defend himself against such a charge?

"What happened exactly?" James asked, poking his head

over the seat from behind. He couldn't bear the idea that something had happened outside his ken.

"Your mother won't believe me, but they happen to have cut down every last tree in Haiti," Geno said. "It's vegetation that holds the topsoil together. So the topsoil washed right into the sea."

"Why don't they plant *more* trees?"

"They can't!" Geno said, too loudly. "Nothing will grow there! I don't think it'll ever recover—not in our lifetimes, anyway."

"How about *my* lifetime?" Milo asked. "I got a longer one than anybody on this airplane. How much you wanna bet?"

"You've got a longer one, all right," James whispered.

Milo tore off the cover of the in-flight magazine, rolled it into a ball, and threw it at James, who ducked so that the ball hit an elderly woman in the next seat.

Geno was still fuming about the topsoil. "It's criminal," he said. "Some kind of international environmental protection agency should be set up. The planet is too small for this kind of thing. Look at what's happening in Brazil!"

Susan put a hand on Geno's forearm, feeling more pity now than annoyance. He'd been like this—hyper, really—ever since the MacAlastair check arrived. He'd been sleeping little, waking from nightmares about Milo or hallucinations about the Rainbow gathering. He had begun to claim that he'd fallen through a time warp. And when Rose Weintraub told him plainly that he was imagining things, he'd quit therapy on the spot.

It had taken a couple of months to wrap up their affairs,

and they'd left the farmhouse in the hands of Charles and Yellow Moon. Now, in early September, they were about to land in Puerto Plata, where they would pick up their car and set off for Samaná. A real estate man whom Geno had met on a previous trip had arranged for them to look at some property there.

The jet's captain—in a crackly, distant voice—announced over the loudspeaker that Puerto Plata was below.

"We're going down!" Milo shouted, alarming the old woman next to James.

Seatbelts snapped, and the silver plane banked, dragging its shadow over a stretch of impossibly blue water. It swooped above a vast field of sugar cane, while a few bedraggled brown faces looked up from amid the stalks and squinted into the sun as the plane landed. It was, for them, an uneventful moment—just another load of *turistas*.

The front hatch of the plane was opened, and the characteristic damp smell of the tropics—the smell of rot—invaded the cabin.

Geno breathed deeply. He always loved landing in tropical zones, just so he could smell that smell.

Susan said, "It's hot."

Milo and James rushed ahead of their parents, nearly toppling down the metal stairs, while outside on the tarmac, a few old planes, vintage 1950s, seemed to drift in from the past. It was a short walk across the airfield to the customs building, which one entered through a long, thatched veranda, where a makeshift marimba band played a Dominican merengue. One of the musicians, a wiry old man shaking a sand rattle with one hand, sidled up to Geno and shook the instrument in his face.

Geno stepped backward, trying to evade his toothless smile.

"You give money!" the man shouted, pursuing Geno with an outstretched hand.

"Not today," Geno said.

The music was a certain lure for James, who remembered this band from their previous trip to the island. He stood beside them on legs grown springy with the beat. Milo (not to be outdone) soon broke into a quick-footed dance that amused one of the bongo drummers, who began shouting and sticking out his tongue.

"Good boy!" he shouted.

"Give money!" another member of the band cried, nodding to a basket on the floor.

Geno gave in, throwing a handful of U.S. coins into the basket.

"More money!" the man shouted. "Paper money . . . not coin! Coin too cheap!"

"That's enough money!" Geno put down his bags and stood there with folded arms, a scowl on his face.

Susan intervened, taking her husband by the elbow. "Come on," she said. "Don't give them your attention."

After customs they were met by Hernando Ruiz, who represented the M&M Real Estate Company of Santiago. Geno had met Ruiz before, and he'd been in touch with him by letter and phone in the past few weeks. There was a piece of beachfront land available in the remote province of Samaná for only twenty thousand dollars, and Geno had an intuition this was the right place to settle. The big selling point of the land was that it lay nearly adjacent to the famous "Bay of Arrows," where Columbus had first met resistance from the Taino Indians during his First Voyage. The Tainos had lined the beach and shot at the Genoese explorer as he attempted to land. It was the primal clashing point between two cultures that would never get along, the beginning of a sad, long history of violence and oppression.

Ruiz, a slight man in his fifties, wore a lime-green polyester suit. He had a big gold tooth in front and was, as far as anyone could tell, the only man in Puerto Plata who wore a tie.

"*Meester* Genovese! *Missus* Genovese!" he said. "I am your delight!"

Susan looked at him steadfastly, the same way she looked at her children when they had revved up to a point where their tiny engines were about to race out of control. "Mr. Ruiz," she said. "It's good to meet you. Geno has talked about you."

"No far, Santiago!" he said, nodding eagerly. "I am your delight, forever."

"Thank you," she said.

"You very sweet wife, I know," he said. "A juicy girl, heh?"

Susan tried to smile but did not succeed.

Mr. Ruiz led them to a rusty old VW bug parked beside the curb. The car had originally been red or, possibly, orange.

"You've got some land to show us?" she asked.

"And a car!" he said. "*Theese* is your car!"

Geno let his fingers drift along the hood. "It's beautiful. But I thought you were going to take us to a car *dealer?*"

"*I* am a car dealer," he said. "And *theese* car belong for you."

Susan said to Geno in a quiet voice, "There's got to be some misunderstanding."

"Let's just take it, honey," he said. "What's it matter? I love these old bugs. Nothing in the world like a VW bug." He crouched on his hams to inspect the frame.

"It's all rusted out," Susan said.

"That doesn't matter down here in the tropics. Cars last forever. Am I right, Mr. Ruiz?"

"Volkswagen never end," he said. "My own sister was driving this car since 1964."

"See," Geno said.

Susan wondered if her husband could really be as naive as he seemed. Was he perhaps putting her on? More likely, it was himself he was trying to convince.

"I make you all so happy," said Mr. Ruiz. "*Theese* land, in Samaná—a dreamboat. A real dreamboat!"

"Really," Susan said.

"Happy, so happy," he said, grinning. "When I tell my wife, she say, 'Hernando, you like make happy everybody.' "

"I'm already happy," Geno said.

The children were chasing each other around a coconut tree with palm leaf swords.

After tasting some local fruit drinks and eating a cheese sandwich, the five of them piled into the car for the longish journey to Samaná. Susan thought it unlikely that they could all fit, but Mr. Ruiz remained optimistic; soon three adults and two children were stuffed into a space designed for a much smaller load.

Susan sat in the back with Milo on her lap and James crushing against her.

"Got enough leg room?" Geno asked, craning his neck to see how she was doing.

"We are not buying this car," she said.

He reached back and put a hand on her knee and squeezed, as if to reassure her. Susan, in no mood for this, lifted his hand away.

Susan began to wonder why she hadn't put up more resistance to this trip in the first place as she dug into Milo's ear with a Q-Tip to remove a bug. Geno had been riding so high since the MacAlastair that she had simply gone along with everything. Now the realities of settling into paradise began to glimmer into view.

The VW proceeded, slowly, through the town of Puerto Plata, with its seats exuding a kind of sulpherous odor. The springs were shot, poking uncomfortably through the torn fabric, and exhaust fumes leaked through rusty spots in the floor. Geno spread a map of the Dominican Republic across his knees and studied it.

"How long will it take, Daddy?" James asked.

"Not long," Geno said. "Two or three hours. Maybe less."

"Maybe less," Mr. Ruiz said. "Traffic depends alway. My wife, she say, go or come, it don't know, depend."

Geno grunted and nodded his head.

"Is he speaking Spanish?" Milo asked.

The road to Samaná from Puerto Plata led eastward along the Atlantic coast through dozens of ramshackle villages, and the meagerness of these places shocked Geno, who was used to the less primitive regions of the island, such as Santiago—which had something of an Old World flare—or the capital, Santo Domingo, which had long ago given in to the modern Third World ambience of high-rise offices, fancy hotels, and surrounding slums.

Caborete, Arenoso, Cabo La Roca, Magante. The Dominicans lived in windowless huts thatched with palm leaves or covered with sheets of corrugated tin. People stood idly in the doorways of huts and smoked Montecarlos—the local cigarettes. Their shanties huddled in the shadows of huge billboards advertising Coke, Seven-Up, Johnnie Walker Black Label, and a variety of local rums.

The overloaded, crumbling VW rolled from village to village along the sun-flooded coastal road. It passed through scrappy wetlands, patches of jungle, and stretches of undulating pastureland where long-horned cattle grazed and offered landing and feeding spots for white egrets, who picked insects off their backs.

Vast stands of royal palm lined the beaches or clustered in elegant rows inland: trees that grew at a fantastic pace, then died and fell over; the vegetal matter they left behind became food for pigs and mice, while their trunks turned quickly into firewood for local kitchens. The palm leaves themselves became thatch for the roofs of peasant huts.

The roads were empty for miles, but when a village was in the offing, motorbikes appeared in great buzzing clusters that swarmed around the rusty VW. Mr. Ruiz would scream, "You bitch of a son!" before dissolving into a long catalog of homegrown insults and fantastic gestures that Milo and James immediately began to imitate in the backseat.

The VW occasionally passed a Honda or Daihatsu pickup—narrow but long-bodied trucks that often ferried a dozen or more people from village to village. There were buses, too: huge crowded buses that invariably featured a blaring radio above the driver's seat. They passed you recklessly, roaring around bends without seeming to worry that somebody might be coming the other way. The merengues poured from their open windows. As Susan said, they were like a headache turned into music.

"It's beautiful here," Geno insisted. What he wanted now was assent. *Yes, it's beautiful*, he wanted them all to sing in chorus.

"Look at those windmills," Susan said, pointing to a series of Dutch-style artifacts on a windy ledge overlooking a sweep of dunes.

"Don Quixote liked to fight with windmills," James said. His picture book version of Cervantes' great tale had been one of his favorite books for many years.

"Where's Don Quixote?" Milo piped.

"Don Quixote, very nice," Mr. Ruiz said. "He was ridden by a very old horse, eh?"

James stared ahead, puzzled.

"Are we going to meet Don Quixote?" Milo asked.

"No, dear," Susan said. "That's just a story. This is real life."

Mr. Ruiz slammed on the brakes, nearly crashing into a donkey, which was slowly crossing the road before the mild prodding of a small boy with a long crooked stick. Its saddlebag was stuffed with coconuts.

The boy waved the stick angrily at Mr. Ruiz, who waved a fist at him through the open window. "Watch you ass!" he yelled. Turning to Geno, he said, "Ass dangerous animal on roads like this."

"He's saying a bad word," Milo said.

"Ass is another word for donkey," Susan explained quietly.

"In Dominican Republic," Mr. Ruiz said, "we very many asses."

By the time they reached Nagua, a fairly large town, the sun had swollen into a red ball and hung just above the horizon. It turned the Atlantic into a stew of blood-bright water.

Milo and James soon slumped on Susan's shoulder, falling into sleeplike stupors.

Geno took out his penlight and studied the map in the growing darkness. The Bay of Samaná was an elegantly shaped inlet with a string of tiny seaside villages with names like Majagual, Los Robolos, Honduras, and Los Cacoos. They were heading toward a mysterious and magical little inlet near Punto Balandra—a famous lair for pirates in the eighteenth century.

"We not farther than we look," Mr. Ruiz said, apropos of nothing.

"Excuse me?" Geno asked.

"Punto Balandra not very near," he said. "Or far."

Night falls in the tropics with unusual fervor, seeping into every crevice and niche; it bathes all growing things in a tangible mist that gives to jungle areas an eerie smokiness. The stars and moon, however, stand out by contrast, and near the coast the moonlit sea has an otherworldly sheen.

The land that Mr. Ruiz was hoping to sell to Geno and Susan was adjacent to the sea, an unimaginably pristine spot that nobody would stumble upon by accident.

The path to the land started between two thatched huts in a village so small that it had no official name. The locals called it Los Angeles because a woman in the town who died in 1956 had once seen half a dozen angels sitting on the roof of her little house and screamed, *"¡Los ángeles! ¡Los ángeles!"* That house had become a low-level shrine, the sight of a putative miracle, and one or two pilgrims a year turned up to say their rosaries below the sacred roof.

"This is Los Angeles," said Mr. Ruiz.

"L.A., we call it," Geno said.

"Dodgers!" he responded, nodding his head, then clapping his hands. "I like Dodgers too much. *Too* much! Better they were Brooklyn, I think, but don't kick a gift horse in the ass, no?"

"The Dodgers?" asked James, drifting awake.

"Are we here?" Susan asked.

"Arrival, not too late, but hotel close."

"The hotel is closed?"

"Yes, but no problem," he said. "I good friend to woman who own."

Geno looked at him skeptically.

"Meester Genovese, you love Hotel Miami."

The Miami was a large shack that doubled as the local delicatessen, bar, and all-purpose hangout. In the "lobby" of the hotel one could buy a plastic bag of hard candies, a burlap sack of plantains, or a bottle of rum. The shelves that covered its four walls were lined with rum, the brightly colored bottles arrayed by volume and brand in discrete series. Two sparsely furnished rooms with built-in bunks at the back were the hotel part.

A veranda with a corrugated tin awning lined the front of the Miami; it sported five patio-style tables surrounded by folding chairs that constituted the only "restaurant" to be found for some miles in any direction. Politics, industry, and the social life of L.A. were conducted here, all presided over by Señora Iguano, a white-haired woman of indeterminate age whose husband had gone off to visit a dying aunt in Miami in 1961—the year Trujillo was assassinated—and never returned.

Señora Iguano had lived with Señor Iguano in Miami for three years in the midfifties, but she missed her native village of Los Angeles horribly and had dragged her husband—a docile man who was nonetheless a wizard mechanic—back kicking and screaming in 1958. Everyone blamed his disappearance on this act of violence, and there was no doubt in anyone's mind (apart from his wife's) that he was fixing cars or refrigerators or *something* in Miami at this very moment. Señora Iguano believed—and told everyone—that he'd been captured by Creole Indians and that, if he ever escaped, he would return one day to Los Angeles for a tearful reunion.

"One day, Señor Iguano—he return," the Señora always said, in threatening tones that kept local suitors and con men at bay.

Geno could feel himself in control now, a peculiar but wonderful feeling. He registered for the two little rooms at the back of the Miami without consulting Susan. There was, he argued to himself, no choice anyway. The boys were put to bed in one room, then Susan and Geno crawled into separate bunks in theirs.

Exhausted, Geno fell asleep instantly, though an hour later he woke with a start. He'd been dreaming, once again, about Milo slipping through the ice, the boy's head caught under the frozen ledge.

"You okay, honey?" Susan had called, weakly, from the top bunk.

"Yeah, I'm just going to take a little walk."

In his crumpled white pajamas Geno stepped onto the veranda, where Mr. Ruiz still chatted, absorbed with Señora Iguano in what he assumed must be a local dialect of Spanish. Glad to avoid them, he walked under a trellis into a small garden and sat on a wooden bench and looked up at the stars, so dazzling and plentiful. The moon whirled like a disk as he breathed in a sweet fragrance unlike anything he could recall. He sat there on the brink of paradise and felt the world like a warm egg just before it hatches.

The brightness of the morning sun nearly frightened Susan, its light palpable and inescapable. Every object seemed illuminated from within, the ground itself exuding a peculiar iridescent shimmer; the air smelled like hot rain, even with a cloudless sky overhead.

"Geno," she said, putting on her sunglasses. "If it's this hot at eight, what's it going to be like later?"

"Ask some mad dogs and Englishmen, not me. I'll be taking my siesta."

Mr. Ruiz was already dressed in the same clothes as the night before and ready to go.

Señora Iguano fed them all at the round metal tables on the veranda of her hotel. Breakfast was a plate of fried plantains mixed with onions—called *mangú*—and papaya or sweet lemons. The second course was a local fudgelike substance known as *dulce de leche*, or "sweet milk." Nescafé was served black and strong.

"Land no far," Mr. Ruiz said. "Beautiful land."

Geno could hardly wait. "Eat up, fella!" he called across the table to Milo, who was poking a luminously blue and apparently dead insect with a piece of straw.

"I'm not hungry, Daddy."

"You'll be starving later. Eat when you have the chance. That's the second rule of travel."

"What's the first rule?"

"Use the toilet whenever you see one."

"Even if you don't have to go?"

"Absolutely."

Susan cut in. "I'll pack something that he can eat later, honey."

Geno was frustrated. "I don't see why the kids can't eat when they're supposed to."

Mr. Ruiz brightened. "My children, they eat only sweetie, but I tell wife, no sweetie too much for small one. Small one—how you say in English?—bite the hand feed them sweetie." He grinned widely.

Geno and Susan nodded.

Within minutes, Mr. Ruiz was leading them like an army patrol down the jungle path, which turned a hard left, then right, then left—a crazy zigzag. At one point a small clustering of shacks appeared on the left, and there were children running about in shorts.

"Good local family," said Mr. Ruiz. "I know personal. Beautiful children—like you own."

The incessant whirring of insects formed a background against which more immediate sounds like swaying ferns, snapping twigs, and groaning bamboo could be heard. Coconuts thudded safely to the left and right of the path.

"Coconut bang you brain, make head ring too loud," said Mr. Ruiz. "Don't forget your head is duck when falls."

"How far is this place?" Geno asked.

"Almost to arrive!" Mr. Ruiz cried.

Milo and James were, of course, delighted by everything they saw. This was an adventure, and they were always up for something that resembled an army maneuver. They had already turned sticks into machine guns and begun a guerrilla attack on some invisible enemy. The ominous *rat-a-tat* of their voices mowed down the background noises.

"Get that fucking Ninja!" James shrieked, leaping from behind a framboyan.

Milo lifted his gun and blasted.

"I don't want to hear that kind of language," Susan said, without conviction. "Look around you, for goodness sake. This place is lovely!"

"Hey, come here! A spider!" Milo cupped in his hands a brilliant yellow insect with legs three inches long and small black spots on its shiny back.

"Don't pick up everything you see," Susan said. "Some spiders bite, you know."

"Spiders don't bite me," said Milo. "I bite them!"

James and Milo found this hilarious and cackled.

"Come on, boys!" Geno was calling, way ahead of them now.

Mr. Ruiz turned to Geno. "Ahead of you—to see. Your land."

The jungle opened boldly into a clearing, and the sea glistened through a stand of royal palm. One could see, just barely, a white pebbly beach with dunes of sand.

"Smell the water," Susan said, coming up behind Geno. "It's beautiful, isn't it?" She put down her knapsack. "I do worry about being in such a remote spot, though. I mean, who will the children play with?"

Mr. Ruiz jumped in. "Many children live here, no problem. Many children!"

"What about electricity?"

"No problem," he told her. "This land is—how you say?—the cat meows!" He wiped a thick lather of sweat from his forehead with a red silk handkerchief. "And *very* cheap. Land not cheap anywhere but here. Here, land cheap. Beautiful land. No much money."

Geno was struck wordless by the aura of this place. He walked alone into the clearing and looked up to see a cloud of pink and yellow parrots rising from a coconut palm. He went on, stumbling down the path for another two hundred yards, moving over a little sand hillock and descending through a dry alluvial wash to where the sea began. Kicking off his shoes, he stepped into the slowly lapping surf to feel the slight but exhilarating draw of the undertow. The water gurgled underfoot, slipping back, exposing a glassy stretch of sand. He could see a school of minnows darken and disappear.

Looking up again, he watched a pelican float on the horizon's edge. And then he saw them: streaks of light poured from the sky—in the shape of long green arrows.

Geno rubbed his eyes. He felt dizzy, giddy. He bent in the water now, on his knees, soaking his jeans to a line just below the waist. He put his face down and let the salt water sting his eyes and fill his ears and wet his hair and shirt. When he looked up, the green glinting arrows were falling into the water, turning the sea around them a milky shade of turquoise.

Geno shook the water from his hair and lifted his hands to the sky. "We'll take it," he said, to no one in particular. "It's ours."

Chapter 24

The meeting took place on the *Santa María* in the captain's musty private quarters after nearly three weeks at sea. They sat around a three-legged oak table stained with wine, poring over charts.

Martín Alonso Pinzón, captain of the *Pinta*, had become uneasy about the journey's length. He knew that Columbus had no idea where they were. Their compasses had for the past ten days ceased to register "true" north, and the North Star seemed to shift erratically in the sky. How was such a thing possible?

Some infernal currents were obviously at work beneath the smooth surface of a glassy sea, drawing the three little caravels across the Western Ocean at breakneck speed. Where would it end?

"I don't like *any* of it," said Vicente, younger brother of

Martín, who captained the *Niña*. "I've been sailing ships for eighteen years, and I've never known the North Star to jiggle. It's the work of the Devil."

Columbus was unperturbed. "It does 'jiggle,' as you say. But I don't see why this should surprise you. We're on the other side of the world. God's universe is various."

Martín sneered. "This part of the world may not belong to God."

The one thing Columbus really disliked about Martín Pinzón was his sense of humor. How, at a time like this, could he be making cracks?

"Our crews must not get wind of this," Columbus said.

"They know already," said Vicente. "Some of them are experienced seamen!"

"Indeed," Martín added. "And they find your calculations ludicrous. You're tampering with the figures, aren't you?"

Columbus rose, furious. "I know what I'm doing, damn it!"

The brothers Pinzón looked at him coolly.

"You must trust me," he said, trying to calm himself. "These men are ignorant, you know. They believe what they're told. We must not frighten them with knowledge beyond their capacities."

Martín flattened his palm on the outspread charts: "So where, if I may ask, do you think we are?"

Columbus brightened. "We've had so many signs of land, Martín. First, we saw a tern, then a bosun bird. Didn't you see them yourself? They never fly more than twenty-five leagues from shore, do they?"

Martín stared at Columbus. Terns and bosun birds often flew a long way from home.

"And then, we all saw that seaweed yesterday," Columbus said, seeming to require no response from his listeners. "It was terribly green, wasn't it?"

"What does that mean?" asked Vicente.

"It means that land is near," Columbus said. "It was torn off a landmass. I've never seen that color of seaweed except near land." He didn't even dare look at them for confirmation. "And furthermore, we've had a windless drizzle for three days, haven't we? Has either of you ever seen a windless drizzle more than, say, forty leagues from shore?"

"A windless drizzle?" Martín asked.

Columbus paid no attention. "And whales! We've had them sprouting off starboard several times, haven't we?" He bent close to Vicente. "Haven't we?"

"We have."

Martín scratched his grizzly beard, which had recently turned white. "You don't think whales are capable of surviving a fair distance offshore?"

"I don't."

Martín shrugged and stood, as if to stretch. Long before they had slipped quietly through the mouth of the Río Saltes and turned hard to port through the gulf channel and toward the Canaries, he had known that his superior officer was a know-it-all and, worse, a bore. What he did possess, however, was a remarkable will. He seemed to believe that destiny had greatness in store for him.

"The men are restive," Vicente said, rubbing his pocked hands together in a way that annoyed Columbus.

"Remind them that our sovereigns have offered a reward of ten thousand maravedis *per annum* to the man who first catches sight of land," Columbus said. "To this, I will add a further reward of one silk doublet."

"That will get their attention," Martín said.

Columbus glanced nervously between the two men.

"And what if they never see land?" Martín, feeling impish, asked.

Columbus said, "Marco Polo says there are 7,448 islands in the Sea of China. All I'm asking is for someone to see *one* of them!"

Martín Alonso Pinzón grinned.

After a glass of port, the Pinzón brothers returned to their respective ships, still dissatisfied.

They sailed westward, silently, for what seemed like months but was, in fact, only another week or so.

On the night of 11 October 1492, around ten o'clock, Columbus (who was sitting in the sterncastle and trying to judge the position of his ships by the stars) thought he saw something flicker on the horizon. Was it a light? Or was he merely seeing things?

He summoned his steward, who said, "It may be a light, sir."

The first mate, José Manuel Torres, was strolling on the deck nearby, and he was eagerly beckoned. He studied the horizon carefully for about ten minutes, saying nothing.

"Don't you see it?" Columbus badgered. "It's like a wax candle, rising and falling."

The first mate said, "I'm afraid I see nothing."

Columbus bit his lip. "I know that land is near, José. I know it!"

He took himself off to his cabin and tried, without success, to fall asleep; at 2:00 A.M. a cannon sounded in the dark: the long-awaited signal!

Columbus rushed up top, soon joined by the whole crew.

It happened that a lookout by the name of Juan Rodríguez Bermejo had spotted land. He cried, "*¡Tierra!*" from the crow's nest. And suddenly, not two leagues off, a New World hove into view.

Its outline—immense and purple—recalled a sleeping Leviathan.

Columbus could feel his knees weaken as he stood there. When he tried to cross the deck, he wobbled like a newborn calf. His stomach tightened. Falling to his knees, he crossed himself and said a brief prayer of thanks.

All sails were lowered, and the ships dropped anchor. The caravels would lay by until dawn.

Suddenly, Juan Rodríguez Bermejo stepped forward, awaiting the audience of Columbus.

"Yes?"

"Sir, I would like to claim the reward. As you know, I saw land first."

"You?"

"Did you not hear me, sir?"

"I heard you, but in fact *I* saw it first. I saw a shining

light in the distance," he said. "It was God's signal. A signal to *me*."

Bermejo's face lost all definition. "Really, sir?" The poor man stumbled. "I mean, sir, I actually saw it . . ." He seemed ready to break into tears.

"Are you doubting my word?"

"No, sir."

"I'm glad you're not."

"I'm not, sir."

"Good."

Columbus claimed the reward for himself.

Chapter 25

"Tres pasitos, tres pasitos," the old woman murmured as she walked among the crowd at the market.

"What's she selling?" Susan asked.

"It's a kind of rat poison," Geno said. "The phrase means 'three little steps.' The rat eats it, takes three steps, and dies."

"Jesus."

"It's also used on husbands around here," he said. "Some only manage one or two steps."

"Ah, they use it on men who fool around, is that it?" She tugged at Geno's hand to tease him. He still never referred to his affair with Lizzie or, for that matter, her relationship with Andrew; once in a while she felt compelled to bring this topic up, but he always pretended not to hear.

They strolled hand in hand past various stalls selling everything from pots and pans to guava fruit and yucca. Susan had slung a rainbow-striped Guatemalan bag over her shoulder, and it was slowly filling up as they ambled amid the clutter of children, women with baskets on their heads, chickens, mules, and old men whose skulls seemed eerily visible beneath their tight black skin.

As if created by God *ex nihilo* on the spot, a small man with an impressively big and bald head appeared at their elbow. "I will take bag, you!" he said, tugging on Susan's bag. "Help you, please!"

Geno was less alarmed than annoyed. He guessed the man was about fifty.

"I am Augusto," he said. "I work for you—*americanos*."

Susan said, "Who are you?"

"Augusto."

"I know you're Augusto."

"You need someone help you to build house? I'm carpenter! Señora Iguano tell me. She say, '*Americanos* nice people, so you work for them. And don't charge too much.' "

It turned out that Augusto, too, had spent time in Florida—as a waiter in a big Miami hotel on Collins Avenue. When the immigration people caught up with him, he was sent back home.

"Señora Iguano is my cousin," he added.

Susan and Geno had already noted that virtually everyone in Los Angeles was, in some way, related. But they nodded hospitably, as if Augusto's connection to Señora Iguano made everything all right.

"Whatever you need me to do, I do," Augusto said. "Caretaker, baby-sitter, carpenter."

"A jack-of-all-trades," Susan said, trying not to smile.

"That's me," Augusto said, grinning.

"We do need a carpenter," Geno said to Susan. "Why not Augusto?"

"Do you know how to build a house, Augusto?" Susan asked.

"I build many houses," he said. "I build you a *casa grande*."

"I don't want a big house," Geno said. "I want a little house. Maybe two little houses. *Simple* houses."

"Like Thoreau," Susan said, teasing Geno, who had been lingering over *Walden* since their arrival.

"I build simple little houses," said Augusto.

As easily as that, Geno and Susan acquired a family retainer, one who took on his responsibilities with a wonderful gravity. He assumed the Guatemalan bag and began negotiating, in rapid idiomatic Spanish, with the farmers. They soon went back to the Miami with the bag overflowing, and the whole shopping trip had cost them close to nothing.

"We can live on air here," Geno said. "Like kings."

Susan looked up at him with frustration. "Sometimes, dear, your enthusiasm is wearing."

"What?"

"You sound like the tackiest sort of tourist."

"Come on, honey."

"I won't 'come on.' You're full of big talk, but when it comes right down to it you'd be just as happy as the next man to exploit these people."

"That's silly."

Susan's voice was angry now. "It's true. You're pissing me off, Geno. Stop being so fucking unconscious!"

Geno looked away bitterly. One of the main reasons he'd come to the tropics was to start over, to become more responsible. To get in control of things. To be conscious. And here was Susan, saying this.

"Nobody build like Augusto," Señora Iguano told Susan and Geno over lunch. "He make houses everywhere in Samaná."

This reassured Geno, and he set off with Augusto and the boys after lunch to scout the property and choose an appropriate location.

"You take advice from me," said Augusto. "Building in Samaná different from America. America complicated. People live *inside* houses. Dominicans, we live outside. Weather too good for indoor life. Sky is our ceiling. Why put up walls?"

Geno pricked up his ears. This was just what he wanted: something simple, a place where he and Susan and the boys could spend this year and, down the road, return for extended visits. He even played with the possibility of leaving this visit totally open-ended. Why not live here for good?

The work began in earnest almost immediately, and Augusto quickly managed to get his family a piece of the action. He had a tall and wildly skinny brother, Néstor, and a pudgy, almost dwarfish cousin, Orígenes. They joined the project that day, emerging from the jungle as if they'd been waiting there, ready for days, to begin.

"I'm a carpenter, too," Milo said.

James heard this and added, "Not me. Leave me out of this."

Geno looked at him coolly. "Where do you plan to sleep, James? On the beach?"

James said, "Come off it."

"I won't come off it. Everyone lends a hand around here. You're not in the States now."

"In the States everyone work hard," said Augusto. "Here, people lazy. Nobody work."

Néstor and Orígenes shook their heads and grinned toothlessly, clapping Augusto on the shoulder. They were delighted to be related to a man who knew English and worked for an American.

James was only ten, but adolescence had been kindling in him for some time; he sulked beneath a large framboyan. A straw hat was pulled over his eyes in defiance and his knees were tucked into his chest to suggest a continuing state of leisure.

"James isn't coming," Milo said to his father. "Do you want me to kick him?"

"I'll deal with him later," Geno said, trying to sound severe. He was determined now to control these boys. To show them who was in charge.

They picked a clear spot on the brow of the hill about a hundred yards from the sea for laying out the foundations of the two little houses, which would be built as rectangles, twenty by thirty feet each. The boys would sleep in one, while Geno and Susan would occupy the other. A veranda connecting the houses would also serve as an outdoor kitchen and dining room. When guests came, they'd bunk in with the boys—to ensure all visits would be short.

Geno relished the prospect of conjuring ways to deal with basic needs of water and light. Like Robinson Crusoe, he would make do with anything at hand; he would fashion a life from next to nothing. There must be ways, he thought, to harness the sun's energy or, if necessary, summon water from a stone.

"Is there a stream somewhere?" Geno asked. "I saw various run-offs from the jungle, didn't I?"

"It's far to walk, too far to make easy," said Augusto. "But I will show you."

They cut through a thick stand of mango trees to where a stream passed; they followed it along for half a mile or so to a cove where the stream formed a mini-waterfall that collapsed into a pool that drained into the bay.

"Beautiful water!" Augusto said, cupping a handful for drinking. "Very sweet." Geno, Milo, Néstor, and Orígenes followed suit.

"This will make a wonderful shower," said Geno. "But you're right about the distance. We still need a source of water at the house."

Augusto said, "No problem, Señor."

"Yeah?"

"We make a cistern," Augusto said, visualizing it with his fingers. "Catch rainwater on roof, then run it to cistern."

Geno's face sank for a moment as he realized how much sense this plan made, even though it also meant abandoning his idea of Tahitian-style thatched roofing.

"I like thatched roofs, you know."

"Thatch is no good. It doesn't catch no rain." He went on to explain that there was nothing quite so wonderful as the sound of heavy rain drumming on a tin roof. "It put you asleep in the rainy season. Very nice to sleep under rainy roof."

Geno sat back on his haunches. "I like that a lot," he said. "We'll drink the rain."

Geno found himself taking control of the building process, and he wondered if maybe he should have been a carpenter or builder all along. Intellectual work was insidious that way: You lost touch with the physical world. He'd always envied the carpenters he'd met in Vermont; they all seemed to have a perfect grip on their experience. They knew exactly how things worked, and that, he felt, gave them a sense of control.

Augusto, however, was the quiet brains of the operation. He knew, for example, that it was easier to dismantle the walls of an abandoned house than to fabricate new walls of interlocking palm wood. The jungle was full of crumbling shacks that had once housed whole families.

"A good floor, a good roof," he said, letting the wisdom of the ages form on his lips. "These are essential to building a house. Nothing else."

A good floor in the Dominican Republic meant a poured concrete floor, to which one might add the ornamentation of an array of white pebbles from the beach. With a tin roof to catch the rain and protect one against the wet, there was little else needed.

Geno worked hard, and he was surprised, and delighted, to find that Augusto, Néstor, and Orígenes threw themselves into the work with parallel energy. Even James and Milo found their father's waves of enthusiasm irresistible and were drawn in. They all worked, shirtless, in the hot sun, with a thick film of sweat on their backs.

Every hour or so, Geno and the boys would cool off in the sea. There wasn't much of a surf in this part of the Caribbean, but that didn't matter. They would swim out just far enough to catch a small wave, then let their bodies hang loosely in the water as it carried them gently back to shore.

The boys loved the wildlife along the shore and jungle fringe: frigate birds swooping overhead, pelicans, and gulls. Just off the dunes were mongoose lairs and trees full of sparrow hawks. Hummingbirds zummed along, just grazing the elephant grass. Snakes cut in and out of the weeds, and manta rays scattered like triangular floormats along the beach. Staring into the oncoming waves, one occasionally caught sight of parrot fish, a foot long, with their rainbow-colored skin and black eyes glinting in the sun.

Susan did not, at first, join the building party. She was still angry with Geno for buying the land without even asking her what she thought, for taking over so completely that any mutuality in the marriage seemed to be gone. Though she hadn't said anything yet, she planned to tell Geno firmly that she would stay in the Dominican Republic for two months—no more. On the other hand, she had never seen him like this before. He woke up early, excited about his day. He was bursting with practical ideas for the houses, for improving the land. And Milo and James were dumbstruck. Their father gave them orders. And they loved it.

After a few days, Susan could not resist the construction site. Quietly she joined "Geno's chain gang" as they poured the concrete floors for both houses and gathered endless smooth white pebbles, which they brought up from the beach in metal buckets slung over their shoulders with hemp.

The frames were necessarily made of wood, and wood was scarce on this island. The horror of deforestation was alive in everyone's mind, and the government rigorously controlled the sale of lumber. But Augusto had a genius for the acquisition of raw materials, and he appeared each morning with an old mule that carried on its back a hoard of necessities: nails, bailing wire, palm wood, dry cement ready for mixing, screws and bolts, doors.

Within a week, the houses were framed and the roofs tacked on. Screens were brought in—one did not need conventional windows—and the doors attached. Within two weeks, the houses were more or less finished: even the gas stove was attached and the cistern dug, cemented, and covered with a metal lid.

The third week of construction was devoted to interior details like bunk beds and bookshelves, while the fourth and final week was left for the outhouse. Geno had found a book in the Barrington College Library called *Sewage Disposal in Rural Areas*, and he Xeroxed the chapter on latrines. Finding exactly the right spot for the outhouse was crucial; it had to be at least a hundred yards from the two houses, and it should have downhill drainage *away* from the living area. According to the manual, a hole twenty feet deep would accommodate a family of four using it daily for fifty years. "Anything deeper would be hubris," Geno said.

Geno, Augusto, and Néstor dug steadily for three and a half days, finishing the hole on the fourth day just before lunch. (Susan imagined Milo tumbling like Alice into a Wonderland of Waste and insisted on an even narrower hole for the seat itself than Geno thought appropriate.) That afternoon, after a big lunch of cassava loaf with an avocado spread, they began constructing a shed around the hole with a traditional outhouse seat inside. By the end of the week the family, one by one, tried it for the first time.

The boys, of course, went first. They were in and out in minutes.

"I couldn't even hear it drop," Milo said. "I let a big turd fall, and I couldn't hear it."

"I heard mine drop," said James.

"Liar!"

"You're the liar."

"Stop it," said Geno. "It doesn't matter."

Susan was next, and Geno waited impatiently outside the outhouse for her.

"You okay, honey?"

"I'm fine."

He waited and waited.

"What's happening in there?"

"You *know*," she said. "Go away. I like it here!"

On the principle that a watched pot never boils, Geno went back to the kitchen with the boys and read the Dominican papers, which Señora Iguano always left on the breakfast table for Geno. He found it hard to concentrate on world events here. Life beside the Bay of Arrows was consuming, and local politics was all that mattered.

Geno's turn to try the outhouse came and he enclosed himself in the dark little world. He sat on the rough seat, listening. It was black in there, and he didn't like it. Already the flies had found this place, and they buzzed in and out of his ear; one flew up between his thighs, and he jumped to shoo it.

"Fuck," he said to himself. For the first time since arriving on the island, he felt a pang of longing for the conveniences of home: a clean bathroom, running water, a conventional toilet, electric lights. Why was he so hell-bent on pursuing this crazy experience? He had never actually liked camping as a child, so it was ludicrous to imagine that he would suddenly find this primitive life acceptable—not for any length of time. Like Rodin's Thinker, he leaned forward and rested his chin on bent knuckles.

Suddenly the room began to whirl. Geno wondered if it were claustrophobia at first, since he'd had problems in elevators and small spaces before. He stood up quickly, sucking in a deep breath, which he held. He dug his fingers into his temples and crouched forward, letting the blood rush to his brain.

He looked up at the ceiling, where he thought he could hear a strange noise—like wind rushing through the tops of trees. The roof slid open, and there was starlight overhead.

Stars? thought Geno.

"Susie!" he called, leaning heavily on the door, which swung open under his weight.

Outside, it was dark. Cicadas throbbed, and bats whizzed overhead. Geno looked toward the houses but all he saw was a campfire.

He crept toward that light, stumbling through some dense undergrowth. Twenty yards away, he crouched behind a large spiky tree and gaped.

A dozen naked Tainos were dancing around the fire, and another one beat rhythmically on a hollow log. The chunky sound echoed across the bay.

Geno closed and opened his eyes. Clearly he was dreaming. Or ill. Or insane.

But these were Tainos who danced before him. He recognized their markings from a book he'd studied in the Barrington College Library. Their long dark hair was smoothed back and tied with thongs. They wore loincloths similar to an Indian dhoti. Colorful markings on their arms flashed in the firelight. Some carried bows, while others brandished clubs. One of them, obviously the cacique, was holding his hand high. Another, the medicine man or behique, was dispensing a drink to the warriors who approached him, one by one, on their knees. Were they taking drugs?

Disoriented, Geno backed away from the fiery scene. He stumbled down through the tall palm trees to the sea, which seemed to roar in his ears, as if his head were pressed to a conch. He knelt in the waves, hoping to wake himself from this wild, horrific dream.

After several minutes of letting his face soak in the cool

water, he looked up and saw it: a caravel anchored in the middle distance, its sails furled. A solitary lamp swung from a post in the forecastle, while a dark figure was leaning over the rails.

And Geno knew that figure by his long shadow, by the way he leaned, chin forward, in the dark.

Chapter 26

Columbus had fallen into his deepest sleep since arriving in the Indies—or wherever he was—in October. It was now Christmas Eve, though he had gone to bed without remembering this.

He was exhausted, having lived off nervous energy since Hispaniola swam into view. He paddled into cove after cove, greeting the natives whenever he could, pushing a few miles here and there into the interior to see if, perhaps, he could get a whiff of the Great Khan's spice-scented world.

Thus far he'd found nothing but jungle and primitive villages. And the Indians were not happy to see him. Indeed, they often fled upon seeing his ships, leaving behind their empty huts. He wondered why they considered him so terrifying; he had not, after all, done anything to harm them.

A few had shouted angrily at him as he set foot on their shores, but these were the exception. Most just vanished into the green thickets. A number of brave ones remained, curiosity outstripping their threshold of terror, and they exchanged gifts with Columbus. One of them, indeed, had presented the explorer with a tribal mask of hammered gold, thus fanning his hopes.

Only a week before he'd written a letter to Ferdinand and Isabella that he hoped, one day, to hand deliver. "Your Highnesses will be delighted to know that in all the world there is no sweeter or gentler people than these Indians," he said. "You should be filled with joy to know that soon they will become Christians and be instructed in the civilized customs of Your Sovereign Realm. There can really be no better people or land in all this world. These Indians, for the most part, possess a most singular and loving character. They speak softly (though a few of them have made threatening gestures, which I shall not dwell on). They are of decent stature, too: men and women alike. And they are definitely *not black* but light brown. Moreover, their attractive houses and villages seem well-governed and peaceful. The people obey their local governors—judges or lords—in a way that makes one marvel, especially given the fact that these rulers speak as softly as their people. And they have elegant manners, communicating with their people by little gestures of the hand and few words. Indeed, we could all learn much from them."

He crossed out that last sentence. One did not tell one's sovereigns that they had something to learn from a tribe of naked Indians. Nor did he entirely believe it himself.

Everything had, indeed, been going well for Columbus until Martín Alonso Pinzón (for reasons of his own) decided to abandon Columbus and his brother. The *Pinta* lifted anchor one morning before sunrise, and the ship simply vanished.

"The bastard wants to get to the gold before we do," Columbus told his gromet, a beardless young servant with small black eyes.

It was impossible to ascertain exactly what the Indians were saying, but Luis de Torres was a gifted translator, and he began to grasp their mellifluous native tongue. One Indian (who called himself Kulaku) had been able to explain to Columbus that a famous cacique named Guacanagarí lived in a nearby coastal village. He was extremely wealthy, and his village was virtually weighted down with gold.

So it came to pass that on this breezy night in late December, just off the coast where Guacanagarí was said to reign in gilded splendor, the *Santa María* ran aground. The ship glided innocently over a sharp coral reef and was deftly impaled. The gromet realized only gradually that something terrible had happened. He woke Columbus, who knew at once what it was.

With the crew roused and called on deck, Columbus gave orders with a cool-headed steadiness. He commanded a longboat to drag an anchor astern to ease the caravel slowly off the reef. The men in the longboat were lowered over the port side of the *Santa María*—only to make a run for the *Niña*.

Columbus shook his head.

The stern of the *Santa María* swung around with agonizing slowness, slicing the keel of the ship lengthwise. Thus gutted, water poured in through the dreadful fissure.

By dawn there was no hope of salvaging the flagship caravel, which listed miserably to starboard, so Columbus ordered his remaining crew to abandon ship; they did so, leaping into small boats that would take them safely to shore.

Columbus did not look back as the *Santa María* was engulfed.

"What shall we do, sir?" the gromet asked as they landed on the lovely beach.

"We shall erect a fortress," Columbus said.

"What's the point of building a fortress in this wilderness?" the young man asked.

Columbus stared at him hard.

"I don't mean to be inquisitive," the gromet fumbled.

"Then be quiet," Columbus said. One always built a fortress in these circumstances. How else could one establish a proper beachhead? How else could one protect oneself from hostile Indians who would surely, in time, object to the fact that Columbus was making off with their gold?

The bewildered crew of the *Santa María* gathered around their captain and listened as he explained to them that it was time to build a fort.

"We'll have a moat and everything," he told them.

One of the men noted, wearily, that it was Christmas.

A huge smile flashed across the captain's face. Yes, God had once again chosen to favor him with adversity. He would, as ever, turn disaster to his advantage; and the heavens would reward him doubly or triply for his perseverance.

"Our fort shall be called La Navidad," Columbus said, kneeling in the sand and crossing himself. "God save the King and Queen of Spain."

Chapter 27

When Geno fainted in the outhouse, tumbling through the swinging door with his trousers hooked around his knees, Augusto quickly summoned Josefina, an immense black woman in her late thirties who lived not half a mile away in a little *aldea*, or settlement, with her six children. She was widely known to have powers of healing, and she brought with her a plastic jar of guanabana juice that improved Geno's health and spirits almost instantly.

Josefina floated above Geno, her big yellow eyes fixed on him like twin moons.

Susan wanted him to see a real doctor, but he refused, saying it was just "heatstroke." The sun was beating down on the outhouse fiercely that day, and Geno had been working outside all morning.

Secretly, he knew that something was wrong. The Rainbow thing, now this. Perhaps even those green lights he had seen when he first looked across the Bay of Arrows. It wasn't only the world climate that was shifting. Time itself was coming loose. Before long, there would be no past, no future. Just a bizarre, eternal present in which everything would be happening all at once.

Josefina, whom he had not met before, devoted herself to Geno while he recuperated. When she heard from Augusto that he liked cookies, she baked him a small basketful of coconut biscuits with chocolate melted over the tops. He would eat them slowly, grunting his pleasure while she fanned him with a big-finned palm and sang Dominican folk songs in a wheezy low voice. Like Augusto, she knew a source of income when she saw one, and she attached herself to Geno and Susan like a limpet. Before long, she was bringing manioc bread in warm loaves every morning, with a bowl of *plátanos* fried to perfection in hot oil. Without even having been asked, she gathered their clothes in a basket every other day and took them to the stream for washing.

Susan was embarrassed by Josefina's lavish attendance on them, but Geno was adamant. "It's all right," he said. "We can pay her very little, but it will seem like a fortune to her. They have no other way of getting money. We're actually doing them a favor, damn it!"

"Give me a break, huh?" Susan said. "It's nothing but exploitation—pure and simple."

"It's not."

"It is."

James and Milo beamed. It wasn't often that their parents engaged in a dialogue at their level.

Josefina's six children were almost always within a fifty-yard radius of their mother. As Geno and Susan soon learned from Augusto, there was no father; rather, there were many fathers, but Josefina was not sure any longer which father was attached to which child. On major holidays, anywhere from three to eight men turned up for dinner, bearing gifts. Nobody seemed to care or count.

The oldest child was a young woman called Olympia, who was fourteen and doubled as a parent. The five younger children, three of whom were boys, ranged in age from three to eleven.

Two of the boys, Jorge and Pio (meaning "Flea"), were exactly the age as James and Milo, and it wasn't long before the black-skinned boys followed the white-skinned boys like happy shadows. They became inseparable, and soon James and Milo chattered away in a language only they and their friends could understand.

When Geno felt totally recovered from his outhouse episode, he decided to establish a routine for the boys that included a number of "schoolhouse" hours. Every weekday morning from nine till eleven James and Milo sat under a huge framboyan on straw mats and did their lessons, working through programmed learning textbooks purchased from an educational firm in Boston. Geno handled the "humanistic" subjects, while Susan—simply because she was capable of doing so—handled science and math.

After breakfast, before and after lunch, and once in the late afternoon or evening, they would go together for a swim. Sometimes, instead of taking a siesta in a hammock, they would fish from a reef throughout the afternoon, returning with a glittery catch.

Josefina remained quietly in the background, sweeping the floors, baking bread, folding laundry, shouting orders at the children. Her Spanish was (to Geno and Susan) utterly incomprehensible, sounding more like Arabic than a language with Latin roots, so they communicated mostly by gestures, smiles, winks, and nods—a method that worked very well.

Susan, especially, developed a fine rapport with Josefina. She admired the peasantlike sturdiness evident in the way she worked, slowly yet certainly. Work—whatever it might be that day—got done around her. Josefina plunged into a pile of laundry without fear, knowing that, within hours, everything would have been accomplished. Within a few weeks, Susan found herself able to hold rudimentary conversations with her in her dialect of Spanish; Geno, amazed, would listen.

Before long, he and Susan developed a counterpointing schedule. He would begin the day at seven, when the boys got up; he saw to their breakfast, took them down to the waterfall for a shower, and made sure they cleaned their little house. The ritual was accomplished slowly, unfolding in a period that Susan used for her own writing. At nine, or whenever Geno had finished his lessons, she took over with the boys. Her tutorials in math, science, and geography lasted until twelve.

By noon, it was time for a swim, followed by lunch, then games on the beach (they were invariably joined by Jorge and Pio, who were enamored of the Frisbee that James and Milo had stashed in their luggage before leaving Vermont). Afternoons began in earnest with a nap after games. James and Milo retreated to their beds, while Susan and Geno slung themselves in separate hammocks. It was a time for sleeping or reading. Often it seemed to rain during siesta time: an intense downpour that watered the garden, filled the cistern, and swept the sky clean for the rest of the day.

After siesta, the children rushed off to play with Jorge and Pio, often migrating to the *aldea* where Josefina lived, and this left Geno and Susan free. She would settle down for another hour or two by herself under a shady tree or listen to whatever stations she could get on her Grundig or, some days, make notes for a sequence of stories about her childhood in Wisconsin.

Geno, for his part, worked on what he called his "projects." He decided, for instance, to build wooden stairs into the path leading from the houses to the sea, making the steep descent to the beach less treacherous. And the garden offered endless possibilities for work: staking out vegetables, weeding, building fences to keep out the kinkajous. The coconut trees dropped so many nuts that one had endlessly to clear and burn them.

"Coconut shells makes very nice house for rats," Augusto had warned, and Susan, who hated rats, conducted elaborate clearings every few days. These led to weekly coconut bonfires.

Geno drew up a list of future projects, enough work to keep him and Augusto and probably Néstor busy well into the next century. These included building a writing studio, installing a shower (the water might be pumped from the cistern into a barrel on the roof), and erecting a windmill on the property's highest ledge that would become the future source of electricity. Geno also thought of creating some kind of gazebo near the beach—a place where swimming gear and the equipment for beach games could be stored. Every day ended with a long walk along the shoreline.

Dinner, which Josefina had largely taken over, followed the late afternoon outing; it was in turn followed by stories. Everyone, including Susan and Geno, went to bed early, since there were no electric lights to extend the day beyond its natural limits, and Geno could not bear to be outside the house in the tropical dark.

The immediate result of going to bed early, for Geno and Susan, was that they discovered each other again as sexual creatures; the loud pulse of the crickets—called *grillos* by the villagers—masked their own intimate and ecstatic sounds, although sometimes Susan got carried away and bellowed her pleasure too loudly.

Milo, who slept lightly, would trot over to see if anything was wrong.

"Is there a robber or something?" he asked one night, standing at the door in an oversized tee shirt that doubled as a nightdress.

"Go away," Geno said.

"I heard noises."

"Mommy and Daddy were just laughing about something. Go away."

"Are you fucking?"

Geno opened the door. "I don't want you talking like that, Milo. Do you hear?"

"That's what James said. He said you were fucking."

"Did he say that?" Susan asked.

"Ask him yourself."

"I'll deal with him in the morning," Geno said. "Now you go to sleep."

Milo walked in his bare feet back to bed.

"They're beautiful, aren't they?" Susan said.

"They're impossible."

"Don't be so touchy. Kids know everything about sex these days."

"If they were girls, I'd be worried."

"That's sexist."

"It's true."

"If they get some girl pregnant in the seventh grade, you'll be worried."

Geno wondered. It seemed such a brief time since they'd been tiny little creatures who burped and whimpered in his arms, light as whiffets.

He rolled over to cradle Susan in his arms, feeling the length of her, naked, against his body.

"Do you like it, Sue?"

"What?"

"Samaná."

"I'm not sure."

"Why?"

"This is more your thing than mine."

"I could live here forever."

"Really?"

Geno frowned, sitting on the edge of the bed now. He said, "I love it here. And just look at us. We haven't been so close in years."

Susan stared at him.

"Christ, we make love practically every night!" he said.

"That's sex."

"I see. You're going to make a fine distinction between sex and love."

"I love you, and I like having sex with you. But—I don't know—I'm confused."

"About what?"

"You. Me."

"What's to confuse? I feel like I've got a grip on things here."

"I admit it, you've got a handle on the boys. I like to see that. But you're in your own world, in a different way."

"You're still pissed off about Lizzie Nash, is that it?"

"That's too simple."

"So explain it to me. I'm simple."

"I wish I could. It has something to do with the way you and I relate. I feel like I've become . . . invisible."

"I see you fine."

"You don't make me *feel* visible."

"Jesus."

"I wish I didn't have to talk like this."

"Me, too."

"But it's better that I do."

He stood now. "For God's sake, Susan, can't you let up? Can't you just let me alone?"

Steel flashed in her voice. "If that's what you want. I'll take the boys back to Vermont, and you can play Henry David Thoreau here by yourself."

"I don't mean that, and you know it."

"What is it that you mean, then?"

"I want to be a man. A goddamn man!"

"That's just a stupid cliché."

"So let me be a cliché. I never had a real father, you know. I don't want my boys to say they never had a man for a father."

"So tell me. What is a 'real' man?"

He sat down now, excited. "That's exactly what I'm trying to figure out, honey. Can't you see that?"

They lay on their backs now, separately, and listened to the jungle noises, the chorus of a billion *grillos*, the exotic birdcalls, the groaning of bamboo and coconut palms. Wind shunted through the vegetation, and the whole world seemed to hum mysteriously: a sign that an abrupt change of weather was in the offing. Then it started to rain: a shower that drummed on the tin roofs, thunderous and fine.

Geno left Susan and the boys in the schoolhouse one morning and took off by himself up the beach. He'd been wanting to go for a long walk for weeks, but life seemed more and more crowded with teaching the children, with building projects, and with working on the Columbus manuscript, which had taken off in directions he could not account for.

Today he decided to walk instead of write.

In Vermont, he'd found walking a solution and antidote to certain kinds of writing problems. A poem in progress often came to an impasse, a point where the text seemed to freeze. Every poem was like a journey, and he would suddenly encounter streams that had to be forded, peaks jutting up from the landscape precipitously that he had either to ascend or cut around, even whole deserts that had to be crossed with little in the way of food or water.

He took a short path through the jungle to a beach just beyond his own, and from there he followed the shoreline westward. The sea was gold-plated this morning, and one could see across the bay for miles. The sand itself was blond and smooth, littered in places with bone-white driftwood, with clumps of bladder wrack like the spilled intestines of a mythological beast: manta rays lay hidden in the sand like landmines, and their whipping tails could startle the unsuspecting walker.

Treading the margin of the glassy surf, Geno found a spring in his walk; he charged on, scaling one particularly craggy reef as frigate birds wheeled overhead in rings. As he came down off that reef, he saw before him a flawlessly white beach. Royal palms crowded up to it, elegantly tall, their leaves yellow in the vertical sunlight, which poured on the world as if there were no more days to come.

As he was crossing the sand, Geno's eye snagged on something hidden among the trees on a thickly wooded hillside: an odd house with a thatched roof, overhanging eaves, and big porches. The structure was, rather, several connecting houses with ramps of bamboo, and it looked more Tahitian than Dominican.

A barbed-wire fence surrounded the property, beginning just off the sandy beach, but Geno wanted a better view. This was, as far as he knew, an illegal maneuver; one could not by law fence in land within a hundred yards of the sea. All beaches in the Dominican Republic were public property. The wire was low enough, however, so that Geno could leap it in one spot where it sagged by putting one hand on a fencepost.

Trespassing, Geno felt guilty; but curiosity overwhelmed his guilt, and he proceeded. He approached the mysteriously alluring house softly, imagining himself a Taino stalking his prey. He stepped carefully, putting his toe down first, letting the full weight sink only slowly toward the heel.

The flower gardens around the house bloomed profusely. They were full of oversized petunias, frangipanis with blond, stalkless flowers, and bougainvillea. There were fat Chinese roses, green crotons, and a row of tamarind with its feathery leaves. A faint wind blew, stirring the orchids that hung beneath the eaves of the porches.

"¿Que 'ta 'ciendo, caballero?"

Geno looked around and saw a man with a shotgun aimed right at him. *"¡Nada!"* he said. *"¡Soy Americano!"*

"¿Que hay?" the man prodded, waving his gun. He lowered his bushy white eyebrows.

"¿Americano," Geno repeated, as if to explain. *"Turisto."*

"You're no bloody tourist," the man said, putting down his gun. "I caught wind of you at the Miami, didn't I?" He was a tall, leathery-faced man with white hair and angular features that included high blushing cheekbones flanked by long white sideburns. His eyes were flinty and focused steadily on Geno.

"Christopher Genovese," Geno said, putting out his hand. "You should call me Geno."

The man shook the hand firmly. "Alec Selkirk," he said, liltingly.

Geno recognized the accent as Scottish, and he felt curiously drawn to the man. He saw in Selkirk one of those rocky-faced and durable Brits who inhabit remote places. The lines in his face bespoke self-sufficiency, independence, and experience. He was a man's man. Not one of those types who had never camped in the woods, paddled a canoe, or hiked alone to the top of a precipice. Geno thought about his father now: there was something servile about Mr. Genovese that terrified his son, largely because he could feel that same servility niggling at him. But Selkirk was a blast of macho. At least that's what Geno imagined as he stood facing the ruddy Scot.

"I was walking on the beach," he said, "down there . . ." Geno pointed meekly. "And I noticed your house. I like it." He worried that he was stammering slightly.

"You're trespassing."

"I'm sorry."

Selkirk drew his lips to one side—a facial tic that betrayed his uneasiness with people. "Have a whisky?"

Geno quickly agreed.

Selkirk led him onto his spacious veranda-cum-living room. The floor was made of tightly bound bamboo, Polynesian style; a teak bar stood in one corner like an altar, with a dozen crystal tumblers tipped upside down on a towel. A gun rack hung on another wall, sporting an array of rifles, while fishing poles ranged horizontally from hooks above it.

A stuffed shark glared from the wall behind the bar.

"You caught that yourself?"

"Ten years ago. It was glorious. Son of a bitch bucked and weaved for three hours."

"I hear there's a lot of sharks in these waters," Geno said, uncertainly. He remembered that the brother of his freshman roommate at Dartmouth had gotten his leg bitten off at the knee by a shark while swimming off the coast of New Jersey. "Do they bother you?" he asked. "I mean, when you're swimming?"

Selkirk's eyes narrowed, and his bushy white eyebrows drew together. "Only if you bleed."

He poured a stiff drink for himself and Geno, filling heavy glass tumblers with Highland Park.

"I'm not familiar with this whisky," Geno said, sipping it. "It's very nice."

"Comes from Orkney—a single malt. My grandfather came from Orkney, too. He wasn't nice, however."

Geno smiled. He had been to Orkney once, as a graduate student, and he mentioned this in passing, though Selkirk did not comment.

The Scot seemed to move with an invisible bulletproof wall around him, and Geno wished he could break through.

They sat facing each other in bamboo chairs.

"How long have you been here?" Geno asked.

"Twenty-four years," he said. "I suppose you wonder how old I am, too?"

Geno looked away. There was something too raw, too frighteningly Celtic, about this man.

"I'm sixty-four. That means I came here when I was forty—about your age, I suspect."

Geno offered a faint smile.

"And you probably wonder what I'm doing here, for Chrissake?" He smiled tightly. "Is that correct?"

Geno said, "I can understand why you'd come here. It's a great place to live and work. The climate is perfect, it's beautiful . . . lots of reasons."

"I'm doing nothing here, damn it. Not a fucking thing," Selkirk said. "It's you *Americanos*, as you call yourselves, who feel the need to *do* something." He picked up a pipe and began fussing with it. "I like to mess about with the house, of course. Built it myself."

"It's a very interesting house."

"Interesting?"

Geno cringed. He spoke too quickly, too superficially, when he was nervous.

Selkirk ignored him now. "It's a continuous project down here—building. You have to rebuild after every fucking storm. Things rot here. The place stinks, really. It's ludicrous." His voice rose on that last word, booming, the thick accent pounding like surf on shingle.

Geno studied Selkirk's face like a painting. The veins in the man's cheeks and nose swirled in purple-red figurations.

"My father was well off," Selkirk added, talking more to himself now than to Geno. "Not rich. But he had a few quid to spare. In the wool trade, which was profitable in those days. I went off as a representative of the family. Bought several farms in New Zealand for the family. That was my second life."

Geno had heard of being born again, but this was different.

"My first life was Scotland. I read Political Economics for a year at the university, in Edinburgh. It was dreadful. That's why I left for New Zealand. Lasted for about ten years."

"Then you came to the Dominican Republic?"

Selkirk merely flicked a hoary eyebrow, pausing ever so briefly to ignore the question properly, then continued.

"I'm an orderly person, you see," he said. "I break everything down into component parts. My first life was Scotland. My second life was New Zealand. But I got itchy feet. I was fucking bored, in fact, so I hopped a freighter to Siam, where I passed the time in interesting ways. After Siam, which you might call my third life, I made my way by land to Turkey. Hitched rides on the backs of carthorses, hopped trains—whatever." He sipped, paused. "I lived in Istanbul for a few years, trading goods. That was my fourth life. In my fifth life I was a planter in Brazil."

Geno loved the use of "Siam" for Thailand. He must remember to tell Susan.

"My father was dead by then, leaving behind the usual pieces of silver. I translated these into the farm in Brazil—

coffee, you know. Bought the farm one year and sold it the next—a helluva profit. One of your American chappies bought it." He smiled blissfully—like an Airedale.

"Your five lives were rather brief."

"I was aiming for Miami, but somehow I got waylaid here. It all began innocently enough. I was a *turisto*—as you so charmingly put it. Found this beach, fell in love with it, and that was that. My sixth life began at forty. It continues."

Geno couldn't resist teasing him. "Six lives down, three to go?"

"Alec. Call me Alec." He gulped the whisky. "That's coming, I know. If I were a religious man, Geno, I should hope that my seventh life would happen up there. Seven, as you know, is a biblical number." His finger pointed to the ceiling. "But I know better. If there *is* life after death, it will be miserable. Fucking miserable. Pray for oblivion, old boy."

Geno shifted uncomfortably. "You must like it here. Twenty-four years in a place like this is . . . well, amazing."

"I hate the fucking place."

"Really?"

"It's the blacks. You've got to keep an eye out every goddamn second. Don't let them rob you, you know. Give them an inch and they take a bleeding mile."

Geno's heart sank. He should have guessed. Selkirk was, after all, the archetype of the British in their colonial outpost mode. On the other hand, he admired the way these British—at least in the nineteenth century—had combined fairness with toughness. That blend of attributes was everywhere in Kipling, whom Geno secretly admired.

"The women are gorgeous," Selkirk continued. "Some of them, that is. Like fucking rabbits, too. Look how many wee bairns they've got."

"Bairns?"

"Kiddies. You haven't read Robbie Burns, I see."

"Ah, yes. Bairns."

"Fucking dishonest, the lot of them. You've got to keep an eye out, or they'll rob you blind. I've had my share of problems, I must tell you." He paused. "Go straight to the police if you have any problems. If you let them get away with anything, they'll take you right over. You're finished."

"Really?"

"I know what I'm talking about," he said. "And you can't get them to do a stroke of honest work. I've got a boy who works for me, Sábato—Sabbie, I call him. Been working here a couple years and he takes anything he can get his hands on. Caught him last week with a bag of sugar. Had to beat the wizards out of him."

"You beat him?"

"I should have put him in jail. But I took a strap to him." He took a long sip of whisky. "I've got a soft spot for the boy."

"You hit a boy?"

Selkirk nodded and called his servant into the room. "Sabbie!"

The "boy" in question was a short man in his late forties,

muscular and fierce-looking. Sabbie waited, listened resentfully to a barked order, then disappeared.

"He'll bring us a snack," Selkirk said. "You hungry? It's almost time for lunch, damn it."

"I've got to get home," Geno said, nervously. "But I enjoyed talking to you."

"Come back, then. I've got other whiskies—and rums. Do you like rum?"

"Yes."

"Damn well better," he said. "Cheap as water around here. Some of it's bloody okay."

Geno stood.

"*Mi casa* and all that," Selkirk said, avoiding direct contact with Geno's eyes.

"That's very kind of you."

Geno politely gulped the rest of the peaty brown liquor. Dizzy, a little flushed, he excused himself with a nod.

"Use the bloody gate this time!" Selkirk hollered. "You're lucky I didn't blow your head off!"

Geno smiled and waved. As he stumbled down the crooked stone path through the garden, he was trying to absorb the fact that a man like Alec Selkirk could have lived more or less alone here for so many years. His racism was dreadful; that much was clear. But one could have expected it from a man of his background. On the other hand, the fellow was admirable in so many ways—tough, independent, and rather kindly beneath the surface. The fact that he was the last embodiment of the British raj fascinated Geno, who had always found this kind of thing curiously seductive when he was at Oxford. He'd met quite a few old colonials who had served in India, in the Far East, in Africa. They were ramrod straight, literate, fair-minded, strong. And they were all sentimentalists, too, devoted to the works of second-tier writers like Housman and Surtees; but there was something charming about that kind of semiliterary taste. It was robust and honest. And that was good.

Chapter 28

Columbus sat with crossed legs beside the medicine man, whose body was painted with bright red and yellow dyes in a geometrical zigzag pattern. He wore a necklace of seashells, and his hair was braided into a long tail. His only body covering was a kind of skirt made of interlacing palm leaves. There was a leather thong around his waist, and from it was suspended a manaca—a hatchet with a triangular blade of polished stone that glistened in the ceremonial fire that leaped, geisering flakes of hot ash upward into the dark sky.

The cacique stood. The bare skin of his legs and chest were covered with strange black markings whose pattern matched those of the medicine man. He wore a bracelet of bone on one wrist. A necklace of gold hung about his neck.

As the cacique began to speak to the assembled company, Luis de Torres leaned forward, trying to grasp his point.

"What's he saying?" Columbus whispered.

"He's talking about the gods. They think that we're gods."

Columbus suppressed a wry smile.

"He's telling them that the heavens have opened, and that our ships have brought us to them for the purpose of showing them a route to some divine residence where their ancestors wait."

"Find out where he got that gold necklace. There must be a mine somewhere."

Luis de Torres frowned. Columbus had so little interest in this wonderful culture.

"Ask him!" Columbus said.

The cacique, puzzled, turned his head to Columbus. He lifted his hands and turned them palms outward—a signal that he could speak if he wished.

"Ask him!"

Luis de Torres stood and cleared his throat. Adjusting his helmet, he asked, in some approximation of the Taino language, about the gold.

The cacique listened patiently, then shook his head.

"Gold!" Columbus cried.

The dozen or so men around the fire began to laugh. The word "gold" struck them as an amusing monosyllable, not unlike a native word for "shit."

Columbus became frustrated. He stood now, boldly, and the Tainos fell silent. He walked over to the cacique and reached his right hand forward, fingering the gold necklace. The long chain was light as air.

"Gold," he said, moving his lips emphatically.

The cacique, no longer smiling, repeated the fierce monosyllable. "Gold," he said. "Gold . . . gold."

Columbus smiled.

The cacique returned the smile.

Suddenly, the medicine man bellowed a strange order, and the rest of the men rose. Several younger members of the tribe began to beat rhythmically on a long narrow drum made from the hollowed core of a mamey tree. A group of men with pebble-filled gourds attached to short sticks broke into a dance around the fire, circling Columbus, his translator, the medicine man, and the cacique. They bobbed up and down, making a weird buzzing sound with their lips, shaking the gourds in counterpoint to the drumbeats.

The cacique and medicine man sat, cross-legged as before, and Columbus took the clue. "Sit down, Luis," he said. "Do exactly as they do."

A large woman in a delicate apronlike costume stepped into the circle. She brought a wooden pipe of sorts to the cacique, who bowed and accepted the ritual instrument.

"Cohoba," the cacique said. It was a sacred rite of the Tainos.

The woman bowed and disappeared.

Luis de Torres became excited, questioning the cacique in rapid Taino; the cacique nodded politely but apparently did not understand a word.

"What did you ask him, Luis?"

"I asked what he was going to do with that pipe."

The medicine man said something unintelligible, whereupon the cacique lit the pipe.

He inhaled slowly, letting the aromatic vapors fill his lungs. The pipe was passed to the medicine man, who followed suit before passing it to Columbus. In imitation of the cacique and the medicine man, he took a long draw on the pipe. The strongly scented vapors burned the lining of his throat and penetrated deep into his lungs. His head began to spin, and he wanted desperately to cough or wheeze, but he supposed that the cacique and the medicine man would not appreciate his doing so.

Luis de Torres was passed the pipe by Columbus. He hesitated, then inhaled rather tepidly, drawing only a shallow breath; almost immediately his eyes bulged, and he exhaled in a rush, coughing and spitting.

The cacique stared ahead, unperturbed, while the medicine man looked nervously around.

Columbus was passed the pipe again, and he repeated the ritual. For inexplicable reasons, he found the smoke less acrid now, and he discovered that he could bear down and hold the smoke firmly in his lungs. A warm feeling spread from his throat to his solar plexus. His scalp tingled, and his eardrums became exquisitely sensitive; soon the rhythmical drumming in the background became palpable and luxurious. It entered his earholes like jets of water.

The black jungle, in the near distance, throbbed as well—the sound of a million cicadas pulsing like a single and great black heart.

Columbus fixed his gaze on the leaping flames, dazzled and dreaming. Gradually he realized that a face was staring back at him from the flames—the face of his son, Diego, floating above the fire!

The small boy beckoned to him.

"Diego!" cried the boy's father.

"Father!" the voice cried, and Columbus recognized the voice.

Luis de Torres observed his captain intensely but did not understand the fuss.

"I love you!" Columbus cried, kneeling before the fire. But the face of his son was now consumed in flames.

Columbus felt his cheeks wet and burning.

He stood, lifting his hands over the flames. The fire flickered in his palms, hot and red.

The cacique touched Columbus on the shoulder.

Columbus turned to face him.

"Gold," said the cacique, forming the word slowly with his thick red lips. The gold necklace was in his hands now, and he leaned forward and fastened it about the neck of the great white god who had come down from the heavens.

The medicine man, behind him, closed his eyes.

Chapter 29

Everyone talked about *la selva*—a particularly dense area of local jungle that was the closest thing in Samaná to a rain forest. In its diminished aspect here, *la selva* was the tropical equivalent of a swamp, a place where nature let itself go.

Augusto was talking about *la selva* one morning when he and Geno were putting up fenceposts around the garden.

"It is so magic," Augusto said, brightening. "When I was boy, I love *la selva*. I go there to pray."

"Pray?"

"I want to become a priest when I was a boy. I pray to God, make me a priest. But God say, no, Augusto, you no priest."

"You'll take me there—to *la selva*?"

"Sure, I take you. Anybody take you. But you must be warn, very dangerous in those wood."

Geno enjoyed it when Augusto made these overly dramatic statements. Everyone in Barrington was so goddamn cautious, understating things in a way that buried them. Why couldn't people speak boldly? Why wasn't exaggeration the delightful norm, not something to be disdained?

"Many pools—waterfall," Augusto said. "Very beautiful."

"You said it was dangerous."

Augusto put down his shovel. "Snakes, too! Very wild animal and poison spider!"

Geno had been happily surprised by the benign aspect of the natural world in Samaná. It had been something that worried him, secretly, all the way down. The possibility that Susan would find life beside the Bay of Arrows too primitive had always been lurking in the periphery of his mental vision; worse, he was afraid it might frighten him, too. If the Vermont darkness terrified him, how might the tropical nights work on his imagination? The notion of all those tangling vines, eyes peeping out from under branches, snakes, and Byzantine insects was too much for him at times, which meant he usually kept it well out of mind.

He'd been careful to say nothing—especially to the boys—about these fears. As he expected, James and Milo took quickly to the landscape. They actually adored the colorful and outsized insects that were part of daily life here. Flying spiders with immense wingspans laced the air, while creepy-crawly things of every shape, size, and color could be found in most nooks and crevices. One of these creatures, an overgrown pink spider with delicate long white legs, was called Pinky by the boys and would often sit quietly on the picnic table between them while they ate.

Susan found it more difficult to think of the spiders in petlike terms. One morning she woke to find a particularly hairy one the size of a large hand, with neon yellow legs and green furry stripes on its shell, poised beside her on the pillow. Her scream, which began as a thin whine and rose to amazing decibels, brought the boys shrieking from the next house. The whole village seemed to have heard or heard about Susan's scream, and Señora Iguano made a little pilgrimage—her only visit thus far—to see them the same morning.

That was the only time Susan reacted quite so violently to a spider, and it embarrassed her enough that she decided to meditate on spiders in a way that would liberate her from a fear of them. She began a program, sitting cross-legged for ten minutes every morning to contemplate spiders. She would invent them in her mind: purple spiders with eyes on long white stems, orange spiders with a thousand frilly legs, mini-crablike spiders, toadlike spiders, centipedes, and tarantulas. Her method was simple: to think of them as friends. After several weeks, she found herself able to imagine petting a tarantula, smoothing its furry little legs and back with her fingers.

One day, at lunch, she amazed everyone by allowing a powder-blue spider with three dozen short red legs to crawl over her hand while she ate. Even Augusto, who had no particular fear of spiders, squealed. "Señora! Spider bite you! Look at yourself! Spider bite you!"

"If you don't hurt them, they won't hurt you," she said. (It was a familiar phrase that she had picked up at Girl Scout camp in Wisconsin, and like so many things she had learned at Girl Scout camp, it was not true.)

The boys loved seeing their mother with a tame spider. Even Pio and Jorge jumped up and down, and Pio imitated Susan by letting another spider, a fat dimpled one with yellow markings over a shiny black shell and black legs, crawl along his arm right up to his neck.

Pio, who had picked up a bit of English from Milo, said, "Spider, he my *amigo*!"

The spider, alas, didn't see it that way and bit Pio, who instinctively smacked it with his other hand, making the brittle creature ooze a clear liquid.

"She bite me!" he said.

"How do you know it's a *she*?" James asked.

"She dead," said Milo, flicking the exoskeleton from Pio's little hand.

That day Geno agreed to go to *la selva* with the boys.

"I take you, *la selva*," Augusto said. "Tricky way only easy if you know. What you don't know, never mind." He pointed a finger at each sweaty temple. "Brain too full, sometime. Brain, it seem to bust. Not good for anybody."

Geno listened with awe whenever Augusto or the other Dominicans spoke English. There was something alluring about their fractured syntax, which—like a Ouija board—offered an endless prospect of serendipitous meanings.

They set off after lunch with a knapsack filled with slices of gingerbread wrapped in sheets of used typing paper—an economy measure thought up by Susan, who was quite taken by the idea that, like their neighbors in Los Angeles, they should let nothing go to waste.

In addition to his notebook, which was never out of reach, Geno put his sacred copy of *Walden* into his backpack; he hoped to read under a tree while the boys played. It was the same copy he'd owned for almost fifteen years, and it had a strange, almost talismanic power to quiet his mind and focus his energies.

They cut through a wide patch of elephant grass just north of the garden area, entering an overgrown thicket roughly half a mile farther along the trail, which began inconspicuously at first—more the hint of a trail than a trail, consisting of a few broken twigs and leaves trampled in the dirt. It was encumbered by fallen trunks that the boys loved to balance on or leap over.

La selva was roughly five miles away—not a long hike, but the terrain was remarkably different from anything Geno had seen before. The ground became soggy at one point, swampy, with deadfalls covering one clearing that emerged and reminded him of the swamps he would seek out in New England—misty regions of decaying woodland, ghostly and silent except for the distant hammering of woodpeckers.

The swamp led to a forested region of tall feathery trees and drooping vines. Bats hung in clusters like blighted fruit from the upper branches, waiting for the dark. Spiderwebs glimmered in the moist air, spun from branch to branch. And wetness was omnipresent and visible, glistening on the infinitely complex vegetation, which included flowers and brush, banana and breadfruit trees, frangipani, and orchids like fantastic blood-soaked sponges. There was a hush over everything, though the bamboo trees groaned overhead like dry old bones.

"Waterfall, this way!" Augusto cried. "When you see it, I think you be surprised how pretty."

The children raced along the path, ahead of Geno, who wanted a few minutes by himself to make notes for a poem. Sitting on a log, he wrote: "A slight wind rustled in the long-necked, sleek bamboo." Then he wondered about the epithet "long-necked." As he paused to think, the sound of the waterfall became apparent; his scalp prickled. An image of Milo falling through the ice drove him to his feet.

When he arrived at the site, Augusto was bending over the cavern with the boys at his side. It was a mini–Victoria Falls—a horseshoe rim, with a drop of perhaps twenty feet. The stream moved slowly toward the edge, a barely perceptible movement of green water that suddenly collapsed on itself, falling in a wide scrim of fizzy light over black rocks that glittered at the bottom like stalagmites.

"Wow, look at the sharp rocks!" Geno said, hoping to snag the boys' attention.

"Danger to fall on them," said Augusto.

"Do you understand what we're saying, boys?" Geno called. "This place is very dangerous!" As soon as he said that, he felt on top of everything: the world, himself, his boys. It felt absolutely right.

"You think I'm gonna jump on these rocks?" James said. "Like I don't care if I live or die?"

"Don't be a wise guy."

"I wanna go swimming," Milo said.

"That's just what I was talking about," Geno said. "I don't like the looks of this place."

Jorge, however, was already scrambling down the edge of the ravine.

"Is that safe?" Geno asked Augusto.

"I don't swim," Augusto said, shrugging his shoulders. "Makes me too wet."

"Come *on*, Daddy!" Milo was tugging on his knapsack.

"All right," Geno said to him, "but let me go first."

He and the boys followed Jorge down the slick bank. At the bottom, they threw off their clothes and waded into the shimmering green pool.

Jorge was already out in the middle, waving and shouting.

"Wait for me!" Geno yelled, diving.

He opened his eyes underwater, but the churning motion of the waterfall had clouded the pool. The water, for all its opaqueness, was cool and fresh.

Surfacing, he flipped onto his back and saw a long vine dangling from a tree that grew almost horizontally from the side of the cavern and reminded him of a Tarzan movie he'd seen as a boy. An image of himself swishing through the air, naked, overwhelmed him, and he swam toward the vine. He grabbed it with one hand and scrambled up the bank. Near the top, not terribly far from the waterfall itself, he leaped into the air, arcing out over the pool. At exactly the high point of the out-swing he let go, soaring through the air, missing the rocks by about six feet when he landed, feet first, in a swirl of water.

The boys were cheering crazily as he swam toward them.

"Daddy, do that again!" Milo cried.

"Bravo!" shouted Jorge.

Augusto was clapping and shouting from the water's edge. "You very good when you swim!" he called. "Me, I drown when I swim!"

James alone seemed unimpressed, making his own solitary dive to the bottom of the pool.

"Do it again!" Milo insisted, leaping onto his father's back.

"It's too dangerous," he said. "Once was enough, sweetie!"

They kept begging, but Geno had already had enough of playing Tarzan for one day. "Another time," he said. "We'll come back again, soon."

He swam to the shoreline now, clambered nakedly up along the ravine, and took out his copy of *Walden*. Below him, Augusto began tossing stones in the water toward the children, who threw back handfuls of mud. The pool, like Henry Thoreau's pond outside of Concord, was a cup of light. It mirrored the surrounding green in a way that enhanced the green, that made the air itself a pale yellowy green.

Geno read:

> *I went to the woods because I wished to live deliberately, to front only the essential facts of life, and see if I could not learn what it had to teach, and not, when I came to die, discover that I had not lived.*

The words, placed like a trail of stones leading the penitent soul through a dark wood, reverberated in his mind.

A shriek startled Geno back to life. It was James.

"Daddy!" a voice cried. This time it was Milo. "James is throwing rocks!"

"I'm not! You threw one first!"

Geno began stumbling, almost crawling toward the waterfall, propelled by Milo's once-broken arm and Susan's potential disapproval. "Fronting the essential facts of life" meant being there to notice them.

One day the mail arrived with a curious postcard:

Dear Geno:

Got the scoop. Nachez did it. He got drunk at my house last night and spilled the beans. Baloo told Botner, who told Agnes. Lizzie is back, by the way. Grad school no go. She's working in Admissions. We miss you. Come home!

Your fellow Boa-deconstructor,
Enid

Geno smirked at Enid's language. What was "it" exactly? That Nachez told Lizzie to pursue the harassment charge? Perhaps Nachez had literally done "it" himself: slept with Lizzie? He sighed at the thought and was happy to be gone.

"They're all so damned petty," he said to Susan, flipping the card to her.

"Life is petty," she said. "You don't think the stuff around here is petty? Like who borrowed a mule from the mayor and didn't bring it back?"

"I guess so."

Susan read the postcard. "Ah . . . Lizzie is back."

"I never thought she'd like grad school. She'll wind up with Outward Bound or something. Leading bike trips across the Andes."

"You should write to her."

"What?"

"Tell her you're sorry."

"You crazy?"

"Just a suggestion."

Geno once again felt he could not fathom his wife.

"Good afternoon, ladies and gentlemen," said Alec Selkirk, who appeared unexpectedly on the veranda in khaki shorts of a military cut and a white shirt.

Susan had planned a long siesta, and the idea of chatting with Selkirk now did not excite her. She had gathered from Geno's description that he was someone to avoid, but Geno greeted him now with surprising warmth.

"This is Susan," he said.

The Scot put out his hand and smiled warmly.

"I'm glad to meet you, Mr. Selkirk."

"Please, Alec is fine."

Selkirk was offered a glass of juice. "Surely you've got a bit of rum on hand," he said.

His forwardness annoyed Susan, but Geno quickly produced a bottle of Don Armando—the best that Los Angeles had to offer. They sat around in Adirondack chairs that Geno and Augusto had recently constructed.

Josefina and Augusto drifted by.

"I've about had it with these people—the Dominicans," Selkirk said. "They can't do anything right. Worse than the Brazilians—by a long shot."

Susan was astonished. "If that's how you feel about them, Alec, why do you bother to live here?"

"The climate. Best climate in the world, don't you think?"

"I don't know," she said. "I'm not even sure I care!"

Conflict, as always, upset Geno, and he wanted to get things back on a better note. "I find the people very friendly."

Susan scowled at him. It never ceased to amaze her how silly her husband could be.

"You only just got here," Selkirk said. "Wait a few bloody years." He took a big gulp of the rum. "I don't mean to say they aren't charming—in their way. Lots of charm, really. But don't try to get anything done." He looked around. "And keep track of your valuables."

Geno cursed his Anglophilia for having been so taken with Selkirk.

"Nothing works in this country," the Scot continued. "Look at the post, the fucking telephone exchange. Baliguer is a madman, you know. He's the nuttiest head of state in the Caribbean, and that's saying something. Built this fucking lighthouse—cost millions—just to impress the foreigners who are coming next week."

"Next week?" asked Geno.

"The pope is even coming—the bloody pope!"

Geno had lost interest in the world at large since arriving on the island. "I'd forgotten all about that stuff," he said. "The quincentennial, of course."

"You should listen to my radio sometimes," Susan said. "They're even talking about the lighthouse in China!"

"Absolutely," Selkirk said, launching into a tirade about the money President Baliguer had wasted on so-called improvements to the city of Santo Domingo, the capital. The gigantic lighthouse—*El Faro*—was built to commemorate what everyone called "the Discovery." And the pope himself would preside over a great ceremony in which Columbus was hailed as the Christian light-bringer, the man who carried civilization to a dark continent. Representatives from all the great nations (and many lesser ones) would attend the festivities, and a fleet of exact replicas of the *Santa María*, the *Niña*, and the *Pinta* would appear in the harbor. Actors dressed as Columbus and his men would wave from the decks.

"The fucking Japs have sent the replicas," Selkirk added. "They probably think Columbus was a goddamn Jap!"

Susan looked around anxiously, worried about Augusto, who was obsessing over a tin pot with a fire-blackened bottom and listening closely.

"It's typical of this country," Selkirk went on. "They waste every resource they have on a frivolous monument, while their people are starving. Bloody idiots."

Augusto burst forward, standing right in front of Selkirk

and shaking a finger. "You be quiet!" he said. "What you say is bad. Very bad!"

The Scot shrank back, as if he could not believe the apparition before him: a black-faced man wagging a finger.

"Your boy speaks English?" he asked, staring at Geno.

"He's not a boy," Susan said.

Milo and James, who had been drawing in their notebooks in a corner, looked up eagerly. The prospect of adults fighting was nothing less than thrilling.

"I'm sorry, my dear. I see I've offended you." He looked at Augusto, then at Susan again. "It comes from living alone, I suspect."

Geno tried to make light of things. "We should have a picnic one day."

"Yes," Alec said, uncomfortably. "Well, I'm away."

"You're going already?"

"I must," he said. "You must both visit me . . . when it suits."

"Thank you," Susan said.

After swilling the last drop of rum, Selkirk left as abruptly as he'd come, slipping off into the woods north of the garden plot.

"What a peculiar fellow," Susan said.

"He's a bigot, but there's something about him I find . . . intriguing."

"You're starved for company, Geno. People who are starved for company are dangerous."

"Do you think I'm dangerous?"

She smiled. "I know you're dangerous."

"What does English say about Japanese ship?" Augusto asked later, as he and Geno worked scraping down a rowboat recently acquired through the good offices of Señora Iguano.

"The Japanese are coming—pretending to be Columbus," Geno said. "It's called an historical reenactment."

"Japan ships come here?"

"They're replicas of the original ships of Christopher Columbus."

Augusto stood and wiped sweat from the wrinkled and mud-filled corners of his eyes.

"You know about Columbus?" Geno asked. He didn't want to offend Augusto, who was sensitive about not being able to read, but he'd noticed that he and his neighbors, especially those who were *analfabetos*—illiterate—knew very little about their island's history or the world outside. They lived in a vivid present, shorn of roots that were neither familial nor tribal. They had all heard tales of New York and Miami, mostly because they had relatives or friends who lived there.

"Colón?"

"Yes, that's the one."

"We speak of the *fukú de Colón* in this country. Everything dangerous when his name is spoke. Nobody like Colón."

"*Fukú*? What's *fukú*?"

"The curse," he said, looking stonily at Geno. "Bad things happen when his name is said."

"Really?"

"Earthquake start, children die, car crashes." His voice seemed to drift through an invisible fog, and he was looking over his shoulder as if the ghost of Columbus might hear him.

"I've never heard of this."

"*Fukú* very bad."

"I believe it."

"Colón is coming? I hear like this at the Miami yesterday. They say he coming."

Geno marveled at his lack of a sense of linear time. He lived, like his neighbors, in a kind of continuous present.

"Apparently the ships that put in at Santo Domingo are making their way along the coast," Geno said. "They'll be here next week."

Augusto's face registered panic and distaste. "Do you like Colón?"

"Of course not! He was the first of the *conquistadores*. He treated your people—the Indians, I mean—very badly. Killed most of them, in fact. It was genocide . . . murder. Many people died because of Colón." Geno waved his hands, as if to make himself more plain; it was disconcerting to find himself talking to Augusto as one might talk to a child, simplifying everything.

"Why did Indian let him do this?" Augusto seemed genuinely incensed.

"They weren't ready for him, I guess. The Tainos were a

mild people. They never thought Columbus would cheat them and murder them."

"I am telling my friends. We don't let him get away with it—not this time."

A light bulb flashed in Geno's heart.

"You know why this place is called the Bay of Arrows?"

Augusto shook his head.

"It's because the Indians who lived here—right here where we're standing—refused to let Columbus land in 1492. They sent him away with a shower of arrows."

"We send him away this time, too," said Augusto. "I will shoot him myself."

Throughout the afternoon Augusto worked beside Geno in a quiet fury, scraping the dry paint off the boat, painting it again. His sun-dried hands, like strange fruit, glistened as he worked. After so many centuries, the ancient anger of the Tainos still smoldered in him, the coals in his heart ready to fall upon themselves and break into gold-vermilion flames.

Chapter 30

The smoke-filled seminar room at Columbia University was silent. Jésus de Galíndez, the instructor, held everyone rapt.

He spoke slowly, deliberately, in a mild Spanish accent, pausing to inhale a Camel.

"I *could* argue," he said. "In fact, I *will* argue that one must see a direct line from Columbus to Trujillo. The desecrations of Hispaniola began in 1492. And it continues in 1956. The *Generalisimo*—believe me, I have lived in Ciudad Trujillo and worked for his government—is cruel, rapacious, cunning, inspired, and utterly *symptomatic*. As you all know, I have written about him in my thesis. I've not argued, as I might have, that he is merely despotic. He is not. He is a remarkable man, and he has done some excellent things for his country. But—ultimately—he has crushed the will of his people. He has turned them into perpetual children." He paused to let the phrase sink in, repeating it slowly. "Perpetual children."

With this, he put his lecture notes into a cracked leather briefcase and dismissed the class with a shy nod. He had already held them half an hour beyond the normal time.

The seminar, which consisted mostly of graduate students, liked his passionate approach to teaching. And they liked him—a neat, somewhat moralistic bachelor in his mid-forties. His hair was inky black and combed back straight. His eyes flashed when he spoke, matching his gold front tooth, which had been capped by a military dentist in Salamanca during his stint with an anarchist wing of the Loyalists.

He liked to reminisce about his soldiering in the Spanish Civil War, about the horrors of General Franco, and about his post–Civil War exile in the Dominican Republic, where he worked as a legal advisor in the Trujillo government's Department of Labor and National Economy. He would soon be considered for tenure at Columbia, which he referred to cynically as "Christopher Columbus University"—much to the annoyance of his students and colleagues, who considered his obsession with Columbus of a piece with his endless chatter about Franco and Trujillo. As his department chairman once said to a colleague in private, "Galíndez exaggerates the power of the individual in history. History is not about individuals."

Trujillo knew all about Galíndez and his thesis, soon to be published by New York University Press. Through one of his operatives in New York, he had already offered to buy the manuscript for a handsome price. Galíndez had written, "*No, gracias Generalisimo*," on a postcard with a picture of a goat's head on the other side and sent it directly to Trujillo. Aware of the presence of SIM, Trujillo's secret police, in the United

States, he had taken precautions, such as doubling the lock on his door at home and purchasing a handgun, which he kept in a drawer beside his bed.

It was a balmy night in March as Galíndez rose from the purgatorial dusk of the subway station near his apartment in lower Manhattan. He felt happy that night. His lecture had gone particularly well that evening, and he had only just heard that his thesis was going to be published. Moreover, he had recently become engaged to a Cuban refugee, whom he planned to marry in June, and she was waiting for him at his apartment.

As he turned onto a side street, a short man with a bright, purple nose stepped in front of him and held a gun to his left temple. Someone else grabbed him from behind, pinning his hands behind his back.

Galíndez thought he was being mugged and said, "Please, take whatever you want!"

They did.

Galíndez was dragged into a waiting car. Once safely inside, one of the men injected a hypodermic into his right arm, just below the shoulder. The effect was nearly instantaneous. Galíndez collapsed.

He was taken to a private airfield in New Jersey, where a small plane was ready to go. An American pilot by the name of Gerald Murphy asked if the cargo was aboard (he assumed it was contraband, but he knew enough not to ask questions).

By the time Galíndez woke, he was halfway to Ciudad Trujillo. His hands were tightly bound, and his mouth was gagged.

If he had any doubts about where he was going, they were

dispelled as soon as the airplane door was cracked: the odor of rot was unmistakable. Having lived on the island for seven years, he could never have forgotten it.

Four big men stuffed him into a dark-blue Olds, and he was driven into the hot night air.

His eyes widened when he recognized his destination: Casa de Coaba, a three-story villa made of teak, mahogany, and oak. It was situated high above San Cristobal on a lush hillside. He knew all about this place by hearsay: it was the preferred residence of *El Generalisimo*, Rafael Trujillo Molinas.

Still recovering from the injection, he was helped to walk up a narrow, glass-enclosed stairwell to a large room on the second floor. The cavernous space was furnished with rattan furniture and personal memorabilia, its walls covered with expensive grass-cloth. The head of a bull hung between two windows, its glass eyeballs staring from each side of its massive skull.

The henchmen pushed Galíndez to the floor, onto the brightly polished Taveres tiles, stopping just short of the *Generalisimo* himself, who was leaning against the mahogany bar with a glass of beer in one hand. Behind him were autographed photos of Cardinal Spellman of New York and Vice-President Richard Nixon, both of whom had recently visited Trujillo at Casa de Coaba. The inscription from Nixon read: "To His Excellency, Rafael Trujillo, America's best friend in the Caribbean." Cardinal Spellman had merely signed his name, writing *Muchas Gracias!* above it.

Trujillo wore an English riding outfit with high black boots; a leather crop stuck out from his right armpit. His bloated face sat on a very short but thick neck, and his sallow complexion was made all the yellower by the banana-colored lampshades.

He put the beer quietly onto a coaster and picked up a copy of his unfortunate visitor's doctoral thesis, which had been stolen from his apartment.

"Bienvenido, Profesor," he said.

Galíndez looked up, amazed and terrified. He was now prepared to make any concessions. Indeed, upon waking in the little aircraft, he had at once decided to offer the manuscript to Trujillo *gratis*.

"I said, welcome!" Trujillo shouted.

Galíndez, of course, was still gagged and could only nod his head.

Trujillo laughed, opening the thesis and reading three or four choice extracts, all of which portrayed the *Generalísimo* in less-than-flattering terms.

"I am unhappy about your attitude, *Profesor*," he continued, ordering one of his guards to remove the gag from Galíndez.

"I'm sorry," Galíndez said.

"I am glad to hear you admit this." Trujillo dumped the thesis onto the floor beside his prisoner. "You admit, then, that it is garbage?"

Galíndez nodded his head.

"Good! Then you will have no objections to eating it."

Galíndez looked up like a dog, wild with fear.

Trujillo kicked the manuscript toward Galíndez. "Eat it, *Profesor*!" he said.

Because his hands were still bound tightly behind him, he could not reach for the manuscript. Indeed, he was so dazed that he slumped forward, and Trujillo responded by whipping him across the cheeks with the leather crop, drawing blood. Galíndez's eyes filled with tears, and he began to whisper, in barely audible Spanish, "Forgive me, Your Excellency."

Trujillo ended the interview suddenly with a kick to the groin, screaming, *"Pendejo! Pendejo!"* at the half-conscious man, who was quickly dragged away.

Galíndez swooned. He did not waken until several hours later when, naked and handcuffed, he found himself surrounded by half a dozen men who smoked Lucky Strikes and chattered randomly about the Yankees and the Dodgers. There was apparently no agreement as to which team was better.

Galíndez watched as his ankles were methodically bound by a long piece of hemp. His captors fed the rope through an overhead pulley, and he was hoisted by his feet, upside down, over a steel vat of boiling water.

Inch by inch, he was lowered into the bubbling vat. Even to his own amazement, he did not scream.

Later that day, his body was thrown over a cliff into the sea, where sharks made short work of what was left of Jesús Galíndez.

Chapter 31

James stepped out of his house, looked around stealthily, and whispered to Jorge: "Come on!"

"Gen' is where?" asked Pio. His little eyes burned like coals.

"He's at the beach—with Mama." James scanned the horizon slowly. "The coast is clear! Come on!"

"Mama will kill us," Milo said.

"And I'll kill you if you open your stinking trap."

"I won't."

"That's right," James said. "You won't.

Jorge expressed his doubts about the whole project—one of the few times he ever resisted James or Milo, who seemed magical to him, like great white gods. But James was firm; he insisted on total secrecy. "The radio is the key!" he added. "We must get my mother's radio if we're really going to stop Columbus!"

On the day when the Japanese caravels were due to arrive, the town of Los Angeles took to the streets excitedly. The guileless crowd milled about in small groups, moving from palm wood shack to shack. Everyone seemed to have a family story about the *fukú de Colón* and how some terrible event was associated with that curse. Buildings had collapsed, babies had dropped prematurely from their mothers' wombs, airplanes had fallen from the sky and crushed whole villages.

Somehow the memory of these disasters did nothing to affect the holiday atmosphere. Some of the women had actually dressed up in their best white muslin dresses with hats made of gauze. A few even dangled parisols from their wrists as they waltzed up and down the dusty street.

The veranda of the Hotel Miami was ablaze with conversation as the leaders of what Augusto called "the revolution" made plans. Only Señora Iguano was against the idea. "If Señor Iguano, he were here," she said, "I tell you, this stupid talk not happen. He very strong man, Señor Iguano." As usual, she added that her husband would return from Miami one day. "I can feel him come across the water," she said. "He very brave man."

Geno and Susan sipped their *café con leche* and listened with amusement. "When Señor Iguano comes home" had become a set answer to certain kinds of questions, such as "When are you going to do something about the smell in that outhouse?"

"Those boys, Augusto and his friends, they make trouble everybody," Señora Iguano continued, mopping her broad forehead. "I remember Trujillo too very well, you know. Nobody say a word in those days—life was peaceful. My husband, Señor Iguano, bless that wonderful man, he work for the government. He say they take boys who protest and shoot them in the brain. Sometimes they shoot the wife, too. Baliguer, you know, he was president for Trujillo. Good friend of the *Generalisimo*. I don't trust anything he do. They say SIM gone, but I don't believe." She sipped from a bottle of Coke. "When my husband, he come back, you will like him. Very intelligent man."

"There's nothing like the SIM now," Geno said, imagining he could argue with her. "President Baliguer was elected by the people. SIM is gone. Maybe the CIA is here—that's always a possibility, since they're everywhere."

Susan rolled her eyes. "The CIA, huh?"

"I'm serious. Just because the Communist bloc collapsed, it doesn't mean they've gone."

"You don't believe what Augusto say to you," Señora Iguano said, defiant now. "Baliguer is trouble, too." She went on to complain about all the money wasted on the ridiculous lighthouse in Santo Domingo. "I vote for Juan Bosch last time. He *very* good man."

Geno could hardly help smiling. The last election had been more or less a draw between two octagenarian relics of Dominican politics. Bosch had been elected president in 1962 in the wake of the Trujillo assassination. Though he had been the first democratically elected president in the history of the country, he had been a socialist and was soon overthrown by the military, who set up (with help from President Kennedy) a puppet government that was "anti-Communist." When this U.S.-backed government was threatened by a coup that would place Bosch back in power, Lyndon Johnson sent in twenty-three thousand American Marines to "maintain the peace" in 1965. Bosch, in his mideighties, was still trying to recover his lost presidency.

"I love Juan Bosch," Geno said. "But he is too old. The Dominican Republic has to find younger leaders in his mold."

"Juan Bosch, he is *intelligent* man," Señora Iguano asserted. "Younger men have no brains. Look around you." She nodded toward Augusto and his friends.

"We will show them!" Augusto cried, raising his fist. He had, by himself, stirred the coals of indignation in the entire village of Los Angeles. The mayor of the village, an elderly man called Miguel Valenzuela, had been convinced that Los Angeles should not submit to the indignities and barbarism of Columbus once again. He sat opposite Augusto in a frock coat, his hands folded on his bamboo cane, his bushy white mustache twitching; the lines of resistance had set firmly in his mud-brown face.

Even Selkirk had made his way up to the Hotel Miami this afternoon; he was sitting with Sábado at a separate table, reading the newspaper and drinking his rum "neat." He had nodded politely to Geno and Susan upon arrival, but he remained apart. Something in his look suggested that he was vaguely ticked off about not being the Only White Man in Town.

Selkirk disapproved of what Augusto had planned.

"Bloody mad," he said, loudly, to Sábado. "I hope they get themselves fucking arrested. Serve them right, it would."

Sábado nodded and grinned.

Señora Iguano spoke quietly. "He very odd man. Nobody like him. But he don't leave."

Susan's face conveyed her dislike of Selkirk, and Señora Iguano was encouraged.

"And he don't pay bill," she said. "Ask the merchant in Samaná. Scotman cheat them all."

Augusto got up and sauntered by the Scot's table on his way to the toilet. He stopped beside him, and Selkirk looked up with a bored expression before turning back to his paper.

A brief, unfriendly exchange in rapid colloquial Spanish occurred between Augusto and Sábado, and this apparently angered Selkirk, who rose and stared into Augusto's face.

The crowd at the Miami was hushed.

"Go the toilet, Augusto!" Señora Iguano shouted.

Before Augusto had to make an embarrassing choice and either back down or challenge Selkirk, a young man shouted from the edge of the jungle: *"Colón llega!"* This was the signal and the stampede began.

A dozen men, most of them under twenty-five, charged into the trees with their handmade bows and arrows. Augusto was their leader, and he led the charge with all the passion of Tecumseh Sherman on his way to Atlanta. They were cheered on by the children and women of the town, some of whom waved brightly colored scarves like battle flags.

Selkirk, abandoned to his newspaper, shook his head. "Bloody nonsense," he said.

"Come on, honey," Geno said to Susan, but he was too late. She was already running.

The three caravels stood in the middle distance, anchored calmly in the large green bay. They were exact replicas of the original ships, and each flew the special banner that Columbus had adopted for his voyage: a green cross on a white field, with a crown on each arm of the cross, one over an *F* for Ferdinand and the other over an *I* for Isabella. The royal ensign of Castile and León was hoisted at the main truck of the *Santa María*, while a variety of brightly colored bannerols and pendants fluttered from the mastheads and yardarms of each ship.

In 1492 most anchorages along the West Coast of Africa or among the Atlantic islands were exposed to violent swells and harsh crosswinds, so ships usually anchored with two bowers and a stern anchor. Today, being mild and unthreatening in every way to the Japanese sailors who manned these caravels, there was no reason for anything but a stern anchor. A short man in a great plumed hat leaned on the wooden tiller that steered the *Santa María*, as if exhausted by his duties. The aft decks of the other caravels were deserted.

A Jacob's ladder on the aft side of the mast of the flagship, which was closest to shore and swung broadside, was dotted with a few bodies, but the sails had already been taken down by the time Augusto's band arrived on the blazing, niter-cracked beach. A small fleet of rowboats was already assembling.

The eager crews of the *Santa María, Pinta*, and *Niña*

emptied into the rowboats, while Augusto positioned his men in the thickets adjacent to the sandy beach. Their makeshift arrows, though not lethal, were designed to do some damage if they found their targets.

The day was brilliant, not overly hot, with the sky as clear as gin. A few gulls hovered overhead, contemplating this historical reenactment with dispassion. The surf rolled landward in a lackadaisical manner.

"Don't fire till you see the whites of their eyes!" James shouted.

"Shoot the man!" cried Pio, who was now absorbing massive daily doses of English from James and Milo.

Geno hushed them. "You'll blow the whole thing, damn it!" he said. "Be still, fellas!"

They crouched behind a bush with holly-bright leaves, not fifteen yards from the rest of Augusto's party. Behind them all, a stand of royal palms swayed in the breeze; on its limbs were haughty-looking pelicans glaring down at a raucous scurry of kinkajous, who chittered like monkeys in the low brush.

One of the Japanese sailors was playing the role of Columbus, but he was slightly overdressed for the occasion. His plumed helmet and harlequin breeches seemed out of keeping with the much drabber garb of his shipmates, some of whom had clearly decided that this particular landing did not matter and wore jeans and tee shirts. One of them—the most peculiar of all—was dressed like a Tokyo businessman in a silver suit with a polka-dot tie and white shirt. His Minolta caught the sun and glittered. He was taking pictures of the landing from another boat, trying desperately to focus on Columbus, who stood in the bow like Washington crossing the Delaware. As the rowboats approached the shoreline, you could hear them shouting at one another in Japanese.

The man in the suit with the Minolta leaped out of his rowboat first, drenching himself to the thighs. Geno guessed that he was a professional photographer sent along to record the caravels' progress for some Tokyo magazine.

The Admiral of the Ocean Sea's boat landed with panache. Columbus leaped over the bow, stumbling momentarily, and marched up on the hot, white sand. A dozen or so mates, also in full costume, landed within minutes; they proceeded behind Columbus along the beach. Another photographer had joined them by now, and there was a fine sense of occasion.

Augusto waited until they had come within easy firing range, then he shouted: *"Tiren! Tiren!"*

The young warriors leaped from behind the foliage and fired. Their blunt-tipped arrows whooshed through the air, and one of them caught Columbus in the kneecap. He began to shriek.

Suddenly Pio picked up a stick, leaped out of the bush, and began chasing Columbus. "Bad man! Bad man!" he yelled, holding the stick over his head like a club.

The photographers rushed to photograph Columbus being chased by a little black boy. The fluttering of the lenses was magical, and the archers knew enough to avoid hitting the people who would record their triumph at the Bay of Arrows for posterity.

The man who was playing Luis de Torres began to shout in a language nobody could understand. An arrow hit him in the left thigh, pricking a hole in his trousers, and he rushed yelping back to his rowboat.

Columbus ordered everyone back to the boats now as he ran, outstripping little Pio. The plumed helmet flew from his head and Pio quickly crowned himself triumphantly. The photographers gathered around, snapping greedily.

As Columbus stepped hurriedly into his rowboat, an arrow shot by Augusto himself stuck him in the rump. *"Chikushō!"* he yelled, pulling the arrow free.

"Yamete kure!" the others shouted, racing in circles around Columbus and scrambling to get into the boats.

Soon the flotilla of rowboats was launched again while a shower of arrows followed them, with Augusto shouting in his most authoritative manner, *"Tiren! Tiren! Tiren!"* Columbus, terrified, knelt forward in the boat with his head covered, although he was soon out of the range of their modest weapons. The rest of the boats followed rapidly, showered by arrows, most of which landed benignly in the sea.

When the Japanese were thoroughly out of range, Augusto's men held their bows in the air and danced in a ring, with Pio grinning on Augusto's shoulders in the brightly plumed helmet. They spent the rest of the afternoon celebrating the demise of the man who had brought so much suffering to their island.

One afternoon a couple of days later, Susan discovered that her shortwave radio was missing.

"The precious Grundig," Geno said. He was reading

Robinson Crusoe—one of those endless classics that he'd never really read with care.

"I happen to like that radio."

"Maybe you left it on the beach?"

"I don't think so." She was bent over the wooden box that she called her "mobile office." It was full of books, papers, notes for stories, letters, and miscellaneous documents. She invariably put the radio back when she was done with it. "Damn it," she said. "Damn, damn, damn."

Geno looked up from his novel. "Maybe the kids took it? They're always messing around in here."

"They wouldn't," she said. "I've talked to them specifically about that radio."

Muttering "Goddamn kids" to himself, Geno went out, closing the door behind him a bit too emphatically. He cut through the palm grove and down the steps that he and Augusto had laid in the steep cliff and across the dunes that led to the water's edge. It was siesta time, but James and Milo had gone to the beach with Augusto for a game of Frisbee.

"Catch!" cried James, sailing the bright red disc toward his father as soon as he came into view.

Geno was not in the mood for games. He watched with a slight annoyance as the glittering circle seemed to pause in the white sunlight, then catch up to itself and zoom past his left ear. "I want to talk to you fellas!" he yelled.

"What's the matter, Daddy?" Milo called.

"Both of you, come here," Geno said.

He waited until James and Milo both stood in front of him—James at chest height, Milo a foot smaller. Augusto stood sheepishly behind James, looking away. He never liked it when Geno became stern like this.

"What's the problem?" James said in his patented wiseguy tone. His rib cage showed through the bronze skin of his chest, and there was a mature look in his eye that surprised his father.

Geno said, "The radio . . . Who knows anything about the radio?"

The boys were deadpan.

"Your mother's shortwave radio is missing. Do you guys have it?" He looked from one to the other. "Or know anything about where it is?"

"No," said James.

"Are you sure?"

"We're sure," said James.

"What about you, Milo? Are you as sure as your brother?"

He could see James staring at him. "Yes," he said.

Geno noticed that Augusto seemed uncomfortable, shifting from foot to foot. "Okay, guys," he said. "Just let me know if you find it. Mama is very upset." He left them standing awkwardly on the hot sand. When he got back to the house he found Susan entertaining Selkirk on the veranda. They were sitting at the table, drinking rum.

"Good afternoon." He raised his drink and nodded. "As you can see, Susan's been taking good care of me."

"How have you been?"

"I never change. It's the secret of my longevity."

Geno grinned.

"That Columbus nonsense is blessedly over," Selkirk said.

"I must say, your gang made right fools of themselves, didn't they?"

"I don't know. It was pretty funny."

"Funny! Didn't you see the papers? It was everywhere." He paused.

"That's great!"

Selkirk took another swig. "I hear you've been robbed."

Geno said, "You mean the radio?"

"Robbery." He said that with a shocking firmness.

"Well, I don't know," Geno said. "Susie's shortwave is certainly missing."

"Bloody thieves, the lot of them. I warned you to be careful. Have you questioned the boy yet?"

"The boy?"

"Augusto. Ten to one he's sitting on it right now. You just can't trust them."

Susan stood up. "That's not possible, Alec. Augusto is our friend."

"Come on, children. Augusto is your servant. You've only been here a short while. What do you know about him?"

"I know him rather well," Geno said.

"Did you know that his father was arrested in Nagua, for instance?"

"Augusto's father?"

"Ten years ago. It's well known to everyone around here. The man is dead now, I believe. But he stole some chickens, I think. It was in the papers at the time."

Susan looked ahead glumly as she sat down.

"I don't believe a word of this," said Geno. "Even if it's

true that Augusto's father was a crook, what's that got to do with him?"

"Nothing, perhaps. Or everything. The point is that you know nothing about this man. I've been here a very long time, and I wouldn't trust him farther than one can spit."

Geno rubbed his hands together anxiously. "I really can't buy that, Alec."

"As you like," he said.

"There comes a point when you just . . . well, trust a man."

Selkirk smiled maliciously. "Is that right?"

Geno lay awake that night, his mind turning from one possible scenario to another. He could not believe that Augusto was involved in such a thing. It was just not likely. They had a perfectly natural and easy relationship, and if Augusto had needed money he would simply have asked. Then again, the man was proud; if he really did need money—to pay for an operation for one of his children, perhaps—there was that infinitesimally small chance that he might resort to stealing. Or was there?

He looked over at Susan, who slept on her stomach. How was it possible that she could sleep so soundly? It was *her* radio, after all, that had been stolen! Why did he, the husband, have to suffer on her behalf?

As he rolled over on his side to try, once again, to fall asleep, he heard a distant but unmistakable sound: a cough. He sat up straight, his head touching the gauzelike mosquito netting that was draped around them. Was he imagining this? He strained to listen through the white noise of crickets and squeaking bamboo as it tossed in the midnight breeze.

He slipped through the netting, put on some jeans and sneakers, and grabbed a flashlight. There was really nothing he hated worse than this: going out alone in the dark to search for trouble.

He stepped outside, his heart throbbing in his neck and wrists. Above him, in the black cathedral of night, the constellations flamed like chandeliers, hummed like neon. The moon was pink, whirling, its face distorted. A light wind hit Geno's face, the same wind that tossed the palm trees, that moaned in the long weeds. A coconut dropped in the grass behind the house, and Geno turned to flash the light on nothing. "Anyone there?" he called, trying not to wake Susan or the boys. "Hello?" He flashed the light in the direction of the outhouse, then turned it on the boys' house. Everything was calm.

As he was about to step back inside, he heard the footsteps. On the path leading into the jungle he saw a figure turn and flee. Instinctively, more like a dog chasing a passing car than a hero in pursuit of a thief, he followed. His family had been threatened, so he had no choice. "Stop!" he called, swishing the light up and down as he ran. "Stop!"

In moments he penetrated the dark jungle, and unseen branches snapped back into his face and stung his cheeks; he tripped on a root and fell. "Fuck," he said aloud. Scrambling to his feet again, he charged up the shadowy path; for whatever reason, he felt sure that this man could not outrun him. Then again, what if the guy were armed? What if he were truly violent? Geno began to slow his pace, but just as he did he saw about thirty feet ahead that the figure had stopped. He was frozen, stuck in midpath, a black but definitely human shadow.

"Stay where you are!" Geno cried, stopping. He did not feel like closing in.

The man said nothing. He clutched something to his breast, as if hiding it.

Geno flicked the light along the narrow trace till it stopped, flush, on the fellow's anguished face. "Augusto!"

Augusto looked down, and Geno followed suit. He could hardly bear to see him. When he looked up, the man was gone.

Chapter 32

Columbus was followed downhill past the Taino village (which had been subdued earlier in the week) by his two brothers, Diego and Bartholomew. It was a ghastly hot day, and the mosquitoes picked at their ears, bit their necks, and made their knuckles swell. In the distance—beyond a wall of mango trees—one could hear the cries of men and women, the barking of dogs, and the shouts of soldiers.

"What's going on?" Columbus asked.

Diego knew, as did Bartholomew. They wanted their brother to see how effectively they had carried out his orders, knowing he could not tolerate equivocation when it came to obedience.

"It's the exactions," Bartholomew said. He was a bit less afraid of Columbus than Diego, who often found himself speechless around his brother.

"What do you mean?"

"We've been having difficulty, as you know. It seems there is much less available gold on the island than previously suspected."

"The place is teeming with gold," Columbus said.

"Maybe so, but the Indians find it difficult to come up with a hawk's bell full of gold dust within the allotted time."

"They've got three whole months in which to satisfy their quota. I can't understand why they complain. The lazy sods."

"They don't complain. They flee."

Columbus sighed. He simply must get the Indians to cooperate. Isabella and Ferdinand had sent him back to the Indies with seventeen ships—such was their enthusiasm for his project. It was obvious to him that what he must produce for his sovereigns was gold.

"We have found entire villages deserted," Bartholomew continued. "They are an extremely mobile lot, these Tainos. Now you see them, now—"

"Oh, shut up," Columbus said.

Diego listened to them talking with amazement. Were they so ignorant of what was really going on? He had himself publicized his brother's decree: every man, woman, and child over the age of fourteen must deliver a "tribute," which consisted of a hawk's bell full of gold, to Columbus every three months. Those living in areas of the island where gold was absolutely unobtainable were to offer in its place twenty-five pounds of spun cotton.

And the system had failed from the outset, since the

Tainos simply took to the hills when pressed. Colonies were now organizing in remote areas, and a burgeoning threat of armed rebellion had to be faced. After nine months had passed and relatively little in the way of gold had accumulated in the government's coffers, Columbus declared that those who refused to participate in the tribute system would be punished. He left the nature of the punishment to Diego and his lieutenants, who had proven themselves adept in the execution of disciplinary measures.

Columbus had been warned, by Fray Manuel Ortiz—a kindly Dominican who was trying to establish a school for Taino children in Santo Domingo near the Admiral's headquarters—that these disciplinary measures had been taken to excess. Fleeing Tainos were often chased into the mountains by dogs, and those captured had their hands cut off.

Now Columbus and his brothers entered a clearing beside the sea. The setting, with its wild flowering shrubs, its long-necked palms and blazing white sand, was so lovely that everyone paused.

At the farthest end of the beach a vision of unmitigated anguish met their gaze.

Thirteen crosses stood side by side, facing seaward.

On each cross, a wretched Taino hung by the wrists. A Spanish guard was busy lighting a fire under each prisoner. Already six or seven were ablaze, the flames bristling, leaping to embrace the Indians at waist level.

One of them screamed for mercy, while the others merely stared ahead or writhed in silent misery.

Not far from where Columbus and his brothers stood, an axman was about to chop off the hand of a young Taino woman. Two men, in chains, watched in terror, aware that they were next on the block.

Columbus approached the axman, who stood and bowed in a way that annoyed the Lord Admiral.

"What has the woman done?" Columbus asked.

"She has encouraged others to ignore the gold quota," he said. "An example is needed."

As a naval officer, Columbus knew the importance of symbolic gestures. He had often punished a man harshly—in public—for refusing to obey orders. But it occurred to him that exacting penalties as severe as this might backfire just now. "Let her go," he said.

"Indeed, Your Exellency," the axman said, stepping toward the naked Taino woman to unbind her legs and arms.

Diego protested. "If we don't let them know that we're serious, we'll lose control of the entire island!"

Columbus looked at Bartholomew, who sighed and squinted into the sun. He knew that Diego's remark was probably correct, but it was too late to change his mind. He had spoken. "Let her go," he said again.

They watched as the newly released woman tore off into the brush like a wild animal, her buttocks flashing.

"Now proceed," Columbus said, waving his hand.

He stood by, expressionless, as the other two prisoners each lost a hand.

Meanwhile, the rank odor of burning flesh had risen in everyone's nostrils, and Columbus decided not to remain on the beach any longer. He most certainly would not inspect the nearby site of the burning Tainos, all thirteen of whom were currently engulfed in flame.

Chapter 33

Geno woke slowly, turning from side to side, uncomfortable. The room was stifling, although it was not yet six. He slipped in and out of a dream in which Fernando Nachez was humping Lizzie Nash behind the Xerox machine in the mailroom of Milton House. Larry Botner was present, but he seemed not to notice, and Agnes Wild busied herself with some copying.

Susan coughed, and Geno woke completely. He sat up and saw that she was solidly asleep, with a light blanket pulled up to her chin. There was a faint smile on her lips, and he grew suddenly curious about her dreams. He touched her cheek, certain that it would not wake her. She slept so deeply in these early hours, sweating like a stone in the wall of a well.

As he stared at the ceiling through the mosquito netting, he could feel the room spinning out of control. Were there a million little cracks in the apparently smooth surface of Augusto's manner that he'd simply overlooked? His fatal naivete had thrust him into an easy acceptance of the world of the Bay of Arrows. Augusto and his cousins had attached themselves hastily to the first source of income that floated into view. But he hadn't, until now, been aware of anything pernicious. He had considered Augusto a friend. They had worked side by side for months. He closed his eyes to see if the room would stop spinning.

Geno put on his jeans and shirt, his socks and sneakers, and went to a patch of jungle behind the house. As he took a long piss into the foliage, he let go of his dreams of paradise, and he determined to take things into his own hands.

He made his way up to Los Angeles along the quiet, dew-speckled path, absorbed in the way the early morning sunlight transfixed the ferns in crosshatched beams of light. In the palm trees high overhead, pelicans called *cras cras* to one another. *What a miraculous place this is,* he thought. He would not, he must not, lose it.

He went straight to Felipe Hernández, a grotesquely thin bachelor of fifty with a twirled mustache and gold-capped front teeth who lived above the small building that passed for a police station in Los Angeles (the jail was roughly the size of an outhouse and adjoined the station). Hernández shook his hand warmly. "I love to see you American," he said. "American nice country. Very good baseball! You like Red Sox, no?" When Geno seemed to hesitate, he added: "Or White Sox?"

"There's been a robbery," he blurted.

Hernández told him to sit on one of the wobbly cane chairs that were lined up against the dirty, mustard-yellow wall. He sat beside him eagerly to absorb the tale that Geno spun; afterward, he assured him that Augusto would be caught and punished.

"I just want him called in for questioning," Geno said. "Mainly, I want that radio back." He paused, then said, "It means a great deal to Susan . . . my wife."

"No problem, Señor, I take this matter myself." Hernández lit a cigarette coolly. "Your wife, I see her. She is—how you say?—very beautiful woman."

"Thank you."

"No problem, Señor." He blew smoke rings into the air.

Geno sat with his hands on his knees and watched the smoke break free of its rings. "It's not actually *certain* that Augusto took the radio," he said.

"It is certain," Hernández said. "Radio good thing. Everybody like radio." He pointed to a radio on a small table beside his desk. "My radio very nice."

"You've misunderstood me," Geno said.

"Thank you, kind sir!" Hernández said, grinning. "You are very nice man!" He pressed close to Geno, and his eyes welled with a great sympathy. "This family must be brought to justice," he said.

Disconsolate, Geno went over to the Hotel Miami to speak with Señora Iguano before heading back to the compound. He trusted her, and he wanted her reassurance that he'd acted wisely. As expected, he found her sitting in the shade of her veranda at the Miami, sipping Nescafé; she listened patiently to his story, only once or twice lifting an eyebrow or curling a lip.

"But this is not true," she said when he had finished, her cup clattering into her saucer. "I don't believe."

"I saw him myself," Geno said. "I chased him right into the jungle."

"I know Augusto many year," she said. "My husband, Señor Iguano—when he come back from Miami, he tell you. Augusto is not a thief. His father was thief, but he not. No." Her fingers trembled, grazing the buttons of her white blouse, checking to make sure everything was secure.

"I'm sorry, but I don't agree."

"Felipe Hernández is bad man," she said, tapping the metal table lightly. "Hernández, he like his job too much—a very bad thing for policeman." She leaned forward as if to whisper, though she bellowed what she had to say. "Felipe Hernández *hate* Augusto. Augusto's sister, Helena. She is very beautiful. Hernández ask her marry one times, many years ago, but she say, 'Go away, you stupid!' She marry somebody else, so Hernández hate Augusto family."

Geno rocked back on his chair. "I can't believe he would let a personal feud interfere with his duties."

Señora Iguano smiled. "You can't believe, huh?"

"I can't," he said, feeling under him a widening pit.

"Well, believe," she said.

It was Saturday morning, so everyone in the village knew exactly where Augusto would be. At the cockfights. Geno excused himself from Señora Iguano and rushed away to head off Felipe Hernández at the pass. He would question Augusto himself about whatever had happened last night. If an explanation were forthcoming, he would tell Hernández to drop everything. Enlisting the help of Hernández had been an impulsive gesture: the product of an early morning fit of anxiety. "Fucking asshole!" he cried, drawing stares from children at the roadside.

The arena where the cockfights were staged was a miniature of the Roman Colosseum, a makeshift bamboo and palm wood amphitheater that tilted fiercely to one side. It was several miles outside of Los Angeles in a dusty clearing, and there was a barbed wire fence around the grounds to ensure that spectators paid the tiny entrance fee. A wizened old man guarded the entrance. He took Geno's fee and pointed a crooked finger toward the arena.

In the amphitheater, cheers rose and fell in waves. Geno had never seen a cockfight, but had always imagined it would be disgusting and cruel, the kind of spectacle that would make generations of ASPCA volunteers writhe in their graves. And he was right.

Fans, most of whom were male, came from the surrounding villages for these Saturday morning cockfights, and they sat shoulder to shoulder in bleachers banked so steeply they seemed to topple over each other. Making his way along the outermost rim of the top circle, Geno peered over the heads of a group of small children in front of him.

Below, like gladiators, the frenzied cocks warily approached each other, cheered on by their equally frenzied trainers. Their heels were enhanced by horny spikes of turtle shell designed to dig into their opponent's flesh. With spikes on their foreheads too, they had been trained to fight to the death.

A scarlet cock and a white one danced gingerly around each other below while a row of surly men in colorful shirts accepted bets. The pale orange Dominican pesos seemed to fly, the fans growing rowdier by the moment, leaping onto their seats, screaming, shaking fists in the air and at each other.

The scarlet cock was in control of the match from the outset; he fell on the white one quickly and mercilessly, fluttering above his hapless opponent, stabbing, stabbing. The white cock got a horny spike in its brain and fell dead in the dust—an instant and disappointingly quick death. The red cock, trained to strike and strike again, continued gouging and demolishing the blood-stained body, its tangle of nerves and feathers quivering involuntarily. The proud owner ran into the arena, then grabbed and held the winner aloft as fans roared and stomped their feet. Everywhere in the bleachers there was money changing hands.

Geno's eye fell upon Augusto, whose cock was next: a brown one, with its claws neatly taped; metallic spikes flashed from its heels and forehead. Augusto was holding it tightly to his chest, stroking it, whispering into its ear as a flurry of last-minute bets was placed.

The opponent was an undersized gray creature, and its trainer was a lame young man who listed toward the center of the arena and set his bird free with a slight upward lift. The bird fluttered in a threatening way, then subsided into a defensive pose. It watched the brown cock warily.

Soon Augusto's cock was attacked in a burst of shuffling wings. Geno could hardly bear to watch as the brown one took three sharp stabs in the side, just below the left wing; it reeled back, staggered forward, and left a trail of blood on the floor. The battle proceeded with cruel slowness, and it looked as though Augusto's cock would never gain an advantage.

The crowd responded wildly, transformed into a single roaring beast, thrilled by the prospect of victory by an underdog; but the gray cock was no match for its larger opponent. It might have struck a hard blow now to take advantage of its momentum, but it became tentative and, seemingly, confused; it hung fatally back, allowing Augusto's cock to recover itself, to begin circling and to descend in a fury of horrible squawks, repeating the action again and again until the gray cock was stabbed, stupefied, and nearly drained of life. The battle ended with a final rush, the bigger cock piercing the smaller one's brain with the deft, almost incidental, flick of a heel spike.

Augusto raced forward, grabbed his victorious bird, and raised it defiantly in the air. The fans roared as Augusto put his lips to the bird's wounds and sucked them clean. He spit the blood into the sawdust.

Geno was struggling to make his way through the crowd to intercept Augusto when Felipe Hernández and three deputies stepped into the ring and handcuffed the astonished man in front of everybody at the cockfight. The place went dead.

Augusto did not protest. He accepted his fate as if it had been ordained, and he was led away to jeers of "*¡Coño, Hernández! ¡ Coño!*" accompanied by obscene gestures, which Hernández and his deputies returned.

Geno watched the arrest with a growing sense of impotence. There was no way to stop the machinery of justice from grinding along in its tracks.

Geno found Susan and the boys in the dining area; they were having a late-morning snack. Because it was Saturday, there was no "schoolhouse," and the boys had slept in late. Milo was eating a muffin at the table beside Susan, while James sat in an Adirondack-style chair with a slice of bread and glass of guanabana juice.

"Where have you been, honey?"

"I went to the police."

Milo looked up. "Can I go next time?"

Susan said, "What's going on?"

Geno plonked himself down across from her at the table, hunching forward. He picked up a piece of bread and spread a thin layer of peanut butter from the last jar they'd brought with them from the States. "Last night," he said, "I couldn't sleep. You know how I can get. And I heard this cough . . . or something. It really scared me."

Susan looked at him over the rim of her teacup. James lifted his chin.

"What was it?"

"I wanted to know. So I went outside with the flashlight. At first, I saw nothing. I was just about to come inside when I caught a glimpse of this man. He was standing on the path—up behind the garden."

"Jesus . . ."

"I chased him into the jungle." Every eye was on him. Even Milo was listening close. "It was Augusto."

"You're certain?"

"I caught up to him. Shined the goddamn light right in his face!"

Susan stood up to release some tension. "What did he say?"

"He ran off into the trees. Vanished. So this morning, I got up early and went straight to Hernández—the policeman."

"Without talking to Augusto?"

"I don't have to talk to Augusto. The police will do that."

"But Geno . . ." Her voice tailed off.

"You think I shouldn't have gone to Hernández?"

"I . . . I don't know."

"Something had to be done, honey." As he spoke, the weight of what he said settled on his shoulders, loosened his posture; he felt as though he was caving in upon himself.

On weekends Josefina often brought something she had baked herself for lunch. Jorge and Pio would appear beside her, and they would soon be circling around James and Milo; little jokes would flare into large-scale games. It was now half past twelve, yet no one had arrived.

"Where's Josefina?" James asked his mother, who was laying out sandwiches on the table—slices of goat cheese over homemade bread. She dipped her knife into a jar of avocado spread that Josefina had brought the week before.

"I don't know."

"Do you want me to get her?"

"It's all right, James. She'll come when she's ready."

But she did not come. Nor did Jorge or Pio.

"This is silly," Geno said, after lunch. He could not hide his anger. "It can't have anything to do with Augusto."

Susan just looked at him.

"I mean, the man stole your radio! He was prowling around here last night like a thief!"

Milo and James turned white and sick. They slunk off by themselves, although neither of their parents seemed to notice.

Geno, too, felt like slinking off, so he went behind the house to find his tools. He and Augusto had been planning to spend the afternoon constructing a shower. Geno had devised a system for pumping water from the cistern into a barrel that was nailed to a platform behind the house. He would configure a trapdoor in the bottom that would release water slowly through a metal plate with holes drilled in a pattern to create the shower effect. By putting a strip of black tar paper across the top of the barrel, he hoped to heat the water by solar power; the result would be—or should be—a warm shower every afternoon, just after they'd all taken their last salty swim of the day.

As Geno worked, he missed Augusto. Several times he muttered aloud, cursing himself for his actions. Yes, he'd taken the situation in hand. He'd done his Selkirky thing. But Augusto might well be innocent. Didn't the man deserve the right to present his case?

His best hope now was that Augusto could explain the whole thing to Hernández, and that all would be well. But he feared he would never regain the trust of his friend, and he knew he couldn't live here without it.

"Want me to help, Daddy?"

Geno looked around at James, who was standing in a sail-white tee shirt and cut-off jeans. His feet were bare and acorn brown. A couple of weeks before, Susan had cut his auburn locks close to the roots, but the hair was so thick that it had already begun to resurrect itself in a fuzzy, russet blur. "Sure, sweetie. Grab that bag of nails, would you?"

All afternoon father and son worked, mostly in silence, on the shower. And by the end of the day, it was finished.

"Wow," said Susan. "This place is turning into a five-star hotel."

Geno said, "Let's just hope the damn thing works. Want to try it?"

"No, me!" cried Milo.

"Hop in," James said.

Geno looked at James. On a normal day James would have screamed bloody murder, since he had devoted his afternoon to the project. Something was either very right or horribly, horribly wrong.

Milo stood under the baroque contraption in his shorts and tee shirt, his eyes shut tight, his chin jutting forward in anticipation.

"Just pull the ripcord," Geno said.

They stood back as Milo pulled the cord. A trickle of lukewarm water fell on his head: hardly enough to wash away a smudge on his brow.

"The holes aren't big enough," Geno said. "Back to the drawing board, James."

James leaped in beside Milo to try the trickle for himself. However briefly, a halo of good feeling had descended upon this family, and they could all sense it. It floated above them, circled like a ring of gold vapor, then disappeared.

"Jorge will like this," James said.

"And Pio too," Milo put in.

But Jorge and Pio, for the first time in months, stayed away from the Genovese house.

Once again, Geno could not sleep. A tower of exhaustion had been adding tier after rickety tier inside him. It puzzled him that Susan had been silent all day. She was not telling him what he'd done wrong. He felt alone with his own actions.

The prickly inward pressure of a full bladder overcame his inertia, so he took a flashlight to the outhouse. In the little shed, with his pajamas circling his ankles, he felt miserably human—a creature subject to a whim, a physical discomfort, a mental or emotional tug. These were the components that made him up, but when he tried to find where they coalesced into "Geno," his own self began to evade him. He was not just the stew of thoughts bubbling in his cranium, nor just the sack of bones that voided into the long black night on a splintery seat in an outhouse by the Bay of Arrows. Was he the sum of his mistakes? Or the blessed whole of his accomplishments?

As he pushed himself off the toilet, he heard a sob from one of the boys which aroused in him a deep paternal empathy. He knew exactly how it felt to be helpless and young, to feel alone and frightened of the world. Back in New Jersey he had spent so many nights awake, afraid. Sometimes he, too, had cried into his pillow, hoping to attract the attention of a parent. But nobody ever came.

In the boys' house, he flashed the light on Milo's bunk, but Milo was asleep. It was James who lay naked to the waist, crying. Geno parted the mosquito netting and crawled in beside him and stroked his back, but James was inconsolable.

"What's wrong, honey?"

"Nothing."

James had been increasingly unwilling to receive affection from his father, and this seemed a great loss to Geno—one of the countless small but remarkable losses that are part of raising children. The boy was incredibly high-strung, and Geno could feel it in James's back: the organic tension in the symmetrical knit of muscles bound tightly on either side of his long spine. His little face—it was still heartbreakingly small—contorted.

"Are you sick, James?"

"No."

"Then what's the matter?"

James lifted himself up on both elbows, turned slowly. He cuddled close to his father, sitting on the edge of the bed in the diaphanous tent of mosquito netting.

"That's it," Geno said, kissing his forehead. "Now, tell me."

"I took the radio, Daddy."

"*You* did?"

"Me and Milo. And Jorge and Pio. We were building a spy station. In the woods. To help with the attack on Colón."

"Ah . . . a spy station." Geno could already feel the new lineaments of his own chastened being.

"But Josefina found the radio, and she got scared."

Geno wiped the sweat from his son's face. "What did Josefina do?"

"She told Augusto to put it back." He paused. "Ask Pio if you don't believe me!"

"Ah."

"And he was bringing it back when you saw him."

Geno sighed inwardly, a long and deep sigh that bloated his lower abdomen with air. He tried to keep from swooning.

"I didn't mean to lie to you, Daddy. I was scared."

"Scared?"

"Yes."

"You were scared of me?"

"Yes." He suppressed a whimper. "You seemed so . . . angry or something. It was in your eyes."

Geno said, "I see. Yes. It was."

"And now Augusto's in trouble."

"Don't worry about that, honey. I can take care of that." He lowered his son gently into the bunk. "I'm glad you told me about this. I'm proud of you. Really proud." He kissed James on the lips—something he almost never did. And he sucked in the child's rank boy-smell, sharp yet oddly appealing.

"I love you, Daddy."

"And I love you, James. I love you a whole lot."

He waited beside the boy until he was breathing deeply, tipping over the ledge of dreams. Then he walked grimly back to his own bed.

Susan was still sleeping hard, but Geno knew it was futile: sleep was a faraway country that he was not even going to try to visit yet. He sat down at the bare table that he used for writing and opened his notebook. The flashlight cast an unreal glow over the blank pages, which seemed to cry out for language. But everything that came to mind fell constantly short of reality.

The freckled face of Lizzy Nash flipped into his mind, swishing to the surface like a marlin, leaping for light. He had no energy to push it back down under. He recalled with dream exactitude that night in her dormitory. "I don't want this," she had said, her voice weak. Her top lip quivered, and he put his forefinger on the lip to still it. He kissed her eyelids, slowly, letting her lashes flutter under his tongue. Her garlicky breath blew hot and strong in his face, and he teased her about it. She put her head on his shoulder, and he ran his fingers through her red curls. The long muscles on either side of her neck stood out like cables, and he rubbed them. "Do you want me?" he whispered. But she said nothing. "I want you," he said, reaching for her small white breasts—the nipples hard, upturned in his palm. He circled them slowly, trying to turn her on. He reached down and touched her navel, then reached lower. A finger opened her, and she was wet inside. Her thighs felt hot. "I want this, Lizzie," he said. "I want you." "Please, no," she said, but her thighs had opened. He pressed his lips to hers, hard. And her lips parted. She let his tongue search the corners of her mouth and let his teeth clatter against hers. She bloomed in his hands like a spring bough of lilacs dipped into a tub of warm water and forced, prematurely, to radiate color, light, and smell.

Geno bent over in his chair, sickened. The images, bright and bitter, flickered in his mind. Yes, she had wanted it. But she also didn't want it. He looked at his hands, the swirl of russet hair just beyond his wrist joint, the large knuckles and long trembling fingers. He turned his hands, drawing his damp palms toward his face, pressing them into his eyes.

In a little while, taking out the stub of a pencil from a jar on the desk, he began scribbling to Lizzie in his notebook:

Dear Lizzy:

I am so sorry. You should know how sorry I am. I did, I still do, feel genuine affection for you . . .

It was hopeless. The white space widened around those letters and the message, so aloof, so impossibly distant; he could not go on. He tore out the page, crumpled it, and threw it into the wicker basket that brushed against his bare ankles.

In a while he slipped through the netting into bed beside Susan, who lay on her back now, her sharp features visible in the moon's ghostly light, which somehow managed to permeate the house even with the blinds pulled down. He touched her cheek lightly, but she did not move. Why had she been so passive about Lizzie?

Her face was held in a gauzelike frame and the silver

streaking in her hair caught the moonlight. Geno saw how mortal she was, and how unlike him. She was another human being, with her own myriad fears, passions, sleights of mind, slants of humor. And all of this had nothing to do with him. She was a foreign body, a distinct and separate creature—one of the billions who inhabited this dying planet. He found himself desperate to know her. To know what she thought, how she felt, what she wanted. And he wanted time. Time to accomplish what, so far, he'd not accomplished in all their years together.

Chapter 34

COLUMBUS IN CHAINS

What could my sovereigns say, then, seeing me
in chains, my ankles bound, these shackled wrists
hard by a wall? The Admiral of the Ocean Sea?
"The Admiral of Mosquitoes!" they were shouting
as they marched me through that raucous mob
of madmen, mountebanks, and traitors, worse.
What else could I expect from men like that?
They're thieves, the lot of them, so let them have
their Bobadilla. I know him, I do—
a courtier and snob, a so-called knight.
Can Isabella know what he has done?
Does she imagine I was sent to rule
a Sicily or Crete, some island kingdom
where the law's dear weight is but assumed?

Some country where the law's fierce love
informs the landscape, shapes the rivulets
and calms the sea, adds justice to the just
and pardons all who seek to understand
its ministrations and obey its forms?

I came to these wild Indies seeking
gold and glory only for my God.
I came to civilize, to bring the law
that Moses brought from those pale hills
in ancient lands where God was spoken
by the sun's clear light, by fiery wings
or flaming bushes, water running over stones.
My God is hard, as I am hardened
by the salty winds that whet their blades
on sunlit boulders of a broken shore.
I've had to kill as David killed:
a warrior for God must do His will.
I do whatever must be done to save
His greater glory: ad majoram dei gloriam!
I came, I conquered. Now they conquer me.
They cuckold me. They strip my body
as they strip my soul. They want to break me,
but they haven't heard that I, Columbus,
am a place apart. I fought my way
from Genoa to Portugal to Spain.
I've launched my heart a thousand times
in deeper waters than they've ever seen
or yet imagined in their blackest dreams.

The moon's blind side is home to me.
I serve my Savior as I serve myself,
without contingency or backward glances,
never giving in to gaps of faith.
No king, no queen, is lord to me.
This Bobadilla, whom they've sent to strip me,
feigned such horror when he landed here.
The hill above the harbor I had darkened
with a row of gallows. I had hung
some mutinous Castilians. What of that?
I should have hung a hundred more.
Their crude rebellion has undone me now,
my rule of law swept out to sea.

I vow: each one of them will pay, and dearly,
for my days and weeks, my months of pain,
these blunt indignities I have suffered lately.
They offend the man whose single mind
has lofted, circumscribed a whorling globe.
I've taken them away from their foul nests
and given them a paradise, imperfect,
but an Eden still. There's gold here, silver,
pearls of liquid beauty, spices, slaves.
What did they want of me except these things?

I shall be rich, but so shall Spain;
the whole of Christendom will share our wealth,
and God will bless us as we rule all lands
with cross and sword. This Bobadilla

doesn't half believe the width, the depth,
of what I promise: world on world,
world within world, these branching kingdoms
where so many children walk alone
without a God, without the law that makes us
whole, that makes us holy, hale, and hard.
They are like Adam and untroubled Eve
in Eden's shade; the serpent lingers
in the shade as well; it always does.
And it will strike and strike again.
These children will be slain without our hope,
the paradise within that angels know.
They'll die and die again a thousand times;
their breath will turn to bitter ashes.
They will spin like Paolo and Francesca
round the blackened center of their hearts.
Perpetual the pain that's born of sin.

Yes, I have sinned. I've done the worst
a man can do. Yet I have asked
my god, Hosannah, for the gift of grace.
They chain me now; they pin my body
to the wall like this: a wriggling butterfly
that has lost its hope of earthly glory.
But I know I'll rise and rise and rise.
I'm part, I'm parcel of the God I know.
They crucify me now, but I'll recover,
recollect myself, becoming light.
The gold of glory will be mine at last.

Chapter 35

The sun was steady overhead, hot and buttery as Geno wiped a thick lather of sweat from his eyes. He stood outside the police station in Los Angeles and listened to the wind as it strafed the nearby grass; it blasted him, stripped him as the wind strips a tree in autumn in New England, leaves nothing behind but a black silhouette of reaching fingers. The connections between the literal phenomenon, wind, and its ghostly analogue, *spiritus*, entranced him. Was this life, then? A gust of consciousness? A whirl of unresolved being?

Some lines from Yeats floated in his brain, going around and around as if spinning on a frictionless circuit: "Turning and turning in a widening gyre / The falcon cannot hear the falconer." He understood those lines, at last. What he could not understand was how, exactly, this life in paradise which he had worked so hard to create had just fizzled in his hands.

"¿Señor, como está?" Hernández asked, beaming as he opened the door for Geno.

"Muy bien, gracias." Geno took his Panama hat off and sat down.

"May I speak English?"

"Of course. I like the English!"

"Good." He set his face into the cheerful gust of Felipe Hernández. "I really appreciate the way you were willing to help me. It seems that my sons—my little boys—were playing a game, and *they* took the radio."

"Very bad, to steal a radio."

"My sons are in trouble," he said, faintly grinning, trying to find the man's distant wavelength.

"No, Augusto is in trouble. Taking a radio is bad."

"But that's what I'm saying. Augusto didn't take it."

"No?" The man's smile was like a weak bridge, the edges tugging up, the middle sagging.

"He was trespassing, yes?"

"Yes."

"That is bad! Is not legal in Dominican Republic." The policeman poured a glass of rum for Geno, who took it for the sake of politeness. He never understood how anyone could drink rum in the morning, though it seemed a common practice in Los Angeles. "Very nice, this rum. Bermudez."

"Thank you." Geno took a swig, and it burned the back of his throat. "I will not press charges," Geno explained. "Is that clear?"

"What you want me do?" the man asked, a sorrowful expression in his eyes.

"Let Augusto go."

"Go?"

"Yes, he's done nothing wrong. It was my mistake."

"Ah, mistake. I see." Hernández stood with his arms behind his back, rocking forward and backward. It looked as though any moment he might tip over completely. "I must telephone my superior in Samaná. He will explain to me."

"Just let him go, Señor!" Geno rose, inflamed.

"This is not good," Hernández said, weakly.

"I will call the police headquarters in Samaná myself if Augusto is not free by the end of the day," Geno said, controlling himself. He knew well enough that one should never express anger in the face of officialdom; it was a good way to get oneself cooked alive in a vat of boiling water. *"Hasta la vista, Señor Hernández,"* he said. *"Y muchas gracias."*

Señora Iguano put a cup of Nescafé in front of Geno. "I told you Augusto not a thief," she said. "No?"

"You did." Geno looked around the café, and he noticed that everybody was turned physically away from him. He had felt the entire village of Los Angeles cold-shouldering him as he walked down the dusty street to the Hotel Miami. "You were right, you know. I should have listened."

"Everyone is angry with you."

"I'm sure they are." He stirred a packet of sugar into the coffee and added cream.

"But Hernández said he will let Augusto go home," she said. "That much I tell you. It is too expensive to keep people in jail anymore. You have to feed a man in jail. This is a poor country." She sat down at his table, and he could sense a great pool of language lying at the bottom of her well—under pressure, like oil. It would spout up, spray all over the café. He'd been through many of these verbal showers since arriving in Los Angeles, and he had come to like them. "I like America better than Dominican Republic," she continued. "More money, more prisons. Not like here. Thieves everywhere. Baliguer, I don't know. He seem not able to control . . . not like Ronald Reagan. Reagan very handsome man. Bush not so good as Reagan—squeak like a chicken. Jimmy Carter, I like him. It's very bad here." The only American president she seemed really to despise was Lyndon Johnson, and that was because he'd sent the Marines to Santo Domingo. "Kennedy, he very good man. His wife, she has a lovely hair. A rich woman." She had no doubt whatsoever that Kennedy had been killed by SIM, Trujillo's secret police, in response to Kennedy's financial and material support for Trujillo's assassins only two years before.

Geno waited for her torrent of conversation to slow, then he cut in. "Señora, tell me. Will the town ever forgive me?"

Her eyes were wide and deep as the Bay of Arrows itself: "Forgive? Geno, the town cannot forgive you. Only God forgive somebody. Only God."

Augusto languished in jail for days, despite Geno's daily attempts to free him. He traveled to Samaná to complain to the chief of police for this district, and he telephoned a lawyer in

Nagua who had been recommended by Señora Iguano. The lawyer reassured Geno by saying, "I take care of everything, Señor!" But this form of reassurance had worn thin lately. He told Felipe Hernández that he would send a telegram to the American consul in Santo Domingo if Augusto were not released within one week.

In the midst of these trials a telegram from Vermont was brought to the compound by a messenger from the village: *"Arrive any day. Charles."*

"What's *this* all about?" Geno asked Susan. Charles was the last man on earth he felt like entertaining at the moment.

"I don't know," Susan said. She was trying to get her shortwave radio to work. Josefina—who had yet to visit them since Augusto's arrest—had sent the radio back via Jorge, but it looked as though it'd fallen into a pot of black bean soup.

"This is ridiculous," Geno continued. "We give your brother our house in Vermont, and now he wants this house, too."

"He's only coming for a visit."

"How do you know that?"

"He mentioned in one of his letters that he might come for a visit later in the spring. I guess he decided to come earlier." She was frowning now. "You don't seem to like reading letters that come from my family."

"That's not true. In fact, your father is fascinating. He's so pure: a nineteenth-century capitalist."

"Just because you don't like my father, Geno, that doesn't make you a Marxist."

"I never said I was a Marxist. I used to call myself a

socialist, but I'm not sure about that anymore." He wiped his sweaty face with the end of his tee shirt. "I'm not really sure about anything."

"Is Daddy a socialist?" asked James. He and Susan had been studying socialism during their schoolhouse sessions that week.

"Are you a socialist, Geno?" Susan teased. "Or has the fall of socialism in Eastern Europe changed your mind?"

"Do I have to justify everything I say?"

"In short, yes."

Geno's patience with her, with everyone, had been stretched like toffee by the Augusto business, and he snapped back at her: "Life is not a seminar." When Susan looked mildly hurt, he said, "All right, I will justify myself. Listen close, children. Your father does not think that socialism—the old versions of it—can work. Small economic communities trading with larger economic communities constitute the future. Look at the ex–Soviet Union: the place has been atomized, but it's a very healthy sign."

"They're starving in Russia," said James. "Isn't that true, Ma? You told us that on Friday."

"I'm starving," said Milo. "Daddy took the last banana!"

"That's the legacy of Stalinism," Geno explained. "Statism."

"Statism?" James asked, plucking the rest of the banana from his father and passing it to Milo.

"Here it comes," Susan said. "Genovese's theory of anarcho-syndicalism."

Geno turned to James, loving the fact that his son was

just becoming old enough to understand his perorations. "Statism is what plagues the United States right now. Governments like to grow. But how can you resist anything of that size? I often wish Vermont was a separate country."

"So do I!" said Charles. "Vermont is lovely."

Everyone looked up at Charles, who stood at the edge of the veranda in white cotton trousers, a white shirt, and a pith helmet.

"It's Jungle Jim," said Geno.

"We are here," said Yellow Moon. "What a most beautiful and exotic location you have found."

"We didn't expect you guys so soon," Geno said.

"I sent a telegram a few days ago," said Charles. "Did you get it?"

"A few minutes ago."

"I sent it a few days ago!"

"It doesn't matter," Susan said, kissing her brother on the cheek. "The calendar doesn't really turn over here. We lose track of time."

"You sound bored, Sis."

"Bored!" Geno said. "Like Yellow Moon said, this place is most beautiful and exotic."

Charles turned to the boys. "Whatcha up to, little guys? Heavens, you've both grown—in just a few months, I can hardly recognize either of you!"

"Hi, Uncle Charlie."

"Hi."

"This is like, like Shangri-la," said Yellow Moon, sweeping a strand of bleached-out hair from her eyes and exposing her broad, almost bulbous, forehead.

"That's it—Shangri-la," said Geno. "It describes this place to a tee."

Yellow Moon missed the twang in his voice: "I have read many books that remind me of this country."

"And seen many movies, I suspect," said Geno.

"I have seen many movies. This is true."

Geno wondered what Charles saw in this robotic woman.

"Have a rum," he said. "The rum is good here." As he said that, he realized he was sounding more and more like Selkirk, or a character in Hemingway.

"Love a rum," Charles said. "But it's a little early for alcohol, isn't it?"

"Not in the tropics."

"I'd like a rum," said Yellow Moon.

"Me too," said James.

"Shut up," said Geno.

"You said in your letter you were coming later . . . in the spring," Susan said, rinsing out several glasses.

"We would have waited," said Yellow Moon, "but it was getting very, very cold."

Geno wondered if Charles knew that Yellow Moon was brain dead.

"It gets cold in Vermont in the winter," Susan said. "I remember it once snowed on October eleventh."

Charles seemed apprehensive now. He had a nervous tic that appeared in awkward situations, and Susan noticed it immediately. His left eye would wink involuntarily, giving the people who saw it the impression that they were being let in on something private.

Yellow Moon, big-eyed, said, "Tell them about the furnace, Charles."

"The furnace?" Susan asked.

"You see, the furnace stopped," Charles said.

Geno, who was pouring the rum, looked up. "Stopped?"

"Yes, it would not run," said Yellow Moon.

"Ah, I see. It would not run."

Susan said, "Did you call a plumber?"

"No. I did not know a plumber."

"You did not know a plumber," Geno repeated, slowly. He turned to Charles. "Surely Charles would know a plumber, wouldn't he?"

Charles winked at him.

Susan was getting more than merely anxious. "Charles!"

Charles shrugged. "I was . . . out of town."

"Where were you?"

"I went back to Wisconsin, to visit the girls."

"And Cicely?"

"Cicely has another . . . a friend." He grabbed the glass of rum from Geno and took a sip.

"Good grief."

"I'm actually quite happy for her."

"What does Mother say about him?"

"He's a bond salesman—Ned Friendly. They know him very well from Green Meadows."

The mention of the Green Meadows Country Club made

Geno's flesh creep. It represented everything he most disliked about America: golf courses, men in plaid pants, women in sickly green or putrid pink sweaters, cocktail parties, anti-intellectualism, snobbery, bad food, as well as a corrosive and self-satisfied, right-wing political correctness. "Entrepreneurship" was their favorite word, the secular equivalent of what Christians refer to as "grace." And they were forever nattering about the tax on capital gains. What *were* capital gains?

Geno stood with his arms folded, looking at Charles and Yellow Moon as if they were children caught with their hands in the cookie jar. "And the furnace broke while you were away, Charles?" he said.

"Yes. That's it."

"And Yellow Moon didn't call a plumber?"

"No."

Yellow Moon offered Geno and Susan a baleful stare, and they did feel sorry for her. She was like one of those "aging children" Joni Mitchell sang about, a walking elegy to innocence.

"So you returned from Madison to find the house well below zero?"

"That's right." Charles grinned slightly. "It was—what was it, dear—ten degrees or so? Imagine that, *inside* the house."

"I can imagine it," said Geno. "What I can't imagine is what happened to the pipes."

"The pipes?"

"Didn't the pipes break?"

"Everything looked all right."

"There was no running water," said Yellow Moon. "I tried to take a shower one day, but there was no running water."

"Did you look in the basement?"

"I went down there one time, but it was very dark."

"Surely the electricity was working."

"I didn't know where to find the switch," she said. "Charles told me not to go down there. Your basement is full of mice." She looked at Geno and Susan with a faintly accusatory squint.

"I dare say, the mice are dead now. Frozen solid."

"We are truly sorry," said Yellow Moon. "We intend to call a plumber when we return."

"When you fucking return?" Geno tried as hard as he could to suppress a rising sense of hysteria. "When you fucking return?"

"We're not going to stay all that long, Geno," said Charles. "We had planned to come later, but the situation at your house was, frankly, intolerable." Indignation flashed in his face. "The weather reporter on the radio said the cold snap wasn't going to last. A thaw was on the way just as we left. They said that right on the radio." He looked at Yellow Moon, who confirmed that the cold weather was meant to pass quickly.

"This is wonderful," said Geno. "I don't suppose, Charles, you're aware of what happens to a house with broken pipes when a thaw comes?"

Charles winked at him again.

"What you seem not to have understood is that frozen

pipes will have cracked everywhere—in the walls, under the floorboards. And when the thaw comes, the water begins to rush through the broken pipes. Do I have to spell it out for you? It'll be Noah's fucking arksville."

Susan said, "Geno is right, Charles. It's probably too late already."

Charles looked immensely gloomy.

Yellow Moon said, "I am truly sorry. I had a premonition about this only a week or two before the furnace stopped. I was meditating, and suddenly a black swan flew into my mind. A black swan."

"That's bad," said Geno.

"We didn't just abandon the house," said Charles.

"No?"

"We left a friend in charge. He said he would get the furnace running again."

Yellow Moon was nodding anxiously as Charles spoke. "He was a member of our circle of meditation."

"That's good," Susan put in quickly. "I was terrified that nobody was there."

"His name is Andrew," Yellow Moon said.

"Andrew?"

"Andrew Ridgeway. Do you know him?"

That same afternoon Geno hitched a ride into Samaná to send a telegraph to Andrew Ridgeway. It seemed inconceivable that the fate of his house in Vermont was in these particular hands, but his life had been taking so many odd detours lately that nothing surprised him. He would now be forced to depend upon this fool's reliability. In a long telegram he told Ridgeway to contact Sam Pickering, the best plumber in Addison County. Pickering charged an arm and a leg just to walk into a room with a wrench in his hand, but he would get the job done.

Later, over dinner, Charles told them how they had met Andrew, who seemed to know everybody in the Rainbow movement. "He's a Buddhist," Charles said. "A very knowledgeable man."

"I like Andrew so much," Yellow Moon added. "His karma is unusual."

"His karma ran over my dogma," James said.

Yellow Moon looked at the boy with big wondering eyes.

"Groucho is alive and well and living in the D.R.," said Geno.

"What's that mean?" Milo asked.

James said, "It's something to do with sex."

"Is that true, Daddy?"

"Ignore your brother, Milo."

James was on a roll now, talking excitedly, fueled by the attention he was getting. "Did you tell them about Augusto?"

"Who is Augusto?" Yellow Moon asked. Her eyes seemed to grow round and yellow.

"Let's not go into that," Geno said. When he noticed the look of frustration on his brother-in-law's face, he added: "Augusto used to work for us. We thought he'd stolen something, but he hadn't. It's a long story. A very sad one, in fact."

"He's in jail," Milo said. "Daddy put him in jail, and now he can't get him out."

"Is this true, Geno?" Charles asked.

"True enough, but I'd rather not go into that just now." He distracted everyone by waving a manila envelope in the air. "I'd like you all to listen up. I'm going to provide the entertainment now." He pulled out a copy of his latest poem, "Columbus in Chains."

"Is Daddy going to read his poems *again*?" Milo asked. He had been half asleep in a hammock, having stuffed himself with curried chicken.

"Yes, Daddy is," said Geno. "Be quiet and listen."

He sat on the arm of one of the Adirondack chairs and read, in a declamatory style, his dramatic monologue, which he described as "part Tennyson's *Ulysses*, part *Samson Agonistes*, all blended with Genovesian rhythms and phrasing."

When he finished, Yellow Moon leaped to her feet and clapped. "Hooray for you!"

"I'm glad you enjoyed it."

"It's very original," she said. "And poetic."

"Poems are supposed to be poetic," said James. "What the fuck did you expect?"

"James!" Susan shot him a look of annoyance. He'd been extremely kind to his brother since the incident with the radio, but his mouth still needed a periodic soaping.

"Sorry," he said.

"It's a very nice poem, Geno," said Charles. "But I thought you hated Christopher Columbus?"

"I do. But Columbus was a human being, and like most of us, he had good sides and bad sides. His bad sides happen to have been extremely bad. But he was an idealist. At least he told himself that he was doing what he did for religious reasons. He wanted to make Spain rich enough to finance another crusade to the Holy Land. The concept of saving Jerusalem from the heathens still obsessed a lot of people at the time."

"You always told me he was cruel, petty, and simple-minded," Charles said.

"I know, I know. I'm aware of all that. But the Left sees him only as a genocidal maniac. In this poem I'm trying to get inside his skin. To see the world from his viewpoint for a change."

They all looked puzzled.

"He *did* have a point of view, you know," Geno said, a little too insistent.

"Hitler had a point of view," Susan put in. "Anyway, you make him out to be far more intellectual than he was. The guy in your poem is more like you than Columbus."

"Hey, I wasn't asking for a critique."

"When you ask us to listen, you're asking for criticism," Susan said.

Geno folded the manuscript and put it away, wondering if his Columbus poem was really so offensive. It was hardly an apologia. He had tried to enter the mind of an *imaginary* persona; he didn't doubt at all that this persona bore some resemblance to himself or, more likely, some antithetical version of himself. Wasn't every poem autobiographical on some level?

"Buen' tard', Gen," said Jorge, who appeared at his elbow in a bright yellow tee shirt that had once belonged to James. He spoke in the harshly truncated colloquial Spanish of the island. Pio stood behind him, his face like a beautifully ripened plum. It was their first visit to the compound since the radio had been taken.

The following Monday Augusto reported for work as if nothing had happened. The first Geno and Susan were aware of his presence was before breakfast; they heard somebody hammering a fencepost in the garden.

"Augusto!" James cried, rushing out to greet him. Milo followed behind.

Geno got up quickly, dressed, and went into the garden to greet him. He could feel the engines of a new life at the Bay of Arrows as they revved inside him.

"Augusto!"

Augusto nodded, never ceasing to hammer the post before him into the soft dirt.

"Please, let's talk. Can we?"

Augusto leaned on the long hammer. "I am here."

"Hernández let you go."

"Last night. He say, 'Okay, you go now.' I don't know why."

"I contacted the chief of police in Samaná."

"Thank you."

Geno could hardly bear the embarrassment. "It's the least I could do."

Augusto had no life in his eyes. It was terrible to see that. "I have much work to do—lose so many day here."

"Don't worry about that. Have some breakfast with us."

"No, I have eat somesing at home," Augusto said, enunciating each word in a meticulous way. "You have you breakfast."

"I must tell you, Augusto. I'm really sorry."

"No problem."

"It *is* a problem," Geno said. He looked at the ground, where a pale lizard flicked its tongue at these vast creatures who dared to disturb its sleep. He'd never before had such difficulty talking with Augusto. His friendship with Augusto used to form a balmy backdrop against which almost anything could have been said. But Geno realized how little had actually been said. He knew nothing of Augusto's family, background, or passions. He had treated him like a child the whole goddamn time.

Augusto said calmly, "I didn't want to get your boy in trouble. But they was already in trouble. Then I was get myself in trouble."

Geno was relieved now, and he said, "I sure got myself in trouble. The whole town of Los Angeles thinks I'm a *schmuck*."

"I don't know this word."

"A bad man."

Augusto shrugged. "You did bad thing, put me in jail without talking to me. If you ask me, I tell you what happen."

"I know that."

"You eat you breakfast now," Augusto said, breaking away from Geno. "I keep working."

"Please, Augusto. Have a cup of tea with us."

"I don't like tea."

"Coffee."

"This is not right day for this," Augusto said. "Maybe another day."

Another day, thought Geno. He would need many days to recover what he'd lost here, if it was recoverable. For all of his disappointment, he felt a grudging admiration for Augusto as he watched him hammer in the fencepost, each stroke boldly and accurately delivered. Augusto knew who he was, and he did not pretend that everything was fine.

A few days later, after lunch, a typical cloudburst settled into steady rain. The compound, the jungle, the whole peninsula submitted to the same dull whispering gray. Thunder, like a cowardly beast, retreated across the bay. Susan and Geno retired to their quarters for a siesta, and Augusto went home to be with his family, taking James and Milo with him.

Susan lay with her head on Geno's chest.

"God," she said, "the tropics can be depressing. When it rains, you feel like there's no way out."

"Remember the movie . . . *Rain*?"

"An old movie?"

"Yeah. It's my favorite depressing movie. The rain never stops through the whole damn picture. Makes you never want to see a cloud in the sky again the rest of your life."

"At least the rain passes quickly here."

Geno said, "I miss Vermont. It's weird, but I do."

"Honey, maybe we should go home." Once this sentence had been inflated, it bobbed at the end of its string like a helium balloon above their heads.

Geno spoke after what felt like five minutes of silence. "We have to, don't we?

She paused. "Apart from anything else, our house is probably breaking into bits by now. Andrew hasn't telegrammed back. Wasn't he supposed to?"

Geno nodded.

There was another long pause, during which Susan wept lightly into her husband's shirt. Geno felt the warm tears soaking through the blue cotton, and he understood her sadness.

"You've been so patient, Susie," he said. His fingers grazed the back of her neck.

"I let you bully us," she said. "At the time—right after we got here—I was just glad to see you taking control. Even that Lizzie thing—I just let it pass."

Geno knew only too well what she meant. "Did I bully them, too?"

"Who?"

"The people . . . here. The Dominicans."

Susan seemed calm now. "That's hard to say. How should one act in a foreign country? Not like Selkirk, of course. But how? It's hard to get away from the old ways . . ."

She rolled onto her back, and Geno propped himself up on his elbows above her. "I don't deserve you," he said.

"You probably don't," she said, laughing slightly. "But you're lucky, huh?"

"I'm very lucky." He leaned his head against her stomach.

Susan said, "If Charles and Yellow Moon want to stay here, that's all right, isn't it? I think they'd like to."

"Of course."

She touched him on the forehead, tracing the outline of his skull with her fingertips. "We have a long way to go, Geno," she said quietly. "But we've started. At least we've started."

Life is normally plotless, a loose jumble of events linked by circumstances beyond the control of the participants in those events. It had always displeased Geno when a novelist, for instance, would suddenly begin picking up the loose threads of a narrative and weaving them back into the text. Couldn't the writer leave well enough alone? Shouldn't a "story" unfold in the imagination the same way it did in life, randomly?

Yet Geno's time in Samaná ended with a whelm of conclusiveness. It was as if the Columbus narrative that he couldn't seem to finish—in poetry or prose—were having its own back on him, seeking revenge by thrusting upon his life the inevitable tidiness of all imaginary contours. As if art insisted, after all, that life participate in its terrifyingly beautiful, often cruel, shapeliness.

Wrapping up his life here with all the energy of Balzac, Geno went into Samaná with Augusto and the boys to reserve the airline tickets from Puerto Plata to Burlington, via Newark, on Continental. He made arrangements with Augusto to become permanent caretaker of the little compound overlooking the Bay of Arrows: for the equivalent of forty dollars per month, Augusto would check in daily. He would have free run of the garden, and his family could live off whatever he grew there. He would also serve as a caretaker to Charles and Yellow Moon, who would be staying on for an indefinite period. "Just long enough to find something to destroy," as Susan said.

On the way back into the village, Geno stopped at the Hotel Miami for a glass of rum while James and Milo rushed off to buy sodas and sweets. It was a weekday, but since relatively few villagers in Los Angeles had anything like work that required them to punch a clock, the Miami was moderately crowded. Miguel Valenzuela held court at one table, his bushy white eyebrows rising and falling as he listened intently to complaints or suggestions from three younger men, each of whom had dignified himself with a bushy mustache that seemed to mirror the mayor's. Geno and Augusto were sitting at another table with Señora Iguano, and Geno was explaining to her that in a few days he and his family were heading back to Vermont. "But we *are* coming back to Los Angeles," he told her.

"When you come back?" she asked, almost defiantly.

"Soon."

"Next month?"

"Not that soon."

"Next year?"

"Maybe." Geno stirred his coffee, disliking his own lack

of precision. But there was no telling what might happen when they returned to Barrington, especially now that Andrew Ridgeway had taken over the farmhouse!

It was a little unlikely that he could go straight back to teaching at the college, although such a thing was not impossible. He knew of a case where a Barrington professor had gotten a job offer from Yale. The guy had gone off shaking his fist at Barrington, saying, "Goodbye, and thank God I'm leaving this dump." A year later he returned with his tail between his legs, and they had taken him back.

As if an angel were passing over, conversation stopped mysteriously and conclusively at every table. Along the dusty white road that led to Samaná, a small figure appeared with a suitcase dangling from one arm. Every eye at the Miami was drawn to the shadowy figure—at first a tiny speck that could have been anyone. As the creature loomed into the middle distance, Señora Iguano began to breathe heavily. She sucked in coarse breaths, exhaled flatly, sucked in, exhaled. Geno, at first, thought a coronary attack was starting. The fingers on her right hand began to tap the metal tabletop rhythmically, loudly, like a war drum.

The approaching figure was clearly a man, and he was obviously running. His small legs scurried under him, as if disconnected from the rest of his body; one could easily believe that once the man arrived, he would step off his legs, thank them, and they would walk away without him.

Señora Iguano was now on the floor, on her knees, crossing herself and muttering a prayer in undecipherable Spanish. Later, Geno would tell Susan that she was speaking in tongues.

The stranger stopped abruptly in front of the Miami, dropping his suitcase in the dirt beside the wobbly railing.

"Señora Iguano!" he called.

Señora Iguano stood now. Her eyes were big as silver dollars. She was crossing herself, unconsciously, her lips moving but utterly silent. At last his name welled up from strange depths in her soul. "Euclides," she said.

Slowly brushing past tables and chairs with the careless deliberation of a sleepwalker, she approached the silver-cheeked and bedraggled stranger; his white suit, gone dusty yellow with travel, seemed to draw her forward. The couple froze in each other's arms.

Now everyone at the Miami was standing, clapping loudly, cheering. Word spread like heat lightning, pranking from hill to hill, and people were by now racing from all corners of Los Angeles to witness this extraordinary event, and even the children of the town, who usually ignored things their parents found truly spectacular, left off their games to watch the reunion of Señora and Señor Iguano. They seemed to know that something was happening today that would be retold, with supple variations and witty embroiderings, over many generations in the village of Los Angeles.

The Creoles of Florida had apparently let Señor Iguano go.

"I don't want to go, Daddy."

"We'll come back," Geno said. He was packing just those things that would be absolutely necessary for the trip home to Vermont. Yellow Moon and Charles had promised to put everything else in a trunk and ship it back in due course. "Do you want to take this conch?"

The conch was a pearly pink-and-blue swirl of a seashell.

"Of course I do!" Milo spoke with the indignation that only small children can muster.

"That's *my* conch," James insisted.

Jorge, who was standing beside James, broke into giggles.

"No, it's not!" Milo shouted, then burst into tears.

James took the shell from the side table. "I said it's mine!"

Geno sank inwardly. Every time he thought he was getting ahead of this thing, he felt himself slip another notch behind.

Pio stepped forward. "It belong to Pio."

"That's it!" Geno said. Pio went over to James and put his hands out, and James handed over the conch. "Here, Pio," he said. "It's yours."

Milo was not as sanguine about the conch as his older brother, and he began to sob. Geno knelt beside him. "Are you kind of sad about going?" he asked, smoothing Milo's blond ringlets with a gentle hand.

"Pio is my best friend," he said.

"That's right. You should feel happy that he's got the conch. Think of it like this: it's something that belongs to all of you. The four of you. And whenever we come back, you can play with it again. Okay?"

Milo wiped his eyes with his tee shirt and nodded; his father's argument seemed to help.

Susan was standing in the doorway, her arms loaded down with bags. "You guys ready to go?"

"Yep."

"Almost."

"Augusto is waiting for us in the village with the pickup. We can't make him wait all day," she said.

Charles and Yellow Moon stood outside in the path, ready to help carry things.

"Come on then," said Geno, lifting Milo to his feet.

The assembly gathered at the foot of the path like a mule train.

"I am sorry to see you leave," said Yellow Moon to Geno and Susan.

"Me too," said Charles. "But you'll be back. Soon as next winter hits in Barrington, you'll start dreaming of arrows."

Geno startled. "Arrows?"

"The Bay of Arrows."

"Ah . . ." Geno put on his most cheerful grimace. "I get it. Next winter, huh?"

Susan stopped herself from adding something like *Or the winter after the winter after* and said, "We'd never give up this place."

This apparently satisfied the children, who lifted their backpacks into position.

Josefina stepped out of the jungle, her wise-set face passive but benign.

"Josefina!" Milo ran to her with his arms out, and Josefina lifted the boy, kissed him, and put him down. She headed straight for Geno, carrying a little box of coconut biscuits.

"Pa' usted," she said. *"Un recuerdit'."*

"Muchas gracias, Josefina." He held the gift in slightly quivering hands.

Josefina dipped her eyes to the ground and stepped shyly backward, but Susan came forward and took Josefina by the hands. Geno, stepping back, watched as they whispered to each other in Spanish, and he envied Susan her access to a woman like this. Men were never so intimate.

He bent over and picked up his own backpack. *"Vamos, amigos."*

The children marched ahead, followed by Yellow Moon and Charles.

Left alone for a moment, Geno and Susan turned for a parting look at their little compound. The sea was aquamarine and glittered in the harsh light behind the vertical black trunks of palm and bamboo trees. A breeze caught and held the elephant grass in the field behind the garden, while the foliage crackled drily in the deep, surrounding jungle. The two houses, linked by the kitchen concourse, were bathed in yellow light, utterly still, as if holding their breaths.

"It's all very weird, isn't it?" Geno asked.

Susan shook her head. "Come on, honey. Everyone is waiting."

As they climbed through the jungle toward the main road, hand in hand, they never saw the little caravels on the horizon as they turned, coming about to head for home.

Chapter 36

The sea swished its tail as the coast of Jamaica hove into view. The two remaining caravels of the Fourth Voyage, the *Capitana* and the *Santiago*, rocked violently from side to side; water sloshed over the already sopping decks; the men, vomiting and swooning as they worked, did their best to bail the foundering vessels, working with pumps and kettles.

A slick norther blew rain slantwise into the admiral's face. He sighed and shook his head. His plan, when the fleet had left Río de Belén on Easter night of 1503, was to call at Santo Domingo for supplies and repairs; from there, he would head straight for Spain. But the *teredos*—nastly little ship-worms that multiplied in the tropics like maggots—had done their deadly work, riddling the ship's vulnerable planking. Two ships had already been abandoned, and the last two were heading into shore. Columbus was quite certain that everyone, including Ferdinand and Isabella, would blame him for the mess he was in. And they would be right. He should have hauled every ship in his fleet out of the water for scraping and pitching at least six months ago. But it was too late now.

The harbor, which Columbus had himself named Puerto Santa Gloria in 1494, was at least a good place to run aground. A deep channel leading into a lagoon was enclosed on either side with protective reefs. And there was a wide view of the seaside approach, which meant that a flotilla of Indian canoes could not easily mount an ambush.

His order had been simple: run the ships aground as close to one another as possible. This had been achieved.

On the south shore of the lagoon lay a sandy beach, and even through the rain Columbus could see that it was a decent place to land. A slight eminence behind the beach would make a decent lookout, and the beach itself shelved steeply into the water. The low shores and straight beach would give the Indians few opportunities to attack from the rear. *This will be no Bay of Arrows!* he said to himself firmly.

The hard work of securing his vessels ashore began in earnest. The caravels were anchored board to board, and all stores were taken ashore; the stone ballast was pitched overboard. Soon a line was stretched from a palm tree to the windlass of the *Capitana*, after which she was bailed as dry as possible. At high tide all hands worked the windlass and sweeps to drag her onto the beach. Before the tide slipped back, she was shored up with fresh-cut timbers from a nearby stand of palms. At low tide, sand was shoveled into the hold for ballast. The exhausted and ill-fed crew slept aboard the safely grounded ship, and the next day they repeated the process with the *Santiago*.

The burden of activity obscured, slightly, the fact that Columbus and his men were marooned and might well never make it back to Spain. The immediate problem, after having secured both ships, was food, since virtually all stores were spoiled or spent. The original complement of 140 men and boys had been reduced to 116, with 12 men having been killed in a battle with the ferocious Indians of Belén; the rest had died or deserted somewhere along the way.

Raúl Méndez, now second in command, said, "We must raid the local Indians. What other choice have we got?"

"They'll chop us to pieces, Méndez."

"Not us!" Méndez drew his sword.

"Yes, even *you*," Columbus said, tipping the sword away with one finger. "I've been here before, as you may recall. On the Second Voyage, they chopped my best men to bits. They're savages, all of them. Not a Christian among them!" He launched into a detailed account of what had happened to him on the Second Voyage.

Méndez, though frantic with boredom, listened politely. He had lost all respect for Columbus personally, but he was in awe of his title. After the Admiral of the Ocean Sea was finished, he said, "I dare say we'll be butchered by our own men if we don't get food. They're sick to death of hardtack."

Columbus looked nervously along the inland horizon. He had a premonition about this island. There was something terribly, terribly wrong here, though he could not put his finger on the problem.

"You're quite right," he said. "Take three good men, a supply of glass beads, some hawk's bells, and a quantity of lace-point. If I remember correctly, they liked the hawk's bells best. There is a lovely cassava bread on this island."

"What about meat?"

"They eat something here called a *hutía*. See if they'll give us some of those."

"I've had them before. They're bloody rats!"

"They taste rather like chicken."

Méndez raised his eyebrows. He was by now exasperated by the admiral, who had become increasingly flippant throughout their arduous journey. At times he seemed utterly disconnected from what was happening around him. Men could die, for all he cared. Was the fellow human? Did he never react, as others did, to the misery that befell those in plain view? Who was this man, Columbus? Did he have any inkling himself?

So here they were, marooned on an island somewhere off the coast of China or Cypango. Furthermore, their only caulkers had been killed at Belén, and the remaining crew would never in a thousand years be capable of building a new ship or, for that matter, even replanking the *Capitana* or the *Santiago*. No ship would be sent out from Hispaniola to look for them, and the odds that another explorer might chance upon them were nil. As far as any rational person could tell, this was their final resting place.

Suddenly a dozen land turtles emerged from the jungle, and the men fell upon them with knives.

"We're in luck!" Columbus said. "It's turtle soup for dinner tonight." He elbowed the dour Méndez. "This spot isn't so bad after all, mate. Cheer up!"

The next day, Méndez and three good men set out in a westerly direction to look for provisions, their packs full of worthless oddments for trading with the natives.

Columbus and his son, Don Diego, decided to explore the eastern side of the island alone, taking with them a modest supply of hardtack and turtle meat as well as fresh water. "We'll not go far," Columbus assured his nervous son, who spent much of his time writing in his diary. "It's important for morale that the men should see that I'm not afraid of the Indians."

They walked for three hours along the coastline, climbing over bright reefs and steep rocks, crossing several beaches. Late in the afternoon, they made camp on one of the most pleasant sandbars that Columbus had seen since first setting foot in the Indies eleven years before.

Don Diego settled down to write in his diary. "A most attractive stretch of sandy beach," he wrote. "Pelicans overhead. Palm trees. A cloudless sky."

Startled, he put down his pen. "My God!" he cried.

"What?"

"Look, Father!"

Columbus already knew what had caught his son's attention, having heard the strange noise several minutes before his son did. Don Diego was not good at noticing things. But what on earth *was* it that they heard?

The two men stood, wide-eyed and deeply frightened,

their swords drawn, as from the nearby brush came three long-legged black men in their early twenties; they wore paisly Bermuda shorts and colorful tee shirts, and one of them carried a huge Sony boom-box on his shoulder. The music that blasted from its speakers was reggae, and the young men danced along the beach toward Columbus and his son as if their swords were made of plastic.

"Are they Indians?"

"I don't know," Columbus said. "They are very black."

"What is that on the tall man's shoulder? A weapon of some kind?"

"A small cannon, I suspect," Columbus said.

The Jamaicans danced around the wary conquerors, flashing gold-toothed smiles and waving their hands in tempo with the music. "Go back home, Columbo," they sang. "Columbo, go back home."

APPENDIX

COLUMBUS AT THE GATES OF HEAVEN
A MASQUE

"Tu non dimandi chè
spiriti son queste
che tu vedi?"
Inferno IV

DRAMATIS PERSONAE

God
St. Peter
Noam Chomsky
Samuel Eliot Morison
Bartholomew de las Casas
Dona Felipa Columbus
Don Diego Columbus
Christopher Columbus

All down the centuries Columbus fell,
then caught his footing, turned to climb;
through many layers he was hauled aloft
by strings of light, half self-propelled,
half pulled by agents who would hear his case
debated at the blazing gates of heaven.
Now he stood in 1992
before the King whom nobody can see,
the Light within the Light within the Light.
The gleaming horizontal wall was white
and wide as anyone could see. The gate
was alabaster trimmed with gold;
seraphic orders lined up left and right,
sweet guardians of the ramp where on a bench
(set out by lesser angels for the day)
the Court of Entrance met to hear this case
which many gossip-mongers perched on high
had waited for with relish all this time.
St. Peter stood upon a little stool
(he was, by heavenly standards, somewhat short)
in zebra stripes by Jean-Paul Gaultier.
The others on the bench were dressed more plainly:
Dona Felipa wore a robe of blue:
the Virgin's color. Don Diego, too,
wore blue as if to point out family ties.
Bartholomew de las Casas came today

in white, pure white, the eternal priest of God;
his head was shaved and shining like a stone.
He loved to smile and smiled at everyone.
Two strangers sat at either side, impatient,
eager for the meeting to begin.
The one was Admiral Morison himself,
historian and seaman, man of letters.
No one loved Columbus more than he.
The other, Noam Chomsky, seemed agog;
the visiting professor had been summoned
from his earthly eminence at M.I.T.
to offer to eternity his insights
(though, until today, it must be said,
he'd always disbelieved in God and heaven).
The wise professor raised his hand now,
and St. Peter nodded.

ST. PETER

All right, let's begin.

PROFESSOR CHOMSKY

Why are we here? It's obvious, I think,
that hardly anyone today in truth
believes Columbus ought to enter heaven.
Heaven is for those who live for justice,
those who try to heal whatever wounds
the world might open. Heaven is a mind
as free as air, a heart committed, and a hand
stretched outward, offered to the weak, the poor,
the lame. Columbus is a murderer and fool.
I see no features to redeem this man;
he wanted only gold and slaves and glory.
And he got all three. On top of that,
he set ill winds in motion that still blow
from Salvador to Cape Town to Iraq;
believing that a hemisphere was his
just for the taking, he assumed control;
he governed badly, I must say, so cruelly
even Isabella blanched when she
found out that he had tortured, robbed, and killed
so many Indians, the bulk of whom
were mild and sweet and innocent of guile.
This genocidal maniac should be
expelled. That's what I think.

ST. PETER

Thank you, Professor.

I wonder if the others here agree
with what you've said.

LAS CASAS

I do, with some of it.

Columbus was my friend—that's fair to say.
But I dissented, given all the suffering
I saw: the women torched like stooks of hay,
the men beheaded, hanged, or burned, the children
left to hide among the starving hills.

DON DIEGO

But surely, if I may just add a word,
my father was a Christian first and last.
He hoped to bring lost souls to God,
and he succeeded. Think of all the lives
secure in glory just because of him!
These Indians he killed: were they not souls
in need of saving?

LAS CASAS

Yes, but let me add

that nowhere in the Bible does it say
that creatures whom the Lord Himself created
should be treated like mere animals—
or worse. I dare say, none of us would kill
a horse or dog for mercenary reasons,
yet Columbus did. A shipload of his slaves
were left to freeze in unprotected holds
en route to Spain. Christ never said
to butcher heathens.

PROFESSOR MORISON

The Moors did that.

DON DIEGO

Amen.

PROFESSOR MORISON

If I may have a further word or two,
I'd like to put this all in context. Nobody
excuses what he did, but in his time
he was no worse—perhaps a little better—
than the rest. He never was a saint:
that much I'll grant. But he had vision.
He conceived the world as one great whole
united by a common love of Christ.

Jerusalem was central to his dream:
the center of the circle he described
within his heart. To liberate the city
God most loved, rebuild the Holy Temple
from its rubble: this was his dream—
fantastic, yes, but perfectly within
the bounds of what men thought was proper then.
Consider his obsession with his name:
the *Christo-ferens*—bearer of the Christ.
He ferried Jesus over blackest water.
The name *Columbus*—it means peace,
and signifies the dove, the Holy Spirit.
In Spain, *Colón*, as he was always called,
meant "populator"—father of new worlds;
he gave fresh life to lost, dead souls.
The gold he sought was not just gold—
the Mines of Solomon were his real goal,
a mystical conviction, to be sure,
but no less real to him for all of that.

DONA FELIPA

I've never heard such nonsense.

ST. PETER

Madam, please!

DONA FELIPA

I'm serious! The man was *made* of lust:
For riches, yes. For women, too. What I
have suffered, knowing what I've known for ages,
waiting for this chance. I shall be brief.
He came to me and feigned such righteousness
that in my innocence I let him in.
He courted with a pleasing, tactful guile.
My mother, bless her soul, was charmed by him;
she pushed him, pressed her wealthy friends
to intervene at court on his behalf.
He took to her, I probably should add;
her ministrations he preferred to mine.
I won't say Christopher was evil; no,
not evil. He was just distracted by a force
within him. I have never understood such men.
They're not their own. A fire inside their head
undoes their judgment, so they hurtle forward
without any thought of those who suffer
from their fiery deeds, their hard-willed acts.
I never knew Columbus. He was mine
in legal terms alone. I hated him
but loved him, too. What was it that I loved?
Or who? I never knew. I still don't know.

ST. PETER

I wonder if Columbus has a word
in his defense?

COLUMBUS

I do, and thank you, sir.
I've listened with a mounting sense of ire.
Professor Chomsky, I have read your work:
it's popular in all the lower regions
I have traveled on my grim ascent
through many circles of the steepest night.
You think of me as Fustian, a self-willed
cad with no high purpose, driven by desire.
Like Saint Augustine, I have had my way
with many women; I regret this aspect
of my early life. Need more be said?
As for my Lofty Enterprise itself,
let history decide. A billion souls
now flutter at the mainmast here in heaven
all because of me. I killed for Christ,
as Saint Ignatius said we must: a soldier
of the cross may sometimes seem unfairly cruel.
If anything, I counted myself kind:
to my brave men, who launched my hopes

that day in Spain five hundred years ago,
and to Felipa, who berates me now
for reasons only God Himself may fathom.
Which of us who's known mortality
is fit to judge the crosshatched motives
that propel a life? I did my best.
On that I'll rest my case.

PROFESSOR MORISON

Well said!

DON DIEGO

My father has a gift for words.

DONA FELIPA

He does.
But words in their embodiment are deeds,
and may I ask St. Peter if intent
bears on the outcome of today's proceedings?

ST. PETER

What one may have meant is half or more
of what one did, but accidental ends
must be accounted for somehow.

LAS CASAS

My Lord,

I find myself confused. What can that mean?

PROFESSOR CHOMSKY

It means this jury needn't vote at all.
God loves Columbus. As for me, I'm going home.
I have a seminar this afternoon.

ST. PETER

My dear Professor, you are right, of course.
We never vote up here, in heaven, though we offer
God our best opinions and we trust in Him.
Democracy is best reserved for mortals,
who deserve the fruits of their poor taste.

GOD

Indeed, they do! Up here it's Me who says
what happens—who gets in or doesn't.
Christopher Columbus, listen closely.
You have learned a little here today,
but not enough. Go back, beginning
where all men and women must begin:
as nobody, with nothing lost or won.
Begin your climb in deep humility,

in sadness. Grieve for every soul—not only
Christian. Grieve for all. That state is wretched
into which humanity is born.
Your life is but a lightning streak that flickers
in-between dark hills—eternal night
on either side. In that bright flash you make
your day, a day that lasts as if forever.
I shall let you try it all again,
my *Christo-ferens*. Go back home.
I shall reconvene this meeting in a brief
five hundred years. My son, attend
to those you gather on your way: all men
and women whom you meet are Me. I judge
you daily, as I judge the world. (I hope,
as always, for a kindly soul to catch
the fire of its redemption, to give up the search
for Something Better, to relinquish all.)
Begin with nothing and with nothing end.
Goodbye, Columbus. And goodbye to all.

The voice was gone, the Light within the Light
extinguished fully, and Columbus found
himself alone in some black field,
a stubble-field with furrows freshly ploughed;
the grape-deep sea unfurled beyond,

a distant boom against imagined shingle.
Wind was blowing from the south like hope,
and birds were singing in a nearby tree.
As the sun came up, a village glimmered
on the farthest edge of what he saw.
But where was he? In Portugal or Spain?
Was this Liguria? He wiped the sweat
that trickled from his brow on his white sleeve
and laced his boots more tightly than before
and set off, chastened, into life again.

THE END